Forgotten Confessions

KT WOLT

Copyright © 2026 by KT Wolt

All rights reserved.
No part of this book may be reproduced, stored in a retrieval system, or transmitted in any form or by any means—electronic, mechanical, photocopy, recording, or otherwise—without the prior written permission of the author, except for brief quotations used in reviews, articles, or scholarly works.

This is a work of fiction. Names, characters, places, and incidents are products of the author's imagination or are used fictitiously. Any resemblance to actual persons, living or dead, events, or locales is entirely coincidental.

Cover design by Samantha Sanderson-Marshall

ISBN: 979-8-9988412-3-1
First Edition: February 2026

Published by KT Wolt
https://www.facebook.com/KTWoltAuthor/

ABOUT FORGOTTEN CONFESSIONS

It's time to take my place beside her and show the world that she belongs to me.

Now that I finally have answers about my parents' murders, I'm going back to the only place I've ever called home.

The one place I'm no longer welcome.

The Oasis.

Harlow Reece has been my secret for far too long. That's about to change. She's fierce, impossible to forget, and deadly with a gun. She thinks she can keep her walls high, but nothing will stop me from tearing them down.

Seven years ago, I walked away from her. My world crumbled, and she didn't wait. A month later, she was with another man: Fletcher Roxwell. Her so-called best friend. The same man who's currently sleeping in the bed Harlow and I once shared.

After everything we had—the confessions, the promises, the moments meant to last forever—she's acting like her betrayal never happened.

But it's time to remind her.

It's time to reclaim what's mine.

And this time, our confessions won't be forgotten.

Chapter One

Logan.

Adrenaline hits different when you're somewhere you're not supposed to be, a place you were never meant to return to. A place you are no longer welcome. The excitement of being there causes your heart to pump harder in your chest. You can feel it throughout your entire body. The tingle, the exhilaration. Knowing what's to come before it even happens. Before anyone else. It's better than any drug in this world.

Three distinctive beeps sound in my earbuds as my screen turns from red to green.

Jackpot.

I waste no time slamming my laptop shut and yanking out the earbuds. A glance at my watch confirms it. Under ten minutes to breach the security system. Nine minutes and forty-four seconds, to be exact. Far too easy, and that only pisses me off. Sure, I've been doing this since I was a kid, honing my skills over the years, but this place? It should be locked down tighter than Fort Knox.

After all, what it holds is far more precious than gold.

I've been scoping the layout for three days now. The day after my sister cleared my name and got me released—the same day I learned my yearslong quest for justice was finally over—I couldn't think about anything else but coming here. Still, I took my time, refreshing my memory, watching the rhythm, and learning the current schedule. A schedule I will be adjusting immediately.

I rise from the porch steps, sling my bag over my shoulder, slowly turn the doorknob, and enter the sleeping home.

The sweet scent of vanilla greets me, and I welcome it. Breathing in deeply, I engulf myself in the familiarity, salivating for another taste. I set my bag beside the old couch and the many memories it holds, quietly slipping through the darkened rooms.

Everything is the same. The chocolate-colored furniture. The wood flooring. The stainless steel appliances. The deep blue paint on the walls. Nothing has changed, yet everything has. I may have been banned from coming back here, but the way my heart thumps against my chest, I know this is where I belong. Where I have always belonged.

And this time around, I'm not taking no for an answer. You don't get this gut-wrenching feeling when something feels so right, only to walk away. No, you claim it. There is no other option.

I already know what I'm walking into when I reach the last door at the end of the hallway. I have spent more time preparing myself for this exact moment than anything else. It's critical that I stay in complete control and not lose my temper. A rage has lived in my body for so long, I can't remember what it was like to feel any differently.

I cross the threshold, my eyesight already adjusted to the darkness. The knot in my stomach finally loosens. My muscles relax. I wasn't right, but I wasn't wrong either. This I can work with.

I stay in the shadows along the outer walls of the bedroom, not making a noise. I round the room, stopping beside the plush bed where the jackass lies. Knocked out cold, still recovering. His long hair is tied back into a man bun. The way he's sprawled across the pillows as if he's king of this castle ignites a fire in me. It would only take a single spark to detonate.

Only *I* will be her king.

Since the explosion, he's been on morphine while he sleeps. I know from hacking into his medical records that this is his last night on an IV, which makes this much easier for me. I remove the syringe from my pocket and push the drug through his IV. This is one show he will not be interrupting.

I step back and turn my attention to the real prize. A five-foot-five live wire that will put you six feet under if you're not careful. She's lying on her side, facing the back of a couch that sits near the foot of the bed. A couch that was never in this room before. The fact that she's sleeping on a couch instead of being in bed with *him* shows the luck we all have tonight. Luck they aren't even aware of. Her chestnut hair is fanned across the pillow, her beauty stealing my breath.

I stand over her, watching her eyelids twitch from the dream she's having. I wonder if she's dreaming about me. About the life we once lived—five years of fierce love and blind faith, back when we felt invincible to danger and were full of hope. Back when nothing could come between us. The sex was out of this world and our love was unbreakable.

Until it wasn't.

It's been seven years since it all fell apart, but sometimes it still feels like yesterday.

We fought every second of every damn day until it finally broke us. My entire world had exploded around me, and she refused to wait. Not more than a month later, she was already in bed with another man. A man she told me was her best friend and nothing more. The same man who is sleeping in the bed we used to share.

After all our late-night confessions to each other... I guess she's forgotten them all. I think it's a great time to remind her. I can't wait to walk down memory lane with this wildcat.

I see the handgun grip peeking out underneath her pillow. I drag out her .357, careful not to wake her, and slide it under the couch. She always has two weapons on her, so I know I'm missing one. But what fun would it be if I took both from her?

She's wearing a royal blue T-shirt and dark gray boy shorts. She's kicked the blanket off her, showcasing her toned athletic legs. Legs that I loved when they were wrapped tightly around my torso and I was buried deep inside her. I could stare at her sleeping body all night long, but even I know she will eventually stir from her beauty sleep and feel that something is off. The sun is going to rise soon, and when it does, it will change everything for her.

She rolls onto her back, letting out a soft sigh. I don't wait another second. I quickly snatch her wrists and hold them tightly with one of my hands as I slap my other gloved hand over her mouth. I lie on top of her, pinning her body beneath mine.

She doesn't disappoint. She's the most intoxicating woman I've ever met. She bucks wildly underneath me, trying to break her hands free. Her sleepy eyes are unfocused and confused, probably wondering how someone could've broken into her home without the alarm going off.

I guess her boy toy isn't as good at security as she thinks he is.

She bites down hard on my gloved hand, a move I was anticipating, but it does no good. The leather protects my skin from her kitten bite.

I lean against her fighting body. Pulling in her vanilla

scent, I drag the tip of my nose along her neck, reach her earlobe, and place a small kiss under it. A growl rips out of her chest, and I can't stop my chuckle at how cute she is.

It must be the sound of my laugh that halts her fight. "Logan?" Her voice comes out muffled under my hand, but I know she said my name. It's the only name that should come from her sweet lips.

"Have you missed me, wildcat?" I whisper softly in her ear, adjusting my grip on her wrists.

"What the fuck? Get off me, you asshole." Her words come out muffled again, but I can catch her drift.

This is great.

She begins to fight again as I adjust my position on top of her. I smile at her reddened face. Her hair is disheveled, and she looks hot as hell. God, how I've missed her—even though I know I shouldn't.

I give her a disappointed "Tsk" and shake my head, then remove my hand from her mouth. "Careful. We wouldn't want to wake your boy toy over there."

As if just remembering she has a man sleeping in her bed, a bed that used to be ours, she quickly looks over. From the couch, she can't see much.

I decide in this moment I'm going to burn that bed come morning rise.

"If you hurt him, I'm going to cut your balls off and shove them so far down your—"

I crush my mouth against hers, silencing her worthless threats. I lose myself in the sweetness of her kiss, cool and sharp like spearmint.

She stiffens at first but quickly gives in, melting into me. This only fuels me further. I deepen our kiss and release her wrists. She slowly glides her hands to my shoulders, then caresses my arms, taking her time. Her touch is soft and familiar, awakening memories of the love we once shared. For a moment, it feels like time has rewound, erasing the pain of our past. Her warmth is a solace I have never stopped yearning for. A reminder that she was and still is everything I have ever wanted. A soft moan escapes her mouth. I press my body closer to hers, letting her know she has the same effect on me.

I run my gloved fingers down her side until I reach the hem of her T-shirt. Wanting to feel her skin against mine, I break our kiss and bring my hand to my mouth, biting the glove and pulling it off my hand. She leans up, capturing my lips again. I grab her hip bone and squeeze gently. My bare hand is running underneath her shirt when I feel a warm, sharp piece of metal press against my neck.

Ah, there it is. I almost forgot. The beauty's second weapon.

I smile, breaking our kiss and resting my forehead against hers, both of us breathing heavily. I push myself onto my elbows, the knife remaining tightly against the side of my throat. "I didn't know you're into knife play."

"I'm about to learn all about it if you don't get the fuck off me."

"Really? I would love to be your first." I lean into the blade. The pressure breaks my skin. A couple drops of blood drip onto her chin and neck.

We lock eyes, challenging each other to make the next move. If her dream is to slit my throat while I lie on top of her, then so be it. Without Harlow, I have nothing. I feel adrift, searching for direction. Looking for a place to belong. If she believes I belong in hell next to the devil, then who am I to argue with that?

She releases the knife, drops it to the floor, and pushes against my chest. I reluctantly sit up, trying but failing to hide my smile as she gets to her feet quickly. *She didn't kill me.* That has to mean something.

She races over to see if Fletch is hurt in any way. *Fucker.* She checks his fluids and feels his head—for what, I don't know. A fever? I think the guy has bigger concerns than a fever. I lean forward, grab the gun I slid under her couch, and pop open the chamber. It's fully loaded. *That's my girl.*

I give the chamber a spin and lock it into place. That finally gets her attention off Fletch and where it needs to be. I stand, adjusting myself without a hint of shame for what she made my body feel, and walk toward her.

"What did you do to him? Why isn't he waking up?"

I glance at good ole Fletcher boy, lying there helplessly. I can't stop the smile that creeps across my face. Karma's a bitch and when you fuck with another man's woman, life can take a sudden turn in the wrong direction.

Everyone believes hate is the strongest feeling. They are all wrong. Love is much stronger, making even the sanest person feel crazy.

"Your precious boy toy is fine. Don't worry your pretty little head." I spin the revolver around my finger before stopping it. The barrel now points at me. "I can't believe you still use this old gun." It was gifted to her by her grandparents. I engraved our initials into the grip many years ago.

She narrows her eyes and moves to take the gun from my outreached hand. She doesn't respond, but she doesn't need to.

"I'm taking a shower, and then we have some catching up to do." I walk out of her bedroom door, whistling.

I would be lying if I said I wasn't nervous about my wildcat holding a loaded gun after the shit I just pulled. Harlow isn't a pushover. Anyone would do great to remember that. Every damn second of every damn day.

I crank the faucets to full blast, ready to relieve myself. I don't think Harlow's interested in helping me out in that department, and it's already been a long night.

Chapter Two

Harlow.

I check over Fletcher's sleeping body again with soaked panties, hard nipples, and blood on my face. I adjust the covers and head to the master bathroom.

A small gasp escapes when I walk in front of my mirror. My eyes are dilated, and my hair is a rat's nest from wrestling on the couch. Logan's blood on me is a hard reminder of how weak this man makes me. He knew there was no way I could do it. Hell, if he hadn't leaned into the blade, he wouldn't have been cut.

I should've known Logan wasn't going to listen to me the last day we saw each other, when we had unexpected sex against my back porch. The sex was hot, making me miss him more than I already had. The moment was intimate, as if we hadn't been separated for seven years.

But on that day, I knew I had to draw the line with Logan once and for all. I had to let go and move on. My last words to him were the hardest I've ever spoken, but they came flying out without hesitation: "We're done, Logan. From this point on, you're banned from the Oasis. If you ever set foot on this property again, I will shoot you myself."

He merely smiled, kissing the tip of my nose, and walked away. Like he knew I was bluffing. Today, he proved he was right. I had the chance to slit his throat, and when I failed to do that, I had a chance to shoot him point-blank. But I couldn't even bring my finger to the trigger.

I scrub my face clean, take a deep breath, and give myself a pep talk to regain my bearings. Then I walk out to the kitchen, passing the closed bathroom door Logan disappeared into.

There couldn't be a worse time for Logan to strut back into my life, and I don't have time for his games and accusations. I have bigger fish to fry, and I have yet to come up with a valid plan to save my own ass.

With the help of my grandparents and Marion Keeyes, I have mastered every business aspect of the Oasis. What I didn't count on was the cost of fighting cancer. It's been taking a toll on me—not only in the pocketbook but mentally as well. The thought alone brings fatigue to my bones.

I grab two mugs and brew coffee, pouring a splash of cream into Logan's cup, on autopilot. I debate making a cup for Fletcher, but I have no idea how long he's going to be out for.

The bathroom door opens, and I lean against the countertop as I grip my coffee cup like a lifeline. Logan appears around the corner in nothing but shorts hanging off his hips, showing his delicious V cut. Physically, he has changed drastically since his parents were murdered. He's no longer the young man I dated for five passionate years; he's now a hardened man who's too smart for his own good.

He smirks. "I like what I'm seeing too."

My eyes jump to his as the realization comes over me that I never put any pants on. I quickly skirt around the countertop, obscuring my bottom half from view. Thank God I'm not wearing a thong right now. Sleeping on the couch in a T-shirt and thong with Fletcher in the same room wouldn't have mattered, but it didn't feel right. Standing here now, I'm thankful I never did.

He chuckles, making his way over to the steaming cup of coffee, and takes a sip. "You remember how I take my coffee after all these years."

My cheeks heat at his observation. There isn't much about him that I could ever erase from my mind. I've tried.

"Topped off with spit, so I hope you enjoy every last drop." My words come off strong and unbothered by his remark, even though I don't feel that way. I'll take any win I can get these days.

Logan licks his lips, staring straight into my eyes as he

raises his cup and takes another sip, this one larger. "You taste delicious this morning, wildcat."

The old nickname kicks me out of the haze he always seems to put me in. "What the hell are you doing here?"

Logan ignores my question as he looks around my home. "You haven't changed a thing since you and my mom remodeled this place."

"Your mom wouldn't take no for an answer."

Logan smiles. He always gives me the same sweet smile anytime I talk about his mother. "And you never changed it. Not even that beat-up couch."

"Hey, that couch isn't broken down. It's broken in." And I wouldn't give it away in a million years. It holds too many great memories with Marion, Kali, and even this asshole. Those words never pass through my lips, though.

"Want to break it in some more?"

I narrow my eyes, remembering the decision he made seven years ago. There will never be a second chance for us because of that. I may have given in to his caveman ways once, but it won't happen again. If he could drop me so quickly back then, what's to stop him from doing it again?

"Never again with you," I respond, tipping my cup back and taking a large gulp. The coffee has just cooled enough to not burn my throat.

"Never say never, wildcat."

I set my cup on the bar that separates us a little harder than I mean to. "What's going on? Why are you here?"

"I wanted to update you on Kali and everything that happened."

I fold my arms across my chest. "I already know everything. Gage filled me in and I've talked to Kali. You could've easily done that over the phone." I lock my shoulders, knowing he isn't going to like what comes next. "I think with Gage protecting Kali now, you and I can finally go our separate ways."

He runs his large hand through his thick blond hair, a look of hurt crossing his face.

A small voice in my head tells me to stop being such a bitch, but I smash that voice into the ground.

"Why is Fletcher here?"

And there we have it: the reason for his unexpected arrival. I should've known the second he made his appearance.

I speak slowly in hopes of making him feel like an idiot for even asking such a dumb question. "To recover."

He shakes his head. "He could recover anywhere. He has no place here."

Placing my hands on my hips, I say, "First off, you don't get to tell me whether my friend has a place here. Fletcher will always have a place with me, whether you like it or not. He's in a damn walking cast. He can't make it up all those stairs at his place and you damn well know it."

"A *friend*, huh?" He leans across the bar, bringing our faces closer. "Is that what you call your fuck buddy? A friend?" His voice rises with each word he spits out.

"Shit, Harlow, can I be your friend too? With benefits like that..."

The sound of my hand slapping his cheek is deafening. "Don't you ever speak to me like that again."

We both stand there, facing off silently.

"Fuck," Logan mutters, pushing off the bar and running his hand down his face. "I'm sorry. You're right. I just feel so fucking lost right now." He lets out a deep sigh and drops his head. "I don't have a clue what's next. I never expected to feel this way after learning who killed my parents and everything coming to an end." He pauses, his voice lowering. "This is the only home I have left."

His words hit my already-shattered heart. *He still looks at my home as his.* Just as Fletcher will always have a place with me, so will Logan. Since his parents were murdered, he's put every ounce of energy into finding justice for his family. Now that he knows their murderer is dead, he doesn't know what to do anymore. My heart aches for a man who has lost too much in his life already.

"I want to help, Logan, I really do, but I can't right now. You don't understand. There's too much going on in my life to have to deal with this shit." And if I can't figure out a way to save the Oasis, I will be killing not only my grandparents' dream but his mother's dreams for the Oasis as well. I can only hope this round of cancer treatment will work. "What about Gage? Does he not have another job he can give you?"

"He wants to take time off with Kali. She's pushing

hard for him to go and reconnect with his mother, so it's only a matter of time before that happens. He said we all could use the break after seven years of fighting."

I don't know what I can offer him. A place to crash? Sure, but I'm not even sure I want to go there. If he does stay, it won't be in my home, and he would need to stay out of my business, which I find hard to believe he will. "I don't have any jobs to offer you right now."

Logan leans his hip against the countertop. "You can't say that. I know all those cottages could use repairs and some fixing up. I can work on those, just like we did back in the day."

Numerous repairs, both small and large, need attention. However, figuring out how to handle them without spending money I don't have is my challenge alone.

"I can't pay you, Logan. My expenses are already higher than I anticipated."

He rears his head back, his widened eyes showing surprise that I would ever think that. "I don't want your money. I'll do it all for free. I just need a place to crash. I can earn my keep by helping, even with Fletch too."

I raise my eyebrows at his last offer. "Really? By what? Keeping him doped up around the clock?"

"Can we do that?"

"No, we can't do that! What kind of person are you?"

Logan raises his hands, laughing. "I was joking, wildcat. Of course I don't want to keep him doped up. His recovery will only take longer if his body isn't in motion."

I roll my eyes at his "real" concern with Fletcher.

"I can help get him back on his feet and teach him exercises to rebuild his strength. You remember what I told you about Kali breaking her leg after falling from a tree?" I nod and he continues. "I went to every appointment she had with the therapist." He taps his temple. "All those exercises are up here. I can help him get back to good in no time at all."

His offer is tempting, and it shouldn't be, but I could seriously use any help I can get. The physical therapist on my staff is off on parental leave for another three weeks. I'm barely scraping by right now—and that's with the large loan I took out. His help on the cottages would be a saving grace. But can I take the chance of Logan finding out about the possibility of having to shut down the Oasis because of all my debt? Before I can answer, I hear the slide of a boot across the floor.

I look up just as Logan turns to see Fletcher turn the corner, his eyes going large when he sees Logan standing in the kitchen. He halts. "Everything alright, Low?"

"Her name is Harlow, and everything's fine." Logan takes note of my disappointed look and attempts to clear the air. "Coffee's strong. Help yourself."

Fletcher glances back at me. I give a reassuring smile as he limps over to the coffeepot. He mumbles under his breath, "I hope this is strong. My head feels as heavy as a cinder block."

I glare at Logan as he smiles brightly back. Meddling jerk.

"What brings you by, Logan?" Fletcher grabs his cup and starts to round the corner of the bar to stand next to me.

Logan quickly sets down his cup. "Oh no you don't," he says as he lifts Fletcher underneath his arms—a two-hundred-pound muscleman like he's nothing—and plants him on his other side.

"Logan, what the hell?" I ask.

"What? You're in panties and he doesn't need to be looking at you. He can stay on this side of the counter."

The ringing of my phone cuts in before I have a chance to tell Logan to go stick it where the sun doesn't shine. I slam the rest of my coffee and head to my bedroom. I don't miss the hard look Logan gives Fletcher as I scurry by. My phone stops ringing by the time I make it in there. I'm hoping this is the good news I have been waiting for. I throw on some jeans and pull my hair into a messy bun. I can't take the chance of Logan or Fletcher overhearing my conversation, so I head to the living room.

"I need to take this call. Behave," I say sternly. I walk out the front door and away from listening ears.

Chapter Three

Logan.

As soon as Harlow steps out of the house, I look over to Fletch, who's watching me warily. It's time to get to work. "Have you done any physical therapy since your surgery?"

His eyebrows pinch together; my question must take him by surprise. "No, nothing yet. I was planning on calling my doctor to get a referral since Harlow's is out on parental leave."

I finish my coffee, not wasting one drop that Harlow made for me. I really hope she did spit in it. It might be the only way I can taste her without a blade to the throat. "No need. I'll be covering your therapy."

"Excuse me?" Fletch's face is as red as my cheek probably still is from the smack Harlow gave me.

I can't blame her. I deserved that. "Yeah. Why do you think I'm here?"

He stands there quietly, staring at me in confusion. Clearly the meds must still be strong in his system. I didn't give him much. *Pussy.* He finally finds his words. "I don't know, to get Harlow back?"

Maybe he isn't as dumb as I thought he was. "Would it bother you if that were the case?"

This asshole has the audacity to laugh, and it takes all my willpower not to knock that smug grin off his face and break his other leg.

"Harlow's been done with you for a long time. It wouldn't bother me at all to watch her knock you down into the dirt where you belong."

I cross my arms over my chest. "Harlow can do to me whatever she needs, and I'll take it like the man I am. I'm the one in charge now. I've already talked to her about helping get your ass back on your feet and the fuck up out of her house."

"Please. You're not in charge. Harlow is."

He has a point. No one can control Harlow. The rest of us can only hope for the breadcrumbs she occasionally tosses at us. I clear my throat. "Let me rephrase. I'm the man of the house, and you will be taking orders from me."

"I'm a man too and the only one staying in this house."

Can he get any more annoying? How the hell did Harlow ever fall for this guy? "Well, congratulations on figuring out you're a man, but you're not the man in charge. I am, and I can make your life a living hell if you fuck with me."

He takes another drink of his coffee—loaded down with too much sugar and cream for any man to be drinking—and sets it on the counter. He leans against the counter to relieve the pressure on his leg. Kali would do the same thing back in the day. "I highly doubt that."

"I broke into the security system you created and installed on her home in nine minutes and forty-four seconds."

"Bullshit."

I shake my head. "I have it all documented on my laptop. You can take a look at it after I finish with your first physical therapy session."

His eyes narrow into slits because he knows I'm not lying. "Only because you have repeatedly hacked into my system. Don't think I don't know it was you, Link." He spits out my alias as though it were garbage on his tongue.

I chuckle. "You would think a man of your caliber wouldn't be able to get hacked."

"Against any other person, I don't have to worry." As soon as he says it, I can tell he wants to take back the compliment he just unwittingly paid me. He may hate me, but he respects my capabilities in technology.

I respect his work as well, but I'll never be dumb enough to admit that.

He tosses his hand in the air, clearly frustrated. "My

point is that you've already hacked into my work. What else could you do to make my life a living hell?"

"Release it to your competitors."

His jaw clenches, telling me I've hit the bullseye. That's exactly why *I* am the man of this house, not him.

"I don't want to do that to you, but if you get in my way, I won't hesitate. You're going to tell Harlow you want me to help with your physical therapy... and we can all get along."

I stare at Fletch as hard as he stares back at me. The tension is so thick, I could cut it with one of Harlow's knives. This is nonnegotiable for me, and if it doesn't work, I may not have other options.

"All right, fine. But if you break her heart in any way..."

I hold my hand up to stop him. "You have nothing to worry about. Now follow me. Let's get your exercises going." I head back down the hallway to Harlow's bedroom, and the sounds of his coffee cup hitting the countertop and his walking cast sliding across the hardwood floor follow me.

By the time he makes it back to the room, I already have the bed stripped.

"What the hell are you doing?"

"Getting you moving. Grab that end of the bed."

He hobbles over to the opposite side.

"Come on, pick it up. I got this side. We're carrying this out the back door."

"This is your form of physical rehabilitation?"

"Don't fucking question me, Fletch. Grab the fucking mattress."

Thankfully he doesn't argue any further as we make our way through the cabin and out the rear door. The opposite end of the door Harlow left through. I've never had to move a heavy fucking mattress with a disabled person, but it's a bitch. We lay it down on the dirt driveway before I order Fletch to head back inside for the box spring. I glance around for Harlow. She's not anywhere in the vicinity, which is good for what I'm about to do.

Fletch reemerges with the box spring and a fine layer of sweat across his forehead. He drops it on top of the mattress and looks to me for direction. *Good dog.*

"Grab the bedding and pillows. I have to head to the shed. I'll be right back." I don't wait for his response. I turn and head down the pebbled path to the beaten-down shed. This building was never in pristine condition, but it wasn't as bad as it is currently. Harlow can refuse my offer all she wants, but it's clear she needs me.

I grab everything I need and make it back just as Fletch is tossing the bedding on top of the box spring. He silently watches me pour a generous amount of gasoline over everything, light a match, and toss it onto the bed. Flames lick across it quickly, and the heat of the fire warms my face. Tension leaves my muscles.

"Have you lost your mind?"

I take Fletch in. He wears his hair long, like that one guy back in the day in the butter commercials. Who was that? Fabio? He's built about the same as me, but I have a few inches on him in height. His attire screams rich little preppy bitch. Nothing that would ever grab Harlow's attention. So why she jumped into bed with this asshole is something I've never been able to understand.

"No other man will be in Harlow's bed but me." I tell him the truth. I want him well aware of what I'm willing to do. Maybe I *have* lost my mind. That's what makes love so sickening. It can make you do things you never would have imagined doing in a million years. I may have been consumed with finding justice for my parents' murder, but that's over now, and I must look to the future before I lose my mind.

Harlow, pocketing her phone, runs up to us, yelling, "Logan! What the hell is going on?" Her long brown hair is tied up in a messy bun and her stunning bluish-gray eyes are locked on mine, filled with panic. She glances around, trying to understand the current situation. She looks completely lost. Join the club.

"I'm taking you bed shopping." I step alongside her.

"Have you lost your mind?" she asks.

Fletch snorts. He just asked me the same question.

I answer her with all I've got, which isn't much lately. "Maybe?"

She runs her small hand down her face, stress etched across her features.

"What's wrong?" I ask. "Who called you?"

The concern in my voice has her dropping her hand to face me. "What? No one. Just a client setting up a time to stay here in a couple of weeks." She looks down at the raging fire. "I can't do this, Logan. I can't deal with your shit right now."

"Hey, there's no shit for you to worry about. I'm going to take you shopping—on me—and buy you a brand-new bed. When we get back, Fletcher boy is going to help me clean this mess up and set up your new bed."

"Why the fuck is my mattress on fire in my driveway, Logan?"

I tuck a piece of hair that has fallen from her bun behind her ear. She doesn't pull away, and I love that. Especially in front of Fletch. It's a huge win, and it takes a lot to not crack a grin. "It might have bedbugs... You know... Because of certain friends sleeping where they shouldn't be."

"Give me a break," Fletch snaps. He's a clean-looking guy, but who wants to think about his naked ass lying in the same bed I will soon be back in?

"Logan, listen..." Harlow lets out a frustrated breath.

I don't let her continue. I already know where this is heading. "Wildcat, you need to stop stressing. I've already worked it all out with your Fletcher boy. He wants me to help with his rehabilitation."

Her eyes narrow, making it hard to see any color in them. Instead of addressing me, she turns to the asshole. "Just say the word and I'll make Logan take a hike, because I know damn well you didn't agree to this."

Now it's my turn to switch my attention to him. I watch him gulp, knowing well the threat I leveled on him. With every second he doesn't answer, I start to question what I actually know about this guy. Maybe he has bigger balls than I expected. I honestly don't want to spill his work, but my want for Harlow in my life is stronger.

"Logan and I talked," he says finally. "We're good. He mentioned he knows some effective exercises I can try, and this actually works better for me. I'd prefer to stay out of the public eye until I'm fully recovered anyways." Then a small smile forms on his lips, and he adds, "Plus, while he's here, he can help you out around the Oasis."

He has no idea I've already offered that, probably thinking he's getting one over on me. I would rebuild every damn cottage at the Oasis from bottom to top for Harlow if she asked me to.

"Are you sure, Fletcher? I can see if I can get a qualified therapist here to help you instead. I can have them sign an NDA before they arrive."

Fletch makes his way around the flaming mattress to Harlow. It takes forever with his limp.

I roll my eyes at his dramatics. I keep myself rooted to the ground, arms crossed against my chest, knowing I can't bulldoze this asshole in front of her. He'd better turn down her gracious offer, or so help me God...

"I'm good, and this..." He pauses, looking over to me, before going back to her. "This is good. I've always preferred to stay out of the limelight and would like to keep it that way, but..."

Oh, that motherfucker.

"If you don't want Logan to stay here, then that's up to you. I'll figure my own shit out. After all, this is your home and you're the one in charge."

This asshole. I want to hate him, but I can't. He's making sure Harlow's okay with everything, and how can I not agree with that? He's smart. I need to remember that. Harlow looks down at the remaining part of her mattress. It's smoldering with springs hissing. I hold my breath.

"All right, if that's what you want. But…" She turns to me and digs a finger into my chest. "You are cleaning this mess up by yourself while I take a shower. Then you're taking me to buy not only a new bed but a matching new bedroom set too."

Damn, I love this woman. She doesn't wait for a response. She turns on her heel and stalks back into the house. Once the door closes, I turn back to Fletch.

"If you think for one second I'm going to let you in that house while she's naked in the shower, you haven't seen anything yet."

He scoffs. "You need to drop it down a few notches. You've got nothing to worry about with me and Harlow."

"You've had a past."

"Yeah, and a present and a future. We're friends, Logan, so you need to back off. You're only going to push her away."

"Is that so? And why would you help me out? We both know the only reason *you're* here is because you want another shot with her too."

He shakes his head as if he's disappointed in me. In me! I was Harlow's first love, and what we shared was way deeper than any relationship she ever had with him. She gave me all her firsts, and in return, I gave her all of mine. We have a connection no one can touch. Not even him.

"As smart as you are, Logan, you can be a real dumbass." He limps away. He doesn't go into the house, though, and instead makes his way down a trail. For that, I'm grateful, because I know exactly what I would've done, and Harlow would have kicked my ass out for sure.

His words circle inside me. Why would he say that? If I were in his shoes, I would be damned if I gave my competition any insight, but the way he just spoke to me... It's as if he isn't here to get her back. But if that's the case, then why is he here? I can't believe his only reason is for recovery.

After I finish cleaning up the mess, I grab my laptop and send him the file showing how I hacked into his security in record time. I also send notes on how to correct it.

Why? I have no idea.

Chapter Four

Harlow.

Climbing out of my new bed isn't easy. All I want is to stay snuggled in the soft new bedding and sleep the day away. But I can't. I need coffee and I need to check on Fletcher.

Despite my arguments, neither of my guys would let me help with setting up the furniture Logan purchased. Not only did he buy me a whole new bedroom set, but he also bought beds for himself and Fletcher. I couldn't believe it. Logan's always been fine financially, and now that he has his parents' inheritance, he's doing exceptionally well. He's never cared for Fletcher. But this? It cracked open a piece of my shattered heart I didn't expect to feel again… but then Logan had to be Logan and piss me off again.

He refused to let Fletcher stay in my home. Claimed

it would work best, what with him conducting physical therapy, if they stayed together. The second bedroom isn't large enough for both of their beds, so instead of squeezing them in, Logan moved them both into Marion's Suite.

I was ready to argue until the sun went down, but honestly? I was over it. Reluctantly, I let it go.

Marion's Suite is just how it sounds. It was hers. She had it completely renovated, incorporating a warm, earthy color palette with the cutest vintage French-style chairs. This cottage is frequently booked due to its charm and coziness. It's the only cottage I have meticulously maintained, preserving every detail as Marion left it.

I had just turned eighteen when my grandparents passed away in a car accident. It flipped my world upside down. Only a couple of weeks after their funeral, an older gentleman I had never met showed up at my parents' home.

He set us down to review the will, revealing that the Oasis—with all its acres and cottages, plus their belongings—was now mine. My parents were furious. They had only received ten thousand dollars each as a token of appreciation for bringing me into the world.

That didn't go over well.

My parents tried to persuade me to sell the Oasis. Subdivide the property and liquidate the assets. They never understood the significance, the beauty, and the hope embodied by the Oasis. After a heated argument, I packed my bags and left.

I had no idea how to run a business, especially one like this. Right away, I double-booked clients at least a half dozen times, once having to opt to let a family stay in my own cabin while I pitched a tent at my favorite pond.

Desperate, I turned to my parents for help. They refused, insisting I should've sold the Oasis right away. I knew if I didn't figure things out quickly, I would have no choice but to close down the Oasis for good.

I'll never forget the day Marion first showed up. The weather that day was wild. The sky was littered with dark heavy clouds, but the sun was still shining brightly in the sky. I was failing miserably at fixing the Gator, which had broken down miles from my cabin. Though the sun was shining, God decided to let loose a downpour right where I was.

Throwing the wrench into the grass, I broke down, unable to stop the tears. I was soaked from head to toe, covered in dirt and grease. I felt defeated. I pulled the hair that was stuck to my face out of my eyes to find a beautiful woman standing close by. She looked familiar, but I couldn't place her.

She was twenty feet away, and apparently it wasn't raining where she stood. The sun shone down on her long blond hair. She was wearing an elegant knee-length navy blue dress. She looked like an angel who had been sent just for me.

Grateful for the rain that was effectively hiding my tears, I trudged over to her.

"Harlow Reece?"

I nodded, wiping my hand clean on my wet jeans and holding it out to shake hers. "Hi. Yes, that's me. What can I do for you, Miss…?"

"Mrs. Keeyes, but please call me Marion. I knew your grandparents." She let out a frantic laugh before making eye contact with me again. "Look, I know this is going to sound strange, so I'm just going to come out and say it." A flush crept across her cheeks, her shoulders dropping. "I had a dream last night about your grandparents, Sally and Jon. They were telling me you needed my help."

She was right. That did sound strange. "What?" was the only thing I managed to mutter.

"My husband James and I did a lot of work with them on firearms."

It hit me as soon as she mentioned firearms. "I remember hearing about you. I found pictures of you and your husband in their—er, my—cabin."

Her smile was soft. "We were much younger back then. Is your Gator broken down?"

I nodded in defeat.

"Jump in." She pointed to the Audi she'd driven up in, idling not far away. "Before this rain ruins my hair. Let's figure out how I can help you."

And the rest was history. She helped me turn the Oasis around quicker than I thought was even possible. We became fast friends, and that's how I met her son Logan. The man who would eventually rip my heart out and leave me behind without another thought.

I park the Gator—a different one from all those years back—and grab the coffee decanter and a bag of supplies before hopping out. I give a quick knock before opening the door, hoping these two haven't killed each other yet.

"Oh thank God," Fletcher mumbles at the sight of coffee.

Logan extends Fletcher's leg and tells him to lift it off the floor.

Fletcher lifts it three inches and holds it in the air for a good ten seconds before he drops it back down.

Logan's hazel eyes turn to mine and he gives a lopsided grin. He's wearing sweats and a white T-shirt that fits tightly around his biceps. "Do two reps of ten and we're done for the morning," he says. He pushes to his feet and crosses the space between us, scooping up the supplies I brought. "Good morning, wildcat."

"Good morning. I'm glad to see you two are getting along." I pull out the cream and sugar from my bag. Logan takes his coffee with a splash of cream, whereas Fletcher prefers a splash of coffee with his cream and sugar.

"I was just getting ready to come see you. How was our new bed?"

I laugh at his boldness. "You mean *my* new bed?"

He shrugs as he pulls three coffee mugs from the cupboard and fixes my coffee just the way I take it. Black as night with a hint of sweetness.

Since he doesn't respond, I do. "It was too nice. I didn't want to get out of bed this morning."

He hands me my cup and I take a drink. "That's great because I'm free the rest of the day. We can go back and spend all day in it if you want." His voice lowers a fraction. "I remember how much you liked to snuggle. You were like a damn leech."

He's being cute, and funny, and Logan, and I hate it. I ignore him and pour Fletcher's coffee while he prepares his own.

Before I can walk over to Fletcher, he takes it from my hand and carries it himself before walking back to me. "What's our plan for today, wildcat?"

I take another large drink of my caffeine goodness. "There are no plans for *us* today."

"That's not going to work for me."

"Yeah, well, you here isn't working for me, so I guess it's only fair."

Our eyes lock, neither one of us budging. He's so gorgeous. That's why I can't have him around. The temptation is too much to handle. My shattered heart still beats heavily when it comes to him.

Logan sets his cup down and grabs my free hand. I try to pull away, but his grip only tightens. "I understand this is new again for both of us, but I meant what I said. Anything you need, I'm ready to knock out."

"Were you serious about helping with the cottages?"

"Yeah, I just need to take a shower really quick and I'm ready to go." Logan raises my hand and kisses the top, then releases it. He puts the cream in the fridge and walks back to me, holding out his coffee cup.

My eyebrows knit together. "You need me to hold your coffee cup while you shower?"

"Nope, just making sure you didn't want to top it off with more of your sweet spit. I have to be honest, wildcat. I might already be hooked."

I laugh and roll my eyes. Sometimes, when everything changes, nothing does at all. "I didn't spit in your coffee yesterday."

"Well, isn't that a shame?" He winks and heads down the hallway.

Heat blooms at his words.

I go into the living room, drop down on the seat next to Fletcher, and close my eyes. The furniture in this room is all plush, upholstered in soft, muted fabrics that invite you to sink into them. The sunlight streams across my face from the large vintage window. This living room is not just a space. It's a haven of comfort and nostalgia.

"I think your ex is off the hinges."

"Nothing new there."

"So, a two-hour lecture on why I'm not right for you is normal. Got it."

I open my eyes and turn my head to face him. "Is he being an asshole to you?"

"It's pretty clear he's still got it bad for you."

I snort. "Logan does what Logan wants to do. Mark my words. The second you're recovered and back at your place, he'll be long gone on the next mission that calls to him."

"I don't think so, Low. He's talking like you two are already back together."

I shake my head. "Because you're here. He doesn't want me and you to get back together."

We sit in silence for a few moments before Fletcher speaks again. When he does, his words are the ones that I was afraid he would say. "Have you ever considered telling him the truth?"

I crinkle my nose at the suggestion. "Absolutely not."

"I don't know. I think it would clear the air around here."

I sit up, set my coffee cup on the aged wooden coffee table, and grab his hands. "Fletcher, there's no way in hell I would ever let our secret out. If Logan can't see the truth, that's on him."

My phone starts buzzing wildly in my pocket, and I drag it out to see my dad's name. Fletcher has no idea about the cancer either, so I excuse myself and head outside for the call I have been waiting for.

"Hey, Dad. Did it work?" I ask, clutching the phone hard to my ear. I desperately need this to work. My funds are draining out of my accounts quicker than I can add to them. When I got the first call a couple of years ago from my dad, I almost didn't pick up. If I hadn't, my mother would've already been six feet under, the cancer taking her away without a second thought. We may not have had the best relationship, but that didn't mean I wanted her to die.

"Honey, we just found out that it has spread from her lungs to her bones."

I almost drop the phone. I don't know if I can afford to give any more money to my father for her treatment. If I do, I'll destroy all my hard work over the years with the Oasis. And then there's Logan. When he finds out I've let part of his mother's legacy fall apart, he'll hate me until his last breath. Guilt fills me almost to the point of suffocating me. How could any daughter hesitate to help out her dying mother just because she might lose her career and piss off her ex?

"Harlow, you still there?"

"Yes, I'm still here. I was just hoping for better news."

"Me too. I spoke with her team of doctors, and they told me about a new treatment that just came out not too long ago. The trial runs have had a 90 percent success rate. We think it's the only option left to save your mother's life… but it's not cheap."

A rock hits the bottom of my gut. Of course it isn't. Since when has anything ever been affordable when it comes to medical care? "How much are we talking?"

"Five hundred thousand."

This time I do drop my phone. Half a million dollars to possibly save my mother's life. Half a million dollars would undoubtedly shut down the Oasis. I've hit the end of my run and am out of options. I pick my phone up and brush the dirt off.

"I don't know if I can get that kind of money," I say

honestly. I'm hit with dead silence as my chest tightens painfully.

Eventually he says, "I see."

I run my fingers through my hair. "Listen, I'll check into some things and see what I can do. Maybe I should fly out there to see her and talk to the doctors myself. I can set up some kind of payment plan."

"That won't work. They have your mom more isolated than she's ever been. They're afraid that if she catches the slightest cold from anyone, it could kill her. She's not doing good, sweetheart."

The reality of the situation makes me gulp. This is bad. "Okay, then we can meet with her doctors and try to figure something out."

"I've put in a request for a meeting. I'll let you know as soon as we set something up."

I woke up this morning in a better mood than I've been in for a long time. This call has killed any hope I had left. My father has refused to let me come out to see my mom. He told me from the start that she didn't want me to see her like this, see how weak she's become.

That's my mother for you. She's always been more concerned with her looks and fine materials than with things that really matter. I couldn't care less about how she looks. We may have had a rocky relationship, but that doesn't mean I don't want to be there for her.

I know what I need to do. I tell my dad I'll forward fifty thousand over to his account and work on getting the rest.

I just hope my contact is still interested in the Oasis and willing to work out a deal. Logan will hate me for good if I make this deal, but so be it. He's going to hate me either way. I can't let my mother die when I have the option to save her.

Chapter Five

Logan.

Harlow and I take off to evaluate the cottages that aren't currently occupied. Some require minor repairs, while others will need supplies. Each time we come across a cottage needing significant work, I notice Harlow tensing up. I don't know her financial situation, but I decide to cover the costs myself. That's what my mother would have wanted, and it's what I want to do as well. Not that I'm going to tell her that. I learned quickly to pick and choose my battles with this wildcat.

After the last cottage is gone through, I take control of the Gator. The property of the Oasis is stunning, with the majestic presence of large, thick pine trees standing tall, the evergreen needles creating a soothing canopy overhead. Traveling along the gravel path, I can't help but notice the vibrant flowers that dot the landscape. I'm sure Kali can name every flower here.

I breathe in the clean air, the scent of pine and blooming flora filling my lungs. I've been in the city for so long now, I almost forgot what it feels like here. It makes me never want to leave again. I can see why my mother loved coming out here so much. I did too, but my reasoning was a bit different. The scenery was nice, sure, but the chestnut beauty stole my breath every time.

When I turn down a path heading away from Harlow's house, I expect her to argue. To my surprise, she seems to relax against the seat. I send a quick thank-you to God and hope this is a good sign.

I dated here and there before I met Harlow, nothing serious. No matter how beautiful the women before Harlow were, it just never felt right. Conversations would fizzle and after a while, being with them felt more like something I was supposed to do than something I couldn't live without.

That all changed the day I met Harlow Reece.

I went back home knowing I had to find a reason to get back to the Oasis. And thank God for my mother. She was the one to suggest I go back to help Harlow with repairs on the cottages, and I didn't hesitate to jump on board. Going through the cottages this morning was like rewinding the clock.

Well, with the exception that we kept our hands to ourselves this go-around.

I pull up to my favorite spot in the Oasis: a lake that's as clear as the blue sky above us. Diamond Lake rests atop a small mountain. It's more like a large pond, but we've all called it a lake since day one. Only one other person knows why this is my favorite spot, and she's sitting right next to me.

This is where Harlow gave herself to me for the first time all those years ago, in this very lake.

We hop out of the Gator and walk along the water's edge as if we have been doing this every day for years. The lake is adorned with a sandy shore that gleams under the hot sun.

Harlow hasn't said much of anything since we hit the trails to evaluate all the cottages, and I think I know why. "Fletch said your dad called. Everything good?"

She glances at me. "Yeah, everything's good." Her smile is strained as she bends to pick a yellow flower.

"I didn't realize you were on speaking terms with them again."

I watch her tiny fingers as she twists the stem around. She looks nervous about this conversation, so I try to put her at ease. She knows I never cared much for her parents because of what they put her through, but I also understand that it's her parents. If she wants to rebuild a relationship with them, I'll support it. But that doesn't mean I won't be having a firm conversation with them as well. "I think it's good that you reconnected with them, as long as they are treating you right."

"They contacted me a couple of years ago." She pauses as though deep in thought, then continues. "I think we all learned a long time ago that you never know what life can hit you with, and it's better not to hold grudges over things you can't change."

I know all about that. It's sad how much in your life you take for granted, thinking it will always be there. Until it isn't. When that happens, it's a cold slap of reality to your soul. I'm still battling that war every day. "Have they come out to see everything you've done to the Oasis?"

She shakes her head and twists the stem so hard that it snaps in two. "No, they moved to the East Coast. They haven't had time to come out."

The small action of her snapping the flower in half speaks louder than any words she's saying. I pull the remaining part of the flower from her hand and tuck it behind her ear. "Have you been out to see them?"

"Not yet." She adjusts the flower before playing a wildcat move: changing the subject. Something she's very good at. "How's Kali doing?"

This is her way of saying she doesn't want to talk about her parents anymore; therefore, I roll with it. After everything they put her through, it's going to take time to rebuild a relationship. "She's good. Better than good, actually. It's like I have my old sister back. She called me the other day saying she ordered paint supplies to start painting again."

A large smile grows across her heart-shaped face. I've dreamed of that smile more times than I can count.

"That's good. I knew she and Gage would be perfect for each other."

I shrug. "Yeah, I guess. As long as he keeps her out of the dangerous part of his life, then I don't have a problem."

Harlow stops in her tracks, causing me to do the same. "Gage would never put Kali in danger," she muses. "I don't think he's going to stick around in that kind of work. He was just as lost as you are now. But with Kali and his mom in his life, I think he's going to head down a different path."

I shake my head. "It isn't that easy. You can't just turn away from the life we've been living for the past seven years. He would lose his mind."

Harlow remains silent. I wish I could read her mind. She turns and marches back toward the Gator. I reach out quickly, grabbing her wrist and pulling her back to me. Her hand automatically lands on my chest above my heart. I know she must feel how hard it's beating for her right now.

"Let me go." She tugs on her wrist.

I don't budge. I need to understand why she got so upset over what I just said. "What's wrong? What did I say?"

She gives another tug, but she isn't trying hard, so I don't let her go. "Nothing. I just need to get back and check on Fletcher."

His name on her lips has the rage climbing through

my body. My jaw tightens as I try to rein it in. "Stop bullshitting me, wildcat. Tell me what's wrong."

She's as stubborn as they come. Her eyes narrow as she straightens her back, ready to fight. I didn't give her the nickname wildcat for no reason. "You think you can just walk back into my life and act as if you didn't abandon me for seven fucking years. That you didn't rip my heart out and walk away without a second thought."

I rear my head back at her hissed words. I do let go of her wrist now. "I didn't abandon you. You fucking abandoned me! You watched my world crumble, and instead of waiting for me, you ran off with your fucking boy toy, Fletch."

Her face is turning redder by the second, but I don't care. We need to get this—all the ugliness, all the lies—out if we're ever going to get past it by some miracle from God.

"If you would open your damn eyes for once in your life," she says, "you would know I'd never do that to you."

I can't believe how easily she can lie to me. And it fucking hurts. Shit, it hurts a lot because I know the truth. "Really? So let me get this straight. You're going to stand here and tell me my sister lied about Fletch coming over for business and not leaving until the next day, looking like he just had sex all night long?"

She crosses her arms and lets out a small huff.

Yeah, that's exactly what I thought. "And not just

once, but multiple times, Harlow. How many times did you fuck him? How many times did you think about me while you were fucking him?"

"It wasn't like that, Logan. I..."

I hold my hand up to stop her from lying any further. If she keeps it up, things will never work between us. "Stop denying it, confess, and let's move on. It's in the past. I get it. I left you high and dry, but fuck, Harlow. My parents had just been murdered. I was lost and pissed at the fucking world." I tug my hand through my hair, feeling like I'm about to combust, all the emotions flowing back into me.

"I know you were, and I wanted to be there for you, but you shut me out. I didn't know how I could help you."

"Well, it sure in hell wasn't jumping in bed with your supposed best friend!" I roar, my anger getting the better of me.

"This is exactly what I am talking about! You never listen to me," she snaps.

We're both losing control.

"Oh, I'm sorry." I put my hand on my chest. "Please, tell me. I'm all ears. If it wasn't like that between you two, then tell me what it was, because I would love to hear what you have to say about it."

She opens her mouth and slams it shut.

The tightness in my chest consumes me. My jaw is already hurting from clenching it. This woman, my wildcat—the only woman who has ever held my heart—can't help but lie to me. It's moments like this that make me wonder what the hell I'm even doing here. She should be the one begging me for another chance. Yet here I am, begging for any little scrap she will toss my way. Love is the worst thing in the world. All it ever does is open you up to being cut deeper. I grind out, "I can't look away from the facts."

She gives a hollow laugh, one with a defensive tone. "Then I guess we can save ourselves all the hassle and part ways now."

"You would like that, wouldn't you?"

She slams her shoulder into me as she stomps by.

"Oh no you don't. We're not done here yet." I try to snatch her wrist again, but she's too quick.

"Yes, we are!"

I reach her, wrap my arms around her waist, and hoist her into the air. She bucks wildly in my arms, but I don't let go. I think we both need to cool down. I walk us straight into the lake and toss her in.

Her whole body goes under. I dive in, coming up right next to her. The water isn't as cold as I thought it would be. When she breaks the surface, her hands start hitting my chest. I don't care. I pull her in and wrap my arms around her body.

Bringing my lips to her ear, I whisper gently, "We both need to just chill out for a second." I hug her close to my body. "I'm sorry. It's hard for me sometimes."

Her body remains tense, but she stops fighting me. We stand in the lake with her hands fisted in my shirt while I rub my hands up and down her back. Eventually, she begins to relax against me. I should hate her for sleeping with Fletch right after we split, but I can't. All I know is I can't have her walking away from me again. From us. Our past is tainted, but I can't stop feeling at home when I'm with her.

She sniffles. I put a finger under her chin and lift her face to mine. Even though she is drenched from head to toe, I see the tears cascading down her cheeks.

"Aw, shit." I pull her to my chest, holding her tighter. The last thing I wanted to do was make her cry. Harlow's tough, so to witness tears on her is rare. "I'm sorry. Let's just forget everything. I don't even care anymore."

This isn't exactly the truth, but I would say anything to stop her tears. I may drop this issue with her, but with Fletch, it'll be another story. He and I will have plenty of time to discuss this all night long.

She starts to shiver, making me feel like a bigger ass. "Are you cold?" She nods. I scoop her up bridal-style and wade to shore. I set her down in the passenger seat of the Gator and circle around to the driver's side.

She's wiping her face and avoiding me when I look over at her.

"Harlow, look at me."

She locks her hands together and turns toward me.

"Tomorrow," I say, "I want to go back to my parents' property, but I can't do it alone. Would you come with me?"

Her eyes widen in surprise. She knows neither Kali

nor I have set foot back on the grounds of the former Keeyes mansion since that day. "Of course. I have a couple of clients arriving in the morning, but I'm free in the afternoon."

I smile, warmed by her big heart. This is what confuses me the most. This is the Harlow I know. The one who would walk across hot coals right next to me without batting an eye. The one who would always stand by my side, no matter what.

"What made you decide to go back?"

I swallow thickly, knowing this is going to sound strange to her. Shit, it has me confused. "I had a dream last night."

She perks up, straightening and turning her entire body toward me. "About what?"

"That it was time for me to go back. I don't know, it wasn't clear." I shake my head as if the action will bring all the details back. "I only remember bits and pieces, but I woke knowing I needed to go there for... something. I just don't know what." I shake my head again. "I know it sounds ridiculous."

Her hand lands on my wet jeans and squeezes gently. "No, it doesn't at all. A long time ago, someone taught me that angels can come through to you in our dreams. Let's do it."

"Who taught you that?"

She drops her gaze to where her hand lies on my thigh. "Your mom did." Her voice is just above a whisper. She meets my gaze. "The first day I met her. She told me she had a dream that my grandparents told her I needed her help."

I lean back into the bench seat. My mother never told me that. I never questioned how she and Harlow got connected. I just assumed it was because our family had done business with the Oasis.

Harlow squeezes my thigh and adds, "So yes, I would love to go with you tomorrow."

I tug her to me as I drive us back to the main house. We may have a lot of baggage, but there's nowhere I would rather be.

Chapter Six

Harlow.

When we arrive back at Marion's Suite, both of us still soaking wet, it's to a silent cottage. My heart races as I rush to the back room. If Fletcher left because of Logan, I'm going to flip out. Thankfully, though, he's knocked out cold in his new bed.

Logan drives me home and parks the Gator. He tries coming in, offering to cook me something, but I can't do it. I have a lot on my mind and need time to work through everything.

I lock down the house, strip, and take a long hot shower. Our heated argument plays in my mind on repeat.

The weight we carry from our past is heavy. Betrayal. Lies. Hurt. We both took part in destroying the only perfect thing we had in this fucked-up world.

I'm not mad at Kali for spilling the beans on Fletcher's secret nightly visits. She wasn't lying when she told him what she saw. She had no idea Logan and I were in a relationship back then. A relationship that was becoming more tarnished with every passing day.

Logan and I agreed back then to keep what we had going a secret, and it was me pushing for secrecy. I had worked too hard for the first few years of running the Oasis to be judged for taking the easy way out.

Word had gotten out that James and Marion Keeyes were donating their time and resources to the Oasis to get it to the next level. If anyone knew I was dating their son, the gossip would have flown around like candy: *Did you hear why Marion and James are helping poor little Harlow? She wasted no time digging her nails into their successful son, leaving them no choice in the matter. She's nothing but a gold digger, half of what her grandparents were. I can't believe they would leave their business to an eighteen-year-old kid.*

Even though I never took a dime from the Keeyes family, no one would have believed that. I couldn't take that risk. I wanted to prove not only to myself but to my late grandparents that I could handle it with everything they taught me. That they had left their pride and joy in good hands. That I was good enough.

My grandma always taught me never to take handouts—but never to turn away a helping hand from a friend either. That's why I let Marion lend a helping hand. We sat down together that first day and I laid out all the obstacles I was facing at the time. One by one, we went through each one, strategizing ways to overcome them. And we did.

I knew Marion was onto Logan and me being more than friends, but she never said a word. She only smiled, pushing us together on projects. It was as if she could see the future before anyone else could.

If only we hadn't messed it up.

My night is restless, so when the sun finally peeks through my blinds, I climb out of bed, ready to conquer the day. I have a text from Fletcher saying that he and Logan will be doing his physical therapy out on the property today and won't be at the cottage.

My clients slated to arrive today all show up on time and without injuries, which is good. Conducting the business I do—thirteen cottages throughout two hundred sixty acres of land where people can stay for whatever reason and have the privacy they need—I have built a large clientele. Some stay to hide out on neutral ground. Some stay to recover. And some simply love the beauty of the Oasis, wanting to take a vacation with their family in safety, knowing they don't need to worry about any bullets flying their way. The bookings aren't cheap. Maintaining a safe haven like the Oasis is costly.

But my mind isn't as focused as I want it to be. It keeps falling back to Logan.

Everything started with him telling me that neither he nor Gage could walk away from their lifestyle. Logan may have been heavily involved in his family's weaponry business, but just as his parents didn't want that for Kali, they also didn't want that for Logan.

He has an opportunity most people never get: to start his life over again. He can do whatever he wants, and I can only pray that he doesn't mess it up. Over the five years we spent together, I learned a lot more about Logan than most people know.

The biggest thing is his love for kids. I went with him countless times to schools that were filled with kids with not much more than the shirt on their backs. He would bring in laptops and hand them out like they were a dime a dozen. He taught them how to use their laptops, the basics of coding, tips on website design, and even ways to create their very own computer games.

I would sit back in awe, observing the way he lit up when he interacted with the kids and absorbing his kindness like a fired gun craves cleaning agents and lubricant. Logan's hands were never made to be covered in blood; they were made for helping kids everyone had given up on.

I finish writing the list of what I would need to buy that I drafted yesterday when we went through the cottages. It's a lot, but if my contact is still interested, I have to keep up with the cottages as much as I can.

Getting in touch with Aleksei Morozov wasn't easy. Not because I didn't have his contact information—I did. But I couldn't risk communicating with him using my computer or my cell phone. I know Logan won't hesitate to hack into my business if he thinks something is off. Just as he hacked the security system Fletcher put in place at my home. Logan's one of the best hackers in the world, so if you want to keep him in the dark, you have to keep your business off the grid. Otherwise, you're offering an open door to all your secrets.

A knock sounds at my door, causing me to jump. Dropping my pen on top of my list of supplies, I wipe my sweaty palms on my jeans. I enter the security code and Logan strolls in, a bottle of bourbon in hand.

I raise my brow in question.

He shrugs. "I need a little liquid courage before we head out."

My heart grows heavy at how difficult this is for him, but it beats harder for how proud I am. This is a huge step forward for him. One I have not seen him take over the last seven years.

"Join me?"

Nodding, I follow him into the kitchen. He opens the cabinet where I've always kept the shot glasses and pulls two down. He chooses the two that he bought all those years ago to celebrate finishing the repairs on our first cottage together. The shot glasses were custom-made but simple. They resemble gun chambers. Mine has "Wildcat" etched on it and his has "Chief."

He pours us each a shot and hands mine to me. I raise it to his, feeling my stomach flutter. "To your parents," I say as his full lips quirk up into a gorgeous smile.

"And to new beginnings."

My face heats. His words make me feel tipsy and I haven't even touched the liquor to my tongue yet. We clink our glasses and tip them back. I embrace the warmth that flows through my body while taking in as much of this moment as I can. "I'm proud of you."

He runs his large hand through the thick blond hair on top of his head, which makes my fingers itch to rub the buzzed sides of his head. He never breaks eye contact with me. "I don't know if I could do it without you."

I wave my hand, dismissing his words. "You don't give yourself enough credit." I grab the bottle and pour one more shot for each of us. I don't know what we'll find by going back there, but I'm grateful to be the one standing next to him when he does.

An hour and a half later, we pull up to his parents' property. Logan jumps from the truck, manually opens the gates, then drives us down the long tree-lined driveway. The dogwood trees aren't in bloom now, but they are still a sight to behold. In a few short weeks, their leaves will turn burgundy. I take notice of Logan's tense posture, his left hand gripping the steering wheel like it's the only thing holding him together. *Maybe I should have brought the entire bottle of bourbon.*

Without thinking, I reach for his right hand. His hazel eyes pierce mine, a silent thank-you passing between us. His fingers close around mine. The simple act of holding hands feels like a spark, making my heart skip a beat.

"The house is gone," he says.

I look up from our locked hands to where the house once sat. "I paid to have the debris cleared about five years ago." It was the least I could do, knowing it would be too hard for him or Kali. Not to mention the fact that they were supposed to be dead.

Logan slams his truck to a sudden stop, releasing my hand quickly. He pulls himself out of the vehicle so fast that I start to second-guess myself. *Crap, he's upset. I shouldn't have done that. I should've at least asked him if it was okay beforehand.* Now it's gone, and the guilt is drowning me.

Before I can process it, he's rounding the truck and opening my door before I can even get my seatbelt off. His face is unreadable as he leans over, unfastening it for me. His hand finds mine, pulling me from the seat with a sudden urgency. Before I can say a word, his lips crash against mine.

It's the last thing I expect him to do. I thought he was mad. I thought I made the wrong decision in getting the ruins of the once warm and loving home cleared out, but as he deepens the kiss, memories flood back in.

Memories of laughter, of shared dreams, of moments when we were inseparable. His touch is familiar, yet it feels new. A blended mixture of past and present.

I can't stop myself from curling my hands into his shirt and pulling him closer. I forget every logical reason my brain says it isn't a good idea to be kissing him back.

When we break away, he rests his forehead against mine as we both take a moment to catch our breath.

"You shouldn't have had to do that by yourself. I should've been here with you," he chokes out, his voice deep and husky.

My eyes burn, but I clamp the emotion down. It *was* hard. I stayed through the whole damn thing, watching every single dump truck haul load after load off the property. When it was finally over, I placed a bouquet of wildflowers from the Oasis where the front door used to be. I've done so every warm month since.

I take a step back, my voice steady despite the knot in my chest. "It was the least I could do for everything you and your family have done for me."

"You won't ever have to do anything like this alone again."

Before I lose my strength to address what just happened, I blurt, "That kiss. That can't happen aga—"

I'm silenced by Logan's finger pressing against my lips. He wraps his hand around mine and pulls me down an old trail.

"Did you go to the underground safe?"

"The what?" It's not lost on me that he completely ignored my stance on the unexpected kiss, but an underground safe? How cool is that? If I can ever get my finances back in the green, I'm putting one in at the Oasis.

He peers over at me as we walk along the grassy trail. "The underground safe. My parents were talking about putting one in at the Oasis as a surprise to you, but then everything happened..." His words trail off, but he doesn't need to say more.

"What's in the safe?"

"You'll see."

I roll my eyes but can't help the excitement of seeing an underground safe. What does it even look like? Is it just a box buried in the ground? Is it like the cellars I have at the Oasis? I think of all the possibilities of what I could use one for. The list is unlimited.

It doesn't take long for us to reach an overgrown area of ivy.

His biceps flex as he drops to his knees and tugs the ivy away. "It's been a while, but I know it's around here somewhere." His fingers fish through the thick ivy until they come to a halt. "Got it." He pulls on a latch and opens a large hatch door that is covered in ivy and dirt. The hatch door is large, I'm guessing four feet wide. He pulls a flashlight out of his pocket and turns it on, highlighting a staircase that leads underground.

Okay, not a small buried safe in the yard like I was thinking. More like a bunker.

I follow behind Logan, gripping the handrail tightly as we make our trek down into the safe. It's darker than night down here and a little creepy.

"Stay here for a second."

I root my feet to the ground and rest my hand on my

.357 in my purse, pleading for my eyes to adjust to the darkness quickly. I hear Logan shuffling around before emergency lights kick on, blinding me momentarily.

A chuckle comes from my right. Logan's eyes are filled with amusement. "No need for your gun down here, wildcat."

"I was looking for my lipstick," I lie and quickly pull my hand out of my purse.

"If you want it back, I'm sure I still have some on my lips."

I ignore him and walk around the safe, astonished by its size. The walls are lined with thick, cold stone and polished metal. My footsteps echo slightly across the smooth, polished concrete floor. I want to replicate this. I can link it to one of the secret underground tunnels my grandparents installed.

The safe has a wide-open floor plan and is well organized. In one section, rows and rows of gun racks display an impressive array of firearms: sleek modern rifles, vintage pistols, and automatic machine guns, all in pristine condition. There are also smaller armaments—knives, daggers, and even throwing stars. All are displayed behind glass in a custom cabinet. Ammo crates are stacked neatly on the shelves, labeled by caliber. This place feels like heaven to me.

Several paintings hang on the walls. Many were done by Kali, most depicting the wildflower garden at the Oasis.

"When did your parents put this in?"

"A long time ago, I was young. I always wanted to play army down here, but I was never strong enough to open the hatch."

I laugh softly, easily picturing the younger version of Logan running around in army paint. Logan walks over to the side opposite me, searching through a desk drawer. I move my attention back to the artwork, and a painting on the wall near the safe catches my attention. I walk closer to see that it contains four very different paintings. I can tell they were separate at one point but were put together to create a mismatched collage.

"What's this all about?" I ask and hear the desk drawer close. I turn to watch Logan slip a small black velvet bag into his front pocket before he walks over to me.

What was that?

He snorts and it sounds hot. I really am pathetic when it comes to him. "That was all Kali right there."

"What do you mean? She painted all these?" I know Kali's work, and only one looks like hers.

"No. After hours of begging, she had all of us sit down and paint one thing we loved the most, but it couldn't be a person."

I smile. Kali prefers to paint only botanicals.

"My father painted the gun. My mother painted the glass of wine, obviously. Kali, of course, painted your field of wildflowers. I painted a code."

"A code for what?"

"The code I used the first time I hacked into Victor

Hemmington's business files. It's not the entire code, of course, but it's part of it."

I turn my gaze to him and smile. He carefully masks his expression, but his rich hazel eyes betray his true emotion. Kali may have had to beg, but I can tell he's happy they did this together as a family.

I lift my hand and trace the code with my finger. It looks like nothing but jumbled letters, numbers, and seemingly meaningless punctuation, but apparently, it's enough to hack into an impenetrable system. As I start to pull my hand away, my sleeve gets caught on the frame and the painting slides off the hanger.

"Whoa," Logan says as he quickly reaches around, grabbing hold of it and preventing it from hitting me in the face.

"Oh God, I'm so sorry. I almost ruined your guys' painting," I sputter as I grip the edges of the frame as well.

"Hey, it's all right. Are you okay? It didn't hit you, did it?"

I shake my head. Logan grabs the collage from my hand, unhooking my sleeve. He turns to hang it back up, but he freezes in place.

I turn to see why. It's a safe within a safe. "Did you know about this safe?" I ask.

He shakes his head and sets the picture to the side, leaning it against the stone wall.

It is a rather simple safe, not large, almost like the

one I have at home. There's a keypad with numbers zero through nine.

"Do you know what the code could be?"

He shakes his head. "I'm not sure. What do you think it could be?"

I ponder for a minute, thinking about James and Marion and what was most important in their life. "Maybe it's your or Kali's birthday?"

He taps his finger to his lips and stares at the keypad. I look back at the pad and think about my code. It's the date my grandparents got married. "Maybe it's the date they got married?"

"No, that would be too easy to guess."

I try to hide my cringe. I know what I will be changing the second I get home tonight.

"But I think you're onto something."

His trembling finger reaches the keypad: 1-0-2-5-6-7. He hits the pound key, and the sound of a latch disengaging has us both letting out a large breath of relief.

"What did those numbers mean?"

"Ten, twenty-five, sixty-seven." He grabs the handle and turns it to open the safe door. "They met on October 25th, 1967. They always brought that up to me over the years, and I never understood why until now."

The door creaks open to reveal only one envelope inside. His hand moves to the back of his neck as he stares inside the safe. I stand on my tiptoes and reach inside to retrieve it.

I read out what Marion's elegant handwriting says: "To our dear son, Logan." I turn the envelope so he can see.

He straightens his posture before slowly taking it from my hands. He runs his finger across the name that his mother wrote years ago. I can only imagine what's going through his mind right now.

"Are you going to open it?"

He clears his throat and slides it into his back pocket. I watch as he closes the safe and fumbles with the painting, placing it back on the wall with perfection.

"Not here. Let's do it at the Oasis," he says. He grabs my hand and we head up the tall staircase, neither of us saying another word.

A single envelope for only one of their kids... and I think I know why.

Chapter Seven

Logan.

We make it back to Harlow's in no time at all. Everything is a blur since we left my parents' property because of the letter from the grave that burns in my pocket. *Is this what I was supposed to find?* While Harlow fixes us a couple of shots, I notice a list she wrote down for supplies she needs to repair the cottages we looked at. While her back is to me, I shove the list in my pocket. After everything she's done for me, there's no way I'm letting her buy these supplies.

After we both take a shot, I lay the envelope on the table before me. Harlow comes over to move the empty shot glass. I take that chance to grab her wrist and pull her down onto my lap.

If I'm going to do this, I'm going to need her as close as possible. She thankfully doesn't argue. I might have crossed that line with her earlier when I kissed her, but holding back wasn't an option.

When I was driving down the long driveway, I thought I would be faced with the burned ashes left behind from the worst day of my life. I don't think my heart has ever pounded so hard in my chest. If it weren't for Harlow grabbing my hand, I would've turned around and headed straight back to the Oasis to drown my sorrows in bourbon.

Instead, I was greeted with a grassy knoll where our home once sat and a bouquet of wilted wildflowers resting in a vase. I know only one person could be responsible for that bouquet.

I don't understand why she did that for me, for my family, while she was hooking up with Fletch. She took the time to handle my parents' home and maintain the property. I might not have said anything, but it didn't go unnoticed. The property should have been overgrown and out of control. But it isn't. I know I have Harlow to thank for that.

This woman is as puzzling as ever, and I won't stop until every piece of the puzzle falls into place.

I wrap my arms around her small waist and tug her against my chest, then reach for the envelope, which reads, "To our dear son, Logan."

I turn it over and run a finger underneath the thick flap, breaking the seal. I slowly pull the letter out and try to control my shaking hands. Exhaling slowly, I begin to read.

Dearest Logan,

Today marks one of the most cherished days in our lives. The day you were born and transformed our world forever.

Watching you grow into the remarkable young man you are today has filled us with immense pride. You have taught us countless lessons about what truly matters, and you have shown us that family is at the heart of everything.

We have decided to close our business, not because we doubt your abilities, but because this was our dream, not yours. Son, you were made for something much bigger than this.

We are sharing this with you on your birthday because we want nothing more than to give you a start toward your dream, so you can run the path you are truly meant to.

48.71890, -121.09296

May all your dreams come true.

Happy 23rd birthday, our sweet man.

I slowly set the letter down, absorbing what I just read. My parents were getting out of the weaponry and armory business. I can't believe it. All those long nights down in the study, going over contract after contract with them. They passed away right before my birthday and I never once saw this coming.

I didn't have a clue what I would read in this letter, but it sure wasn't this. I blink my eyes hard a couple of times, seeing if the carefully written words will change what they spell out, but they don't.

I drop the letter on the table just as Harlow adjusts on top of me to stand. I tighten my grip around her waist, pulling her to me and dropping my forehead to her back. I need a minute to take this in, and right now I feel as if my entire world has been flipped upside down... again. She's my only anchor in choppy waters.

It can't be true. I don't understand. When I think about my parents every day, I never think about the business side of things. I've always focused on the memories filled with our family time. Now, I try to focus on those last few months and what was going on with the business.

We were going through all the contracts one by one. That wasn't uncommon; we would occasionally go through the contracts to make sure everything was operating as it should be. But the more I think about it, the more I realize that everything we were doing was different.

There was never talk about renewing any of them, only noting the end dates. I figured they wanted to know when each one ended so a new contract could be written up by their attorney. But that wasn't the reason at all. They were looking at when they could truly walk away. My stomach knots at that thought.

They got out too late.

"Logan," Harlow whispers, her soft voice calming

the storm inside me. "I think those numbers are latitude and longitude coordinates."

Everything in my body feels heavy, but I manage to pull myself up and look over her shoulder. She's holding the letter. I grab it and take in the numbers scrolled across it. I completely overlooked those, too hung up on the rest to even give them a second thought.

She's right. That's exactly what they are.

"I think that's where your birthday present is." She grabs the envelope and turns it upside down, a small key sliding out. She drops the key into my hand.

None of this makes any sense. "I doubt anything is still there. It's been too long," I say as I examine the key closely. It's a simple one. It could go to anything.

"I can pull it up on my phone and we can go check it out."

I shake my head. "It's late. Let's go tomorrow."

"Do you need another shot?"

"No, I'm going to call it a night." I lift Harlow from my lap and stand behind her. She puts the letter back into the envelope and hands it to me, her face downcast.

I tip her head up to see wet red eyes. "Hey." I pull her to my chest, and she wraps her arms around my torso. "It's okay. Please don't cry."

"I'm sorry. I just... I just miss them both so much."

"I know, wildcat. I miss them too."

Her chest rises as she takes in a wobbly breath. "I should be comforting you. Not the other way around."

"You've helped me more than you realize." And I mean it. If she hadn't come with me, I wouldn't have found that hidden safe. I wouldn't have ever known about any of this.

We release each other and I miss her warmth immediately. I'm about to ask if I can stay with her tonight, but her next words stop me.

"Come on. I'll give you a lift in the Gator. I need to check on Fletcher anyways."

Fletcher Roxwell. The one man standing in my way to Harlow's heart. I had planned to have a conversation with him last night, but he was already out cold. I think tonight might be the perfect time. It'll help get my mind off things.

"I'm going to walk back. I need to clear my head. I'll check on Fletch for you."

"But—"

"Please, Harlow. Just give me this tonight. If he needs anything from you, I'll let you know."

She hesitates for a moment and finally nods. "Okay. If you need anything, let me know too."

I kiss the tip of her nose and stalk out of the house. My thoughts are swirling quickly. I can't keep up. The only thing grounding me is Harlow, and the only thing in our way is Fletch.

The moment I step outside, I'm breathing in damp, heavy air. Full of tension. I can't clear my head. Not with Fletch still in the picture. My footsteps grow heavier as I walk toward the trail. Her warmth still touches my body.

The way she looked at me lingers in my veins, but it's tainted by the weight of what stands between us.

I break into a run, needing to shake off the circling thoughts. The night is muggy, the dark sky covered in clouds, blocking out the moon. It matches my current mood. My shoes crunch against the gravel path as anger builds slowly inside. I can't stop thinking about him holding her, kissing her... fucking her.

Twenty minutes later, I slam the front door closed behind me, but it's not enough to shake the chaos happening in my head. I don't feel any less unhinged. If anything, I feel worse.

Fletch's head jerks up in surprise as I stalk into the living room. He wasn't expecting my arrival to be so violent. "Where's Harlow?"

"Not worried about you," I say, dropping down onto the couch across from him.

He has his leg propped up on the table between us, his laptop on his lap. He clicks a few buttons and closes the laptop, setting it next to him. "She said she'd stop by when you two got back."

"I guess she changed her mind."

His eyes narrow. I'm sure he's already tired of my bullshit. Well, good, because I'm over his bullshit.

"Anyone ever tell you how much of an asshole you are?"

His question makes me smile, and I must look deranged because he gulps hard. "Has anyone told you that you're overstaying your welcome?"

Fletch drops his leg from the table and rolls up his sleeves. He leans forward and grabs his cell phone from the wooden table. "I'm calling her."

My jaw tightens. I use a carefully controlled tone. One that will make him understand I'm not playing games anymore. "Why'd you do it?"

His brows dip together. "What are you talking about?"

"You took advantage of her. When we were rocky, you swept in and exploited it. She was vulnerable and you didn't wait one fucking second to cash in on it."

Understanding washes across his face, causing me to grind my teeth harder. He drops his phone and runs his hand through his long hair. "I wasn't trying to take advantage of her. It was just bad timing."

I cock my head to the side. "Bad timing? That's your excuse?"

"It isn't an excuse. It was just what it was. Believe me. I can see how selfish it was of me to put Harlow in that situation."

"You don't feel too bad about the situation, considering you're still standing in the way."

A laugh rips from his chest and I clench my fists. "I'm not standing in anyone's way. If Harlow doesn't want you back, that's got nothing to do with me."

"Bullshit!" I roar, standing quickly.

Fletcher gets to his feet, but he's slower. By the time he's standing at full height, I have his shirt wrapped around my clenched fingers. I slam him up against the wall. "She's mine! I don't care what happened between you two. She always has been and always will be mine. I'm giving you three days to get the fuck out of here before I take you out myself."

"I'm not going anywhere. She means more to me than anyone in this fucked-up world. I won't stop loving her," he spits, his face beet red.

I lose all control in that moment. I don't hesitate. My fist slams into his cheek, and we tumble to the floor. Fletch rolls on top of me, hitting me hard in the ribs, making my next breath harder to take in.

I came back looking for a fight, a way to release all my frustrations. It seems Fletch needs that too.

I roll us, slamming his shoulders against the hardwood floor. His head bounces as he struggles for control. I punch him right in the same spot I originally hit him. "She fucking loves me!" My voice sounds unrecognizable.

"I fucking know that, all right? I know she fucking loves you!" Fletch yells right as he punches me in the face.

I stop.

Breathing heavily, I heave myself up against the wall and lean against it, wiping blood off my lower lip. For someone who occasionally sports a man bun, he's tougher than he looks. Fletch slides up next to me and leans his body against the wall, rubbing his jaw.

"Fuck, man, you got a hard right hook," he says.

I laugh. "You're no walk in the park either," I say.

Both of us give weak, fake smiles.

He releases a gush of air. "Listen, man, I'm not here to get into a relationship with Harlow. She's nothing more than a good friend. Anyone with half a brain can tell who owns her heart."

I drop my head into my hands. Harlow's never going to forgive me for starting a fight with him. This entire situation is fucked up and nothing makes sense anymore. The letter, my parents planning to close up shop, the geographic coordinates that probably lead to nowhere because it's been seven fucking years, and now this. "I don't think she's going to like me for much longer once she gets a look at your face."

"You're not looking too fair yourself."

I huff in agreement. I've got no doubt that once the adrenaline leaves my body, the aches will make an appearance.

Fletch sighs. "It was bound to happen. I think we both needed to get this shit out of our system. When she comes by tomorrow morning, I'll talk to her."

"And why would you do that?" I've done nothing but be a dick to him since I set foot on Oasis soil.

"Because I owe you one. Those files you sent me on hacking into my security system. You were right about how to correct them. I already made the changes and updated the software on Harlow's house today."

Nodding, I stand and hold my hand out to help him up. I walk over and pick up the envelope that must have fallen out of my back pocket when we started to fight.

Blood smears across it. I toss it on the table and head to my room, exhaustion hitting me hard. I'm going to need my rest tonight. I have a feeling I'm going to be working hard on taming a certain wildcat by sunrise.

Chapter Eight

Harlow.

My mind is jumbled as I race through my home, getting ready. I can't find the damn supply list I made for the cottages. I thought I left it in the kitchen, but it apparently grew legs and walked off. I feel unfocused. Only one thing will clear my head. I need to go to Marion's Suite and check on Fletcher. At least that's what I tell myself, but I know it's only partially true.

I desperately need to see Logan. When he left last night, I could tell he was barely holding it together. I wanted to ask him to stay the night with me, but I couldn't bring myself to do it.

He may have broken my heart all those years ago, but the heartache I will cause him if Aleksei and I reach an agreement over the Oasis will be even worse. That doesn't mean I can stop worrying about him. I still love him. He still holds my heart and I would do anything to help him through this. I know he's lost and confused.

His mother's letter took me by surprise. I had no idea they were planning to close that chapter of their lives. Marion never once hinted at it. From the way Logan's body went stiff underneath mine, he didn't have a clue either.

I'm ready to look up the latitude and longitude coordinates this morning. He's probably right that whatever they had planned for him isn't there any longer. They died less than a week before his birthday. They probably never got the chance to complete it. I just hope that the unknown doesn't kill him inside. If I were in his shoes, it would torment me until my final breath. But not knowing? That would be even worse.

I take the steps up to the front door and give a quick, light knock, then let myself in. The smell of bacon hits first, but that isn't what stops me in my tracks. It's the scene playing in front of me.

Logan is standing at the stove, his lower lip split and swollen, his eyes cast down on the frying pan. There's a small bruise on the side of his chin. Fletcher's sitting at the table, his laptop open. His eye is black and blue.

What the fuck?

Neither of them seems to notice me. They keep going about their morning like they didn't beat the shit out of each other last night. That has to be what happened, right?

"Make it fingerprint-accessibility only and you got

that one in the bag," Logan says, stirring something in the pan.

Fletcher leans in closer to his computer. "Shit, man, you're good."

Logan shrugs like it isn't a big deal. I look around, trying to make sense of what has happened. Nothing in the cottage looks out of place or like there was any kind of scuffle.

"What the hell is going on?" I say, walking into the kitchen area and dropping my bag on the table. Both men whip their heads toward me, but my gaze locks onto Logan's. I know without a doubt that he was the one who started the fight last night. This isn't Fletcher's MO.

"Good morning, beautiful," Logan says.

Fletcher chimes in. "Logan just helped me troubleshoot my latest prototype. I was stuck on how to integrate the locking mechanism and—"

I hold my hand up, halting his words. "You can stop right there. What the hell happened to both of you?"

Logan brings over a plateful of eggs, bacon, and hash browns and sets it down in front of me. "I hope you're hungry," he says, giving me a wink.

As if on cue, my stomach growls.

Fletcher chuckles. "Good call. She's always been easier to handle with food in her stomach."

They share a laugh. I roll my eyes but don't argue. I'm starving and I have a feeling I'm going to need all my energy for whatever shit is going to come out of their mouths. Logan sets up plates for Fletcher and himself before sitting down next to me.

I remain silent as I eat; I blame my shock over these two. They carry on with the same conversation they were having when I first came in. I feel like I've woken up in *The Twilight Zone*, listening to these two talk each other's ears off. Every time either one looks my way, I narrow my eyes and slam my fork into my food.

I knew if Logan gave Fletcher a chance, they would make fast friends. After all, they're both into computers and whatever crap they do on them. Fletcher might be on the right side of the law, while Logan is without question on the other side, but you would never guess it from their banter.

The breakfast is so good that I want to lick the plate clean. Logan has always been a great cook and used to make some of the best dishes I've ever tasted. Feeling happy as a fat cat on a sunny afternoon, I push my plate away, lean back in the chair, and cross my arms. They pass glances between each other.

"Okay, you two, spill."

Logan clears his throat. "I punched Fletch in the face last night."

"And I punched him back in the face," Fletcher adds.

I close my eyes and rub my forehead. "That much I can tell. Why did you two punch each other in the face?"

They both sit silent for so long, I wonder if they're even planning on telling me. They're making me feel like the parent of two kids who don't want to confess.

"We were playing a game of truth or dare," Logan finally says.

If looks could kill, he would be dead on this kitchen floor.

Fletcher coughs, trying to conceal his laugh. He turns his attention to me, his expression serious. "You need to tell him, Harlow."

His words hit me like a freight train because I know damn fucking well he didn't just say that right in front of Logan. I want nothing more than to slap him upside the head.

Logan whips his head back and forth between me and Fletcher, clearly not understanding. His gaze finally locks on me. I look down at my jeans and drag my hands up and down my thighs. My anxiety is already kick-starting.

"Tell me what?" Logan's tone is even but guarded.

"Do it, Harlow, or I will," Fletcher says, his voice low and firm.

I shake my head, not believing this. "No, Fletcher. I'm not doing it and neither are you. This is only between us and that's how it's going to stay. I made you a promise and I won't break that for anyone."

Fletcher grabs my hand and Logan growls.

"I'm serious, Low. I'm done hiding from everyone. It's time we come out with it. I'm tired of living in secret."

I peek through my long lashes toward Logan to find him vibrating with anger and about to lose his shit.

Fletcher gives me a reassuring nod. Releasing his hand before Logan rips his arm off, I turn to face Logan, who looks like he's holding himself together by a thread. His eyes drill into me.

"Fletcher's gay."

Logan stays locked in place. The only part of his body moving is his eyelids as he blinks once, twice, then three times slowly. "What?"

"You heard me. Fletcher and I never hooked up. He would come over to meet with his boyfriend and do, you know, whatever." I wave my hand. "But then Kali took notice while living here, and I decided to neither admit nor deny what she was thinking. I made a promise to Fletcher that I would never tell another soul he was gay. I don't break promises. So there. Now you know."

Logan leans back in his chair, hopefully taking a moment to reflect on how much of an asshole he's been to Fletcher over the years for no reason at all. "You're really gay?"

"As gay as you can get."

Logan's head snaps back to mine. "And you two never hooked up?" Apparently, we just overloaded his brain, because he's a lot slower than usual.

"Nope." I hope he's feeling two inches tall for all the fights and arguments he's started over absolutely nothing.

A wide smile sweeps across his face. He leans toward Fletcher, slamming a hand to his back and making him grimace. "Man, that is fucking great! Wow," he says, standing and putting his hand to his chest. "I thought you were going to say you knocked her up and I was going to have to bury you six feet under."

"Logan!" I hiss, coming to a stand and putting my hands on my hips. "Apologize right now!"

Logan seems undeterred by my tone because his smile never leaves his face. "Dude, thank you! I don't think I've ever been so happy to learn someone is gay."

"Logan!" I yell again.

Fletcher stops me. He rises out of his chair, slower than both of us, but still showing improvement. "It's all right, Harlow. I know he didn't mean it like that." He turns to Logan and holds out his hand. "Truce."

"Shit, anything for you, brother," Logan says as he knocks his hand away and pulls him in for a hug.

My phone comes to life in my bag. I pull it out to see Gage McCollin's name flashing across my screen. I step away into the living room, giving these two knuckleheads their moment.

"Hey, stranger. How's life treating you?"

"Better than words can explain. I saw my mom again and met her boyfriend."

I smile, knowing Kali has been working hard to orchestrate that. "It's about damn time."

"Listen, I don't have much time. My little lion just got in the shower. I was wondering if you know where Link is. I've been trying to call him all morning and can't get through."

I look over at them. "He's talking with Fletcher right now."

"I thought those two didn't get along. How's his leg?"

"As good as can be expected. He'll be back to good in no time at all. I know you're in a rush. Give me a second."

I walk over and hold the phone out to Logan, his eyes dropping to it and lifting back to mine, silently asking who it is. "It's Gage. He's been trying to call you all morning."

Logan's eyes turn wide and he quickly snatches the phone from my hand. "What is it? Is it Kali? Is she all right?" I watch the side of his neck grow redder the longer he listens. "Fuck, man, I don't know. Isn't this a little fast?"

I can't hear what Gage is saying, but I can hear him talking a hundred miles a minute.

"Fuck, man, she's my little sister." Logan paces back and forth, his hand rubbing the back of his neck.

A smile reaches my lips. I think I have a good idea of what this conversation is about. I may only be hearing one side of it, but I would bet my .357 that Gage is asking for Logan's permission to marry his sister. I give my hands a little shake, trying to release some of the excitement building inside.

"Yeah, man, all right. But if you do anything to..." His words cut off.

Now I don't have a doubt in my mind. I bite the inside of my cheek to stop from squealing in excitement. I turn to Fletcher. He's thinking what I'm thinking, judging by the large smile on his face. Kali worked for Fletcher for years and he knows her well. He's happy.

Logan finally disconnects the call and walks over to me. He holds out my phone, but I can't take it from him right now. My hands are threaded tightly together like I'm praying. Which I guess I kind of am.

Logan's lips twitch before he says, "He's going to ask Kali to marry him."

Everything inside me rushes out. I scream and jump into Logan's arms, hugging him tight. *I knew it, I knew it, I freaking knew it!* Kali is the light to Gage's darkness, and together they're an amazing couple. Logan laughs and squeezes me back before letting me slide down his body. I probably shouldn't have done that, but I don't think I could have stopped myself if I tried. "Logan, oh my God! That was so sweet. He called and asked permission to marry your sister."

He chuckles. "I think it was more along the lines of demanding it, but he knows if I'm not there, Kali won't do a thing."

I smile. I know Gage well enough to surmise that nothing would get in his way to Kali's heart. "Oh my! Planning this wedding is going to be so much fun. Did he say if they are getting married in Ireland or in the States?"

Logan looks down at me warmly. He knows I love his sister like a sibling. I always wanted a sister, but my parents weren't even happy with having me, so I guess it's good they didn't have any more.

"He's planning on asking her and then surprising her with all of us there. He wants to marry her on the same day. He told me he wants us to get our asses to Ireland as quickly as possible. He'll send a plane to pick us up."

"What day is this happening?"

He smiles. "Saturday."

I shriek again, biting my hand. Why? I have no clue. I'm just so happy right now. That's four days from today. "We can try and find what your parents left you and surprise Kali with that."

"Oh no, wildcat. We won't have time for that. I need to get as many of those cottages repaired before we leave."

My shoulders droop. There's no way I am letting him chicken out of this. We're traveling to those coordinates to make sense of things. Before I can even make my argument, Logan says, "The weather will be changing soon. We'll do it first thing when we get back."

He kisses me on my nose and walks back into the kitchen. I smile a genuine smile for the first time in a long time.

I've been glowing from the inside out since this morning. I watch the mail carrier approach from down the road. I check around, making sure Logan isn't nearby. Last I knew, he was working on one of the oldest cottages on the property, which is a couple of miles from where I'm currently at. Which is good. He can't hear the conversation I'm about to have.

Old Man Joe comes bumping along the track and finally reaches me.

"Miss Reece, I've got word from Mr. Aleksei Morozov. He's requested your presence to talk over a deal in private as you requested, but he wants it done in Russia."

I rock back on my heels as Joe hands me a stack of mail and I slide him money. His services aren't too outrageous, and keeping this negotiation off the grid is worth every penny.

"Please let Mr. Morozov know that I will be visiting Ireland in a few days and will be staying at the Menlo Park Hotel. If he's serious, he can meet me halfway. Have him leave his number with the front desk attendant. I'll call him when I get there to set up a place and time."

Old Man Joe nods and takes off down the road. I turn on my heel and walk back down my driveway. I come around the corner to discover that Logan is back. He's loading more wood into the trailer. He's shirtless and his pants hang loosely on his hips. The man is built like an oak tree. I want nothing more than to climb him like the wildcat he claims I am.

But I don't. I step out of view and watch his muscles flex with every load he picks up. Guilt starts to fill my lungs, making my skin damp from sweat. If I can score a deal with Aleksei, I might be left with a fraction of the Oasis. If I'm lucky.

My phone vibrates in my pocket. I pull it out to see that my dad is calling.

An hour later and a hundred grand less in my pocket, I hang up.

Chapter Nine

Logan.

It takes just under ten hours to get from Seattle, Washington, to Dublin, Ireland. By the time Fletch, Harlow, and I arrive, we're all beat like we ran a damn marathon for a week straight. Gage wants to keep our whereabouts unknown to Kali until he can reveal the surprise. That's fine with the three of us. We all crash hard in our rooms at the Menlo Park Hotel.

Today is the big day. Or maybe not. There's no telling whether Kali will accept his proposal. I'm more than happy if she tells his ass no. It's not that I don't like Gage. In spite of our recent misunderstanding, he and Conner have become great friends of mine. I understand why he did what he did to me and I've forgiven him. But she's still my little Kali-Allie, and it's hard to give her away.

Even though Gage has already swooped in. Just not under oath yet.

I shower quickly. Our plan is to meet up at Harlow's room, which is one floor above me and two above Fletch. Then we can head down to the ballroom before Kali and Gage arrive. Aric is here as well, but we have yet to see him. There's profoundly no rush in that reunion. He may be in the works of taking down his father, but I still can't bring myself to trust the manipulative asshole. As I slide into my suit, my mind wanders to the revelation my little wildcat and Fletch revealed to me about his sexuality.

I almost didn't believe it. Fletch being gay? Inconceivable! My stereotypes clouded my judgment, making me feel like an even bigger asshole for trying to categorize him based on superficial traits. But he's a good man, one I now consider a close friend.

I always felt that we share a unique bond; our minds work in tandem on complex codes and software that often seem like an arcane language to the uninitiated. But over the past four days, we've plumbed new depths. Our conversations delve deep into realms that would leave most people bewildered. With Fletch, there's a comforting familiarity. His revelation has only strengthened our connection. Not only because I'm now aware that he's not a threat to my attempts to rekindle my relationship with Harlow, but also because it revealed the depths of his character and the courage it took to share such a personal part of his life with me.

His help with the repairs to the cottages before we left has been tremendous, helping me work through the to-do list faster. The contractors I hired will keep things moving along. By the time we get back into town, another three cottages that are currently occupied should be vacant. We should have no problem knocking those out in a week's time.

Guilt over how far the Oasis has slipped over the years weighs heavily on my chest. I take full blame. If I had trusted Harlow, I would never have walked away completely, leaving her alone. She looked after my sister and took care of my parents' property while buried in her own responsibilities. I haven't come close to groveling enough. She's keeping me at arm's length, but I catch her watching me often. Whenever she's near, I know it. Call it a sixth, seventh, or eighth sense. I don't know. All I know is I can feel her presence the second she walks into my orbit.

Like the evening after she told me about Fletch. She didn't realize it, but I knew her bluish-gray eyes were on me as I loaded lumber into the back of the trailer. I caught her just after she hung up from talking with her father. The entire day, she had been laughing and joking like the Harlow I know. But after her conversation with her father, she became... depressed. Her bounciness was depleted, and her smile didn't return the rest of the day. I know she's trying hard to reconcile her relationship with her parents, but at what cost is it worth it?

She already works nonstop, and her situation with

her parents isn't helping. The Oasis isn't a full-time job. It becomes your life. It is your life. Two hundred sixty acres is a lot of land to maintain. Even with her employees, those thirteen cottages are no walk in the park.

But I love it there. Maybe even as much as Harlow does. I just wish whatever her parents are saying to bring her down comes to an end soon. I might need to intervene, but being that I've been on thin ice lately, I choose to put that on the back burner. For now.

The letter also lingers in my mind, along with the coordinates, which I haven't been able to bring myself to look up yet. Harlow begged me to plug it in and drive to the location. It's been seven years since my parents were killed. If something ever was waiting out there, it's long gone by now.

Besides, we didn't have time. Especially with Gage's unexpected call demanding our presence. I have enough guilt hanging on my shoulders, making it my number one priority to get those cottages renovated as quickly as possible. Anything to help shift the weight from her shoulders onto mine.

My mother saw something in Harlow the day she met her. I see the same thing. She may hold a tough exterior, but her heart is as pure as the mountain air or the water in my favorite lake.

I'm sure when we get back, Harlow will be on me again to take a road trip to whatever it is that my mother and father had planned. But I know how it will end—with us sitting at a dead end. A dead end I don't want to face. The truth of the matter is that they died before my twenty-third birthday, so even if they did set something up, there's no way it's still there.

I adjust my tie and head out early, hoping to catch a few minutes alone with Harlow. As the elevator door dings and slides open, so does the one next to it. I walk out and almost straight into a sight that makes my heart stumble.

I'm used to seeing Harlow in her normal clothes, which consist of cut-up jeans and classic rock T-shirts. So when my eyes land on her, my breath is stolen from my lungs. Harlow's in a long dark purple dress that has a slit up the side. Her chestnut hair is curled and pulled back in a fancy twist. The curves on this woman are enough to drop any man to his knees and beg for only a moment of her time.

I'm officially the biggest jackass known to humankind for messing up my chance with this woman.

"Logan. You're early."

I cock my head to the side, assessing her flushed skin. "Where were you?"

"Oh," she says as her hand moves to her sparkling necklace. "I had to run down to the front desk."

Something seems off. "Is everything all right?"

She smiles and it dismantles me piece by piece. God, I'm pathetic. "Yeah, of course. My blow-dryer went out and I ran it down to the front desk to get a replacement for tomorrow."

I look down at her empty hands and raise an eyebrow.

"They're bringing one up later. Is Fletcher ready?"

I shake off the feeling that something isn't right. It's most likely jet lag. "He's on his way." And as if the timing couldn't be worse, the elevator dings and Fletch walks out. I like the man, but damn, can't he be late for once in his life? I was really hoping to get some one-on-one time with Harlow, but it looks like that's going to have to wait.

We all head down to the ballroom and make our introductions to Gage's mother Angela and her boyfriend Cillian. I give a nod to Conner. He's talking with Gage's younger brother Ashton. Aric stands next to Angela, looking like the arrogant son of a bitch he is. Gage really pulled out every stop in hopes that my sister will say yes. Still, given Kali's past relationship with Aric, I figured he would be the last person here. But knowing Kali and how she sees the good in everyone, Gage must have lost that battle.

The ballroom is expansive, with high ceilings and crystal chandeliers. The walls are adorned in rich, deep tones, with delicate gold-leaf detail framing the tall windows. Gage spared no expense for Kali. Renting out this place couldn't have been cheap. The thought brings a smile to my lips.

Harlow pulls open her clutch and cusses under her breath.

"What is it? You forget something?"

"I think I left my phone at the front desk."

I check my watch. I still have plenty of time to make it there and back before Kali and Gage arrive. "I'll run and get it now."

Her small hand wraps around my arm. "No, it's fine. I can grab it afterward."

"Nonsense, wildcat. I got you." I give her a kiss on the cheek and walk out without waiting for her debate. That woman can argue until the sun comes up if you allow it.

The lobby is slow, with just one man standing at the counter. I walk up to the young receptionist who is typing away on her computer. She does a double-take, her typing coming to a halt. She takes her time to check me out, her tongue running along her lower lip.

I want to tell her not to waste her time. No other woman can make me stray from my wildcat. But I choose to ignore her. Gage and Kali will be here soon.

"Harlow Reece thinks she left her phone down here. Has anyone turned it in?"

The young lady's cheeks darken. "Yes. I put it in the back room. I'll grab it now." She turns to the other man standing at the desk. "Excuse me for one second, sir."

I turn and lean against the counter as the man next to me takes a step closer.

"You know Harlow Reece?" he asks. His Russian accent is unmistakable.

I side-eye the man and stand to my full height immediately. This guy is built like a brick house and apparently knows my woman. Not that it's unusual. Harlow knows a lot of people because of the Oasis. She probably has every major player on speed dial.

"Yeah. Logan Keeyes. And you are?" I ask, holding my hand out.

He grips it tightly, as if trying to show me rather than tell me. "Aleksei Morozov. Do you know where she is?"

I look him over again. He's wearing a three-piece suit, his dark hair cut short to his head. I don't remember meeting him before, but again, that means nothing. Harlow's contacts stretch across the planet. "Are you here for the wedding?"

"Yeah. I've got a date."

Realization hits me. He must be here for Fletch. I know he was talking with a guy out here about meeting up. I know this because I hacked into his computer during our flight. I was bored and it was a long flight. Digital trespassing seemed like the logical thing to make time pass.

"The phone, sir," the young woman says as she slides the phone across the counter.

"Thanks." I take it and slip it into my pocket. "Follow me." I don't wait for his response and turn to head back to the ballroom.

His heavy footsteps tell me he's right on my heels.

We make our way into the ballroom, thankfully free and clear of Gage and Kali. We walk over to Harlow and Fletch, who are toasting glasses of champagne.

"I found your date," I say to Fletch.

He chokes on his champagne and starts into a coughing fit. I give a hard hit to his back and hand Harlow her phone. Her eyes reach Fletch's date and she pales instantly.

What the fuck?

I look at Morozov, but his gaze isn't on Fletch. They're on my woman. "Hey, asshole. Eyes off my wildcat."

Harlow holds her glass out to me, and I take it. She grabs this asshole's arm and storms off.

What in the ever-loving fuck is going on?

I take a step to follow, but Fletch halts my progress, slamming a hand to my chest.

"Don't do whatever you're thinking. She'll lose her cool if you crawl ten feet up her ass."

I turn back to him, my voice low and rough. "What the hell are you talking about? I'm not letting any man walk away with her. Especially one who looks like that." I'm as straight as an arrow, but even I can tell when a threat is looming.

"You need to chill out. This guy is probably here to do business with her, not hook up. Fuck, man, you need to rein in that jealousy before you lose her for good."

I drain her drink in one go and slam it down on the table. I look Fletch dead in his eyes. "You're going to need to knock me out to stop me from going after her," I spit, getting ready to turn and follow Harlow. But before that's possible, I am knocked back by his fast fist to my jaw.

That motherfucker just threw one of the hardest hits I've ever felt. I would laugh if I could, but apparently, I have bigger things to handle. Like not getting my ass kicked in front of everyone here. I stumble backward, gasps breaking out around us from the other guests.

I don't give a fuck.

I charge Fletch with everything I've got, and we slam to the floor. It feels like déjà vu as we tumble to the floor, throwing cheap shots at each other.

"You don't even know who the fuck this guy she just walked off with is," I hiss.

"You dumb fuck! You have her heart, and all you have to do is not fuck it up!"

I slam my fist into his face, cutting him above his right eyebrow. "Don't tell me what the fuck I have to do. I thought he was here for you."

Large arms wrap around me, tugging my grip from Fletch.

"What the fuck, Link?" Conner says as he rips my body back. "Get your shit together. They're going to be here any second now."

Aric materializes, takes hold of Fletch, and shoves him back. They probably think we are fighting over Harlow. Which would be correct, but not for the reason they're thinking.

Fletch cracks his neck. "You think that asshole is my type?"

I shrug Conner off. "Fuck, man, I don't know. He's tall, dark, and gloomy. Figured that was right up your alley."

Fletch lunges for me again, but Aric holds him back. If someone had asked me years ago whether I thought Aric would come into my life and do something to help, I would have knocked out their front teeth and laughed in their face. Guess I would have been wrong.

"You both need to chill the fuck out. I don't know what's going on between you two, but any second, Kali is going to walk through those doors, and you are the last thing she needs to worry about."

Aric's severe words hit home. The fact that this asshole is showing me up with his straight thinking has me seeing red, but I don't react. He's right. This is all about my little sister finding her happily ever after. I would hate myself for the rest of my life if I messed up her special day.

And as much as I hate to admit it, I know Fletch threw that cheap shot to help me, not hurt me. He did exactly what I asked him to do. I grab his champagne flute off the table, slam the rest of his drink, and throw it against the wall behind me. It shatters.

Fletch shakes his head and says, "Nice, you asshole."

I ignore him and keep my eyes focused on the corner where Morozov and Harlow disappeared. It takes all my willpower not to walk around that corner, but I know he's right. I've been working hard to regain Harlow's trust. If there's one thing I know about her, it's that a clingy man is not her type.

I work to compose myself. Fletch does the same. "Sorry," I mutter under my breath.

Fletch gives a nod.

I stalk off to the other side of the room with Conner. I need to cool down and get a better view of this corner.

Chapter Ten

Harlow.

"What the hell are you doing here?" I whisper-yell at Aleksei, not wanting my voice to carry to the other guests. I drag his large ass around the corner and down a long hallway. "We were supposed to meet tomorrow morning."

"I'm a man of little patience and the only one I know of who's interested in the Oasis."

His Russian accent is thicker than I imagined, but he speaks impeccably. I place my hands on my hips, not only because I'm mad beyond belief, but because I once read that the way for a woman to feel more dominant in a man's world is to take the superhero pose. It works.

"I have what you want. Let's not forget that." I jab my finger into his hard chest. "Overstepping will make me walk away. I would rather give up everything I've worked my ass off for than hand it over to an entitled asshole like yourself."

Aleksei's frigid gaze sizes me up. He slowly licks his lips as his eyes flash with something I'm not interested in tangling with.

"Rumors give you no justice, Miss Reece. You are more than the queen of darkness."

What the fuck is he talking about? Queen of darkness? Ha! If only he knew the real me: the one who wears holey jeans—not because they're in style, but because I don't have time to go shopping—and whose life consists of cleaning guns and caring for the grounds that make up the Oasis. "You need to go."

Aleksei takes a step closer. One step is all it takes to close the short distance between us. I keep my feet planted when all I want to do is shove my .357 underneath this asshole's chin and take care of him myself.

"You're the one who asked for this," he says, his deep voice rumbling from his chest.

"No. I told you I'd meet you tomorrow fucking morning. You have no idea what kind of shit you just started by showing up."

He cocks his head kind of like Logan does, but not as sexy. I'm sure he has women lining up to get a piece of him. Why wouldn't they? He's tall, dark, and if I'm honest with myself, edible. He has a square jawline with dark stubble, black hair that is shaved short, and brown eyes that hold danger and power.

"As I said, Miss Reece, I'm a man of little patience."

He tucks a stray hair of mine that must have come loose from my twist behind my ear. I slap his hand away. I don't need a knight. I already have two who butt heads on the regular. Dealing with a third would push me over the top.

His lips twitch. "So, which one is it? The long brown-haired brute or the blond warrior?"

His question forces me to take a step back. He only had a few short moments with Logan and Fletcher. I'm flabbergasted that he read the situation so fast.

"The blond. His name is Logan and if you want to keep breathing for longer than the next sixty minutes, I highly recommend showing some respect."

Aleksei's full smile appears for the first time and it's almost blinding. "I'm only here for business, Miss Reece." His eyes sweep over my body. Nothing about his look is screaming business. Before he can make his way back up, I slap him across the face.

His jaw clenches.

I'm sure he isn't used to this queen of darkness.

Welcome to hell, asshole.

"You listen right now, and you listen closely. I don't need you. I can walk away from this arrangement and not lose a wink of sleep." I'm lying through my gritted teeth, but I'm hoping my squared shoulders and steady gaze make him think twice. "You want to stay for this celebration? Fine. But you will follow my rules. One, no business talks around other people. Whatsoever. If you utter one word, this deal is off. And two, if you fuck with anyone who's currently here or about to arrive, I will fillet you from head to toe then feed you a bullet for dinner. *Capiche?*"

We stand locked into a calcified glare. This is my life he's fucking with. I'll be damned if he throws it upside down more than it already is. Seconds tick by, but it feels as if it's been a lifetime.

"Fine. But I'm not here to pussyfoot around. I'm here to make a deal."

Good enough. I need to get back to the party before Logan comes rushing around the corner. I turn on my heel and stomp back into the main ballroom, but when I reach it, my steps slow.

What the hell? I left for two seconds.

I take in Logan first, who looks pissed and is now standing on the opposite side of the room, leaning against the black grand piano. At first glance, nothing is amiss. But on closer inspection, I can tell his hair has been fixed and the skin below his eye is red and swollen.

My eyes snap to Fletcher's, because who else could be involved but him? I'm proven right when I notice his perfection is disturbed and a red line of blood runs across his eyebrow.

These two are going to be the death of me.

I head toward Fletcher because that's where my drink should be, but all I come across is an empty glass, and the other one is missing. Just as I reach him, my eyes screaming at him in silence, a server appears from my left with another tray of champagne.

I grab a glass, as do Aleksei and Fletcher. Ten seconds later, the main doors to the ballroom open. Kali and Gage appear and we all yell out, "Surprise!"

This is going to be a long night.

The wedding was nothing short of magical, with every detail perfectly curated, from the glimmering chandeliers to the delicate floral arrangements that filled the air with sweetness. Gage and Kali's love was evident in every glance they shared.

Seeing Kali as happy as she is now—as happy as she was before her world crashed down—is a blessing. I remember the long dark days after she first moved in with me. I didn't know if she could pull herself out. I did everything I could, but nothing worked. Not until the day I handcuffed her wrist to mine, forcing her to run and breaking down her wall.

Seeing her now, shining like she has always been meant to, I realize I can't take credit for everything. Gage may have stormed into her life like a hurricane, but he brought out more of her light, and her shine is incredible.

I glance over at Logan, who's in conversation with Conner and Gage. Those three have created a bond with one another that I doubt can ever be broken.

As if aware that my eyes are on him, Logan turns his attention to me and winks. The gesture is small, but I take it as if I won the lottery.

Aleksei showing up unannounced could have revealed my financial problems and the fact that the Oasis won't be completely mine anymore. Thankfully, Aleksei didn't stay long and told me to collect the paperwork he brought about the Oasis at the front desk.

"Want to dance?" a familiar voice whispers into my ear.

I turn to Fletcher with a smile. This man has been my best friend since we were young. I couldn't imagine my life without him. "I'd love to."

Fletcher takes my hand and leads me to the dance floor. Gage and Kali are locked in each other's arms next to Cillian and Angela.

"You want to tell me what happened during the five minutes I was gone?"

Fletcher's smile is warm as he peers down at me. "Why aren't you giving Logan another chance?"

His ignoring of my question doesn't go unnoticed, but it works in deterring me. "I can't. We've been through too much. You've seen how he is." I laugh and quickly add, "And then toss me into the equation. We would destroy each other in no time at all."

Fletcher's smile doesn't waver as he twirls me around his hand and brings me back to him. "The greatest love is never that simple. I thought if anyone knew that, it would be you."

Fletcher is such a romantic. It's one thing I love about him. Nothing great is received easily. If you could obtain anything great with ease, you would never appreciate its value. If you want something bad enough, you have to make sacrifices and work harder than the next person.

"Logan and I aren't young anymore." My response might be weak, but it's all I have. Fletcher has no idea how my business is about to fail and, in doing so, will fail Logan and his parents.

"And yet no one else has ever caught your heart like he has."

And no one ever will.

I don't realize I said those words out loud until Fletcher responds, "Exactly. So what's holding you back, Low? What's stopping you from a love most people can only dream of?"

I've always told Fletcher everything. Every little challenge I've ever faced. Everything except my current one. If I did, he would demand to help me, and I can't accept that. He has enough on his plate with his own recovery. To have to deal with my money problems and the unyielding cancer rocking my mother's body would be too much.

"It's too late, Fletcher."

"It's never too late."

I feel a small hand wrap around my arm. "Fletcher, hi," Kali says. "Harlow, I have to pee and need help in this poofy dress! I think my bladder has at least ten gallons in it, maybe twenty. I can feel it crying inside me."

I laugh at her pained expression. Fletcher steps back as she leads me off the dance floor to the restroom.

I help her with her dress, which Gage already had ready for her to change into. She looks like a princess. Her mother would be gushing in tears if she were here today. I turn my back while she does her thing.

"All right, start spilling," she demands, yanking her dress back down over her hips with the grace of a drunk octopus. "What the heck is going on? Are you in one of those three-way relationships I keep reading about in gossip magazines?"

I have no idea what kind of magazine she's reading, but clearly not the same ones I do. "What? No, of course not."

"Who was the tall, deliciously dangerous man with you earlier?"

I laugh and hold back an eye roll. "It was just Oasis business."

"You and Fletcher then. Good. You two are cute together. I always knew it, since I first started staying with you. I can't believe you two waited that long to eventually go public with your relationship," she says, heading toward the sinks.

Before, I would never correct her, but after everything I just went through, I speak up. "We're just friends."

"Uh-huh." She wags her eyebrows.

I shake my head and laugh. "I'm serious. Fletcher and I have never been with each other. Not like that." I don't know why I feel the need to tell her. Maybe because her brother is back in my life and I don't want her to think that we had a fling behind her Logan's back. Regardless, I need to make it clear that there will never be a me and Fletcher. "Fletcher is gay."

Her mouth drops open, then snaps shut like that of a puppet whose strings just got yanked. It takes her a moment to catch her bearings. "You're just messing with me, aren't you?"

"I promise I'm not," I say, grabbing a cloth towel to wipe my hands with.

Fletcher told me after we came out with the truth to Logan about his sexuality that he was done hiding his true self. He told me to tell Kali the truth if she cornered me about us again. He was done hiding behind me. It only took two bottles of wine to convince me.

The door vibrates, and a loud pounding rocks the other side of the bathroom door.

"Little lion, you okay?"

Gage. The man who never had time for a woman is now living his life wrapped around the finger of an incredible woman.

"Coming!" she yells, then turns to me and says, "We're not done with this conversation."

The door busts open and Gage strides in.

"Gage, what the hell? This is the women's bathroom."

"Harlow," he addresses me.

I give a small smile.

He turns his attention to his bride, wraps his arms around her, and pulls her to his large chest. "When are you going to learn, little lion? I don't care where you're at, when I need a kiss from my wife, I'm going to get one." Their lips crash together and Kali wraps her arms around his neck.

Smiling, I take a few quiet steps and exit the room. The love they have for each other is addictive and has me seeking out Logan. I enter the ballroom but don't see him anywhere.

I deflate and make my way toward the balcony doors, needing some fresh air. The moment I open the French door, I'm hit with Logan's masculine scent, a mixture of spices.

His back is to me. I slowly close the door and slide the lock. Music still seeps through. I'm only a step away from him when he turns his body to face me.

With love in the air tonight, I want to grab a slice for myself. Even if I can only afford to take a bite.

Logan grips the balcony railing behind him as his eyes level with mine. "Who was he?"

The question is simple enough, but it's one I don't want to dive into. Tonight is all about love and forgetting all my problems. I want to remember, if but for a second, what it feels like to be free again. To be his again, even if it's only for one night.

"Business." I lift to my toes and kiss him softly. He stiffens briefly before melting into me, our tongues dancing to "Perfect" by Ed Sheeran.

His strong arms wrap around my waist. He pulls me to his hard chest and deepens our kiss with a throaty growl. In this moment, I feel as if I am floating. As if all my worries and responsibilities have disappeared and it's only him and me under the full moon.

"Take me, Logan, just for tonight," I beg.

He doesn't argue. He whips me around to the balcony rail and slowly drags his hand through the high slit of my dress. His rough fingers slowly glide under my panties and across my aching clit. I lean back against his chest as a soft moan escapes me.

I open to Logan, letting him explore my body as I fall into a state of ecstasy. Logan is the only man I've ever been with and probably ever will be. I greedily take everything he gives me and let myself go. Letting the pressures of my mother's cancer go, letting the fate of the Oasis go, and falling into pure bliss with the only man I will never stop loving.

Chapter Eleven

Harlow.

By the time we landed back in the States, we were all thoroughly exhausted and crashed hard for twelve hours straight. Well, at least I did. Logan wanted to join me, but I sent him along with Fletcher. I savored every moment of the one night I allowed Logan in Ireland. It was unforgettable. But now, reality has come calling again.

The quick trip was both fun and tiring. After the wedding, we spent a few days exploring the rolling green hills, visiting historical castles, and enjoying the warm hospitality of the locals.

We also learned that Kali and Gage are going to live in Ireland. Logan wasn't too thrilled but wisely kept his thoughts to himself. As he should. It was Kali who pushed to set roots down across the pond. I can only hope that they visit home often. I miss Kali and her elaborate stories. I saw the bond between Kali and Angela, Gage's mother, growing strong. Angela may never replace Marion in Kali's heart, but she's doing a wonderful job filling the hole.

I reluctantly pull myself out of bed and get ready for the day. Another cottage should be open for Logan and me to work on. I'm ready to get this done as quickly as possible. I want Logan to check into the geographic location left in the letter by his parents.

By the time I get to Marion's Suite, Logan is nowhere to be found. Fletcher tells me he went out to the Hidden Hedge cottage, so after a brief chat, I hop back into the Gator and head that way. This cottage holds a lot of history for Logan and me. It's also the one that needs the costliest repairs.

As I climb out of the Gator, I note Logan's black truck parked in front of the cottage. A ladder is set up along the side. I catch a glimpse of him up on top of the roof.

How did he get all these roofing supplies here? He never said a thing about buying anything for the cottages. Setting my coffee down, I take a deep breath and climb. I'm not one for heights.

I peek over the edge of the roof. Logan is hammering nails into the new shingles he has laid out. When did he have time to purchase these? He's almost finished, which tells me he didn't sleep twelve hours like I did. Shame runs through me. I'm the owner of the Oasis, the one who should be getting my ass up early and working. Not the other way around.

He's wearing worn-out jeans and a deep blue shirt. I watch his bicep flex every time he brings the hammer down. I swallow the lump that forms in my throat over the thought of those biceps wrapped around me the night I gave in to temptation. I wish I could relive that night every night for the rest of my life.

How good they felt around my waist while he gave himself to me on the balcony. How I trembled in his arms as he took me again in the shower back at the hotel. How those arms carried my soaking-wet body to the bed where we spent the rest of the night tangled in one another.

By the time the sun came up the next morning, we had only gotten a few hours of sleep. I could feel the impact of our sex on my body and felt wonderfully sore and lethargic. He, on the other hand, was full of energy, reminding me of our earlier years together.

He reaches for another shingle, wiping his forehead as his eyes jump to mine. "Wildcat."

My cheeks flush at his nickname as if it's the first time he called me that. Shyness shivers through my body. I give a pathetic "Hey" in response.

His smile appears. He drops the hammer, stands, and makes his way over to me. "What are you doing up here? Did you get over your fear of heights?"

The fact that he remembers such a small detail about me makes my heart thump hard in my chest.

He glances at my death grip on the ladder, giving out a light chuckle. "I guess not. I'm almost finished. Why don't you climb down? I'll be there in a couple of minutes."

My phone starts ringing in my back pocket, scaring the crap out of me. I jump at the sudden noise.

Logan's hands slam to the ladder. "Whoa, wildcat. Easy now. You're okay. I won't let you fall."

I press my head up against his ankle and exhale roughly. I feel his hand rub down my back before reaching my ass and pulling out the little device that almost brought me tumbling to my death.

He looks down at the screen and back at me. "It's your dad."

It's all he has to say to kick-start my heart to what must be an unhealthy rate. "Don't answer it!" I screech just as his finger hits the button. There's no way in hell I can allow Logan to speak with my dad. It could uncover every dark secret and unravel my world.

And it turns out I'm not ready to give Logan up yet.

I look down at my white knuckles, pleading with myself to let go of the ladder, but I can't get my body to do what my mind is screaming. Logan brings the phone to his ear.

Shit!

Logan doesn't say anything, and I can faintly hear my father call out my name.

"Mr. Reece, it's been a long time."

It's not hard to hear my father's next words; he's yelling. "Who the hell is this?"

Logan laughs and looks over at me. I give my best pleading look, but it doesn't seem to work.

"Aw, now you're just hurting my feelings. I thought you would never forget the bad boy who stole your daughter's heart."

I can't hear my dad's response, but Logan smiles at me before responding, "The one and only."

My hands are starting to sweat, and I silently curse myself for getting into this situation. I look down to try and figure out a plan but quickly look back up. I might as well be at the top of a ladder against the Empire State Building for the way my body is starting to shake. I may be deathly afraid of heights, but I'm even more afraid of my father spilling my financial issues to Logan.

He must notice my shaking because he latches onto the ladder again with a firm grip. "You seem to have forgotten that I don't answer to scum like you," he says while he smiles down at me.

Oh. My. God.

My father has been in turmoil since my mom's battle with cancer, and Logan doesn't have the slightest clue about that. I narrow my eyes into slits, hoping to get the message across. It doesn't work.

He plops his ass down completely and leans back on the shimmering-hot shingles like he's on a damn beach. "Let me make this perfectly clear to you. I'm back in

Harlow's life and I'm not going anywhere. Harlow told me you all have been starting to rekindle your relationship, and I won't get in the way. *But* if you hurt her in any way, use her in any way, hell, look at her in a fucked-up way, I will personally make sure that won't ever happen again."

Logan's voice is low and lethal, his threat to my father raising goosebumps across my skin. He pauses to listen and then responds, "I don't care if you haven't heard a word about me from your exquisite daughter. What we do is none of your damn business."

Oh fuck. I drop my forehead to Logan's thigh, wishing the world would suck me up and take me far away. His hand dips into my hair. He caresses his fingers gently through it. How can he be so calm with me but deadly with someone else at the same time?

I embrace his touch right now because it's the only thing stopping me from having a heart attack.

"It's been a real pleasure talking with you, Mr. Reece. Harlow will call you back in a few. Don't forget what I said. I wouldn't recommend taking it lightly." He ends the call and drops my phone on the rooftop. "Hey. You okay?"

I shake my head, refusing to look up at him, and mutter, "They're going through a lot right now. He doesn't need the added stress on his shoulders that you just brought him."

His hand freezes in my hair, and I feel him pull away with an ache, missing his touch already. It took me years to build my walls, and now he's stormed back into my life, toppling them as if they were children's building blocks.

His fingers touch below my chin, gently raising my face to meet his gaze. "Then tell me. What's going on with them?"

I stare into his hazel eyes, trying to think of what I can say without giving away too much and leading him to dig deeper. "Life. And all the bullshit that comes with it," I reply generally. His tight expression shows he isn't satisfied with my answer, but thankfully, he doesn't press further. He stands, grabs my phone, and slips it into his pocket.

"What... What are you doing?" I ask, hugging my body the ladder as tight as I can.

"I would never let anything happen to you, wildcat. I'm going to get behind you on the ladder. We can scale it together."

"But how can you do that with me on top?" I'm in full panic mode right now, my voice coming out in a high pitch. The thought of falling off this damn ladder is tipping me over the edge.

Logan wraps his hand around mine as he easily swings his leg around my body. I slam my eyes shut, not wanting to witness our fall to our deaths. My breathing has quickened as if I just got back from a five-mile run. I feel like I'm going to pass out from fear at any given second.

His hard body leans against mine. Slowly all the fear

starts to drain out of my limbs. "Let's take this slow, okay? I'm going to take a step down, and then I want you to take a step down. We'll be back on the ground before you know it."

I swallow roughly and nod, not really having a choice in the matter. Logan takes his time with me, his body pinned against mine as we make the slow trek down the rickety ladder. I keep my eyes closed, so when Logan's hands wrap around my waist and tug my grip from the ladder, I can't help but squeal in surprise.

My feet hit the grass. He pulls me into his large arms, wrapping the same biceps I was just admiring moments ago around me. I instantly melt into him. The safety I feel in his arms is something that has never changed and never will.

He pulls me back, assessing me closely. "You okay?"

I take a step back, wiping my sweaty hands on my jeans, unable to make eye contact because, well, that was as embarrassing as it gets. And to think people call me the queen of darkness.

"Yeah, I'm sorry. I shouldn't have climbed up there."

"I'm glad you did."

My eyes jump to his in question. "You are?"

He gives an adorable lopsided grin, one of my favorite Logan smiles. "It's always a good thing to face your fears head-on. It shows how courageous and brave you truly are."

He pulls out my cell and hands it back to me. "I'm

going to finish these last few shingles. Don't go anywhere."

His lips brush against mine for a simple kiss, and he turns back to the ladder and climbs up to the roof.

I stand stunned for a moment before my phone starts ringing again. It's my dad. I'm not looking forward to what he has to say now.

"Hey, Dad," I say, trying to sound nonchalant and not like I'm about to have a breakdown.

"What the hell are you doing with Logan Keeyes? You know that piece of shit isn't any good for you." His voice is sharp like broken glass. "I don't care what kind of promises he's made or how charming you think he is. You're better than that."

"Dad, stop. Logan's just here to help me out around the Oasis."

A laugh that sends shivers through my body comes across the line. "That's right. That's the normal Keeyes MO. Always riding to your rescue. Are you still having issues with the Oasis? Your mother and I tried to warn you about taking it over."

"It's not like that, Dad. He's in town for a few days helping out." If my dad would give Logan a chance, like an honest-to-God chance, I know he would love Logan as much as I do.

"Did you tell him about your mother's condition? You know we don't want anyone knowing."

"No, of course not." What I want to say is how good

it would be for both of us to have a support team, but I keep my lips sealed tight. We've already traveled down that road and there was nothing smooth about it.

"You know how much stress I've been up against with your mom's health. Having to worry about my only daughter getting hurt again by the same man is extra stress I can't afford. I have so much on my plate, and I need to know that I can count on you. That your mother can count on you."

Guilt rises in my throat, and I swallow it with a gulp. This is exactly why I didn't want Logan to answer the damn phone. I knew my dad would go off the rails, and he needs his energy focused on my mom and getting her back to health. "I can come there, you know. Help out with whatever you need."

"Like how you flew across the pond on an impromptu getaway?"

I open my mouth to respond, but nothing comes out. It takes a moment to collect myself. "How did you know that?"

"I know this is hard for you to understand with our history, but I care about you," he says roughly. "A father's job is to always look after his little girl, even when she's a grown woman and thousands of miles away."

I start pacing back and forth, trying to wrap my mind around this. "Then why don't I come out to visit? We can work through this together."

"Oh, sweetheart, I've been praying for that too. I think soon, but right now, your mother can't have visitors. I'm buried in paperwork and trying to keep everything afloat. I'm working on it, though, and it'll happen soon. I was just calling to let you know that we received the money you transferred over, and your mother got her first dose of these new trial meds. It's going to take a little time to see whether her body rejects it, so stay close to your phone."

Hope blooms. They have already started treatment, even though I haven't been able to get all the money. "That's great news."

"It is, sweetheart. Now you take care, and I'll be in touch. And Harlow?"

"Yeah."

"Stay away from Logan. I don't think I can stand watching him break your heart again. My heart is too weak with your mother as it is."

With those last words, he hangs up. I walk over to the porch stairs and drop down. The banging of the nails going into the new roof above me lets me know I still have a few minutes to get myself composed. I drop my head into my hands and fight the burn in my eyes from holding back tears that are begging to fall.

How did my life become so hectic? I worked hard to get where I am today, and yet it feels like every step I take forward, I jump back three. Life can be so cumbersome, closing every door that opens before you can even reach it and see what is inside.

My father's words play on repeat through my mind. He doesn't need the extra stress of Logan back in my life, and I can understand why. Logan destroyed me. What he doesn't get is that I need extra support too, and right now, Logan is my rock. Otherwise, I might have already crumbled to the ground.

    I heave out a breath, uncertain what to do.

Chapter Twelve

Logan.

I find Harlow with her face buried in her hands on the front porch of the cottage. I sit down next to her and nudge her. "Hey, Evel Knievel, you forgot something," I say.

She lifts her head and looks at the coffee mug I'm holding out to her. She left it at the bottom of the ladder. A small smile breaks apart her lips. She takes the mug. Her cheeks may be dry, but her eyes are red. The last thing I ever want to do is hurt her in any way. I think I've done enough, accusing her of having a fling with Fletch and destroying the only good thing left in my life.

"Evel Knievel?"

"Hmm, you're right. How about Spider-Man—wait, my apologies—Spider-Woman? Scaling that twenty-foot ladder to rescue your man in distress was no light task."

She snorts and shakes her head. It wasn't a laugh, but I'll take it. "I didn't save you. You had to save me."

I notice she doesn't argue the fact that I said *your man*. My smile grows larger. I like the fact that subconsciously she knows I'm hers. Deep down in that locked-up heart of hers, she knows we are far from being over and this is only the beginning. "That's where you would be wrong. That sweat wasn't from the work I was doing." I flex my arm, showing off my muscles. It might be petty trying to show off, but I will pull whatever shot I can to get her attention.

She unknowingly licks her lips as she drinks me in.

Before I get too distracted by everything that is Harlow, I continue. "These guns can handle anything coming their way. Mountain lions, hurricanes, ungodly tall ladders… But that sweat was from the distress of being alone way up in the clouds."

She rolls her eyes. "Now you sound like Kali."

I shrug. "Who do you think taught her?"

We share a smile.

Harlow takes a drink of her coffee. "How did you get the supplies to reroof this cottage?" The question is one I saw coming, but one I was hoping to avoid. This woman can be as stubborn as you can get when offering money.

"I ordered them before we left for Ireland and had them delivered while we were gone." I also had two construction companies here doing work throughout the Oasis during our getaway, but she won't be hearing that.

"How much do I…" she begins to ask, but I shut her down with another quick kiss on the lips before standing. She has yet to stop my unexpected kisses with a slap to the face. Or her .357 resting under my chin, which I'm well aware she currently has on her. I could feel it when we were descending from the ladder.

"There's more. Come on." I hold out my hand to help her up. Her unique bluish-gray eyes peer up at me in suspicion, but her hand still reaches for mine. I weave our fingers and pull her up. We take the remaining steps up the front porch. I swing the door wide open and gesture for her to enter first.

She eyes me warily, then crosses the threshold of the cottage that means more to me than any other. I have no idea if she remembers our history here. Regardless, I could never forget it. I felt like I won the lottery that day, and I did. Just not with money.

A small gasp slips from her thick lips as she takes in all the work that has been done. She spins in a circle, her eyes jumping from the refinished hardwood floors to the fresh paint on the walls to the new appliances. I'm definitely bringing the construction crew back out here. "I don't understand. I didn't sleep *that* long. How did you get all this done so quickly?"

"A guy I know brought his crew in and did the work while we were gone." I choose not to inform her that multiple cottages were redone while we were away. I would prefer to live another day.

"This had to have cost a fortune."

It did. Especially with the short time frame. But I have more money than I can spend in a lifetime, and it was money well spent. I can see my mother right now, jumping up and down in excitement at this moment.

I'm trying, Mom.

She walks through the kitchen entryway. Her fingers glide across the countertop on the exact spot that changed both of us forever. I use my long strides to reach her, wanting her to relive this memory with me. I grab her hips just as she turns around to face me. I lift her onto the counter in the same spot where it started for us all those years ago.

"You remember." It's not directed as a question to her, more as a statement of relief that she does. Her red-tinted cheeks tell me she hasn't forgotten one confession we gave each other that day.

"How could I forget all those smooth moves you were putting on me?"

"Damn right. I had to pull out all the stops to get you to kiss me for the first time." I open her legs and step between them. I brush her long chestnut hair away from her heart-shaped face. "You're still the most beautiful woman I've ever seen." Her lips beckon me with a magnetic pull. "I need to kiss you again."

Her eyes glaze over with need. I lean closer. The world around us seems to dissolve. I brush my fingers against her jawline, tilting her head in a tender gesture. Our breath mingles, creating an electric charge between us.

When our lips finally meet, it's a slow, deliberate connection that sends my blood pumping harder. Her mouth parts, inviting me to explore deeper. I wrap my arms around her waist, pulling her flush with my chest. I can feel her heartbeat sync with mine.

Her hands find their way to my hair, tangling in the strands as our kiss deepens. My body goes up in flames from the simple taste of my wildcat. It's as if time stands still. In this moment, nothing else exists but the two of us.

Sure, the one night she gave me in Ireland was any man's fantasy, but this right here is deeper. More intimate. She's giving herself to me at the same spot our lips first touched. I did everything to earn that kiss, and the reward was better than any gold medal. Until the day she cuffed me to the old iron furnace in the Lavender Lodge. Now *that* was the best day of my life.

I slide my fingers through her thick hair. My teeth playfully drag at her lower lip before my grip grows possessive, more intense.

Her soft moan tells me all I need to know. She might not say it with words, but I know she loves my mouth on hers, my hand fisting her soft hair, and everything else that makes us a done deal. She still loves me. I can feel it.

My cock throbs hard, and I'm about ready to snatch her little ass up and take her to the bedroom when she breaks the kiss. She pants audibly as she presses her forehead to mine. We both remain silent, the only noise coming from our labored breaths.

"Um, if I remember correctly, I got to second base before I let you off this countertop."

An unstrained laugh comes from my wildcat as she leans away from me, amusement dancing in her eyes. "I think you had plenty of time with my tits in Ireland."

I grin, my chest expanding. "I'm thinking I need a reminder."

She laughs as she pushes me back and hops down.

That's okay, wildcat. I've always loved the chase.

She makes her way to the other side of the kitchen but stops at the newly installed bay window. "How much do I owe you?" she asks once again. It doesn't surprise me.

My response comes out quickly; I was already prepared to answer. One thing I have learned about Harlow is that you always need to be on top of your game. "I'm covering the cost of this."

She pops her hands on her hips, an argument about to break out.

I don't give her a chance. "You let my mom remodel Marion's Suite. I think it's only fair you let me do the same. With the memories this cottage holds for me, I've picked this one to make my own."

Her face stays blank, making it hard to read what's going on in that head of hers. I'm about to elaborate further, but her next words stop me. "Okay, but only if you give me payment for doing this behind my back."

My eyebrows come together. Did I hear her correctly? "You want me to pay you for doing this?" Hell, if that's what she needs from me, I will happily drain all my bank accounts into hers.

She looks around before bringing her eyes back to mine and nods. "Yeah. I think it's only fair."

"Done. How much do you want?"

She shakes her head and makes her way back to me. She's making no sense. Asking for money after I just forked out a shit ton to get this done fast has me stumbling. This isn't like Harlow, but again, it's a sign of why I need to be on top of my game with this wildcat. She loves a curveball like no other.

"I don't want your money."

"Okay..." I respond, still not following her and probably looking like a complete jackass.

Her eyes meet mine, and I know, I just *know* I'm not going to like what comes out of her mouth next.

"For payment, I want you to go to those coordinates your parents left you. It's either that or I'm paying you back for all the work you've done... with the cost of labor."

Fuck. I run a hand through my hair. I was hoping she would drop that. "You realize that whatever they had planned was probably never set up at the location, right? They died just before my birthday. Seven years ago."

Her finger reaches my chest and she swirls it right above my pounding heart. There's nothing fair about this. I feel my cock growing in response to her touch. An intoxicating vanilla scent overloads my senses. I know exactly what she's doing.

Her words come out husky and hot. "Maybe, maybe not, but there's only one way to find out."

I lean against her, unable to stop myself, and trail my nose along her neck.

A giggle comes out of her as goosebumps erupt over her skin. She pushes me back. "What do you say, chief?"

Oh, she's really pulling out all the guns on this one. I can't remember the last time she called me the nickname she gave me the first day I showed up to help her with repairs on the cottages.

Grabbing her hips, I pull her against me and look down into her mesmerizing eyes. This woman is a drug I can't quit. "Only if you come with me."

Her eyes light up. I love seeing the excitement in her, even though she just tricked me into something I'm not sure I'm ready to face. I don't know what I'm going to find, if anything.

What am I even saying? Nothing is going to be there.

I won't allow myself to hope. I don't know if I can take it. But then there is the other side of the coin. What if there *is* something there? I don't know what I expect to find, but if Harlow is willing to be by my side, I can take on anything.

"Clean yourself up, chief, and I'll meet you at your place in a couple of hours." She lifts on her tiptoes, kisses me on my cheek, and bounces out of the cottage. This wildcat is going to kill me.

I walk into Marion's Suite to find Fletch typing away on his laptop. He gives a nod and tosses back the rest of his drink. Even after cleaning up my mess at the Hidden Hedge cottage, I have some time left before Harlow shows up.

I take a seat across from him. I need to feel him out. "What do you know about Harlow's parents?"

His typing slows to a stop, and he looks back up at me in question. "Jack and Robin? Not much. I know they live somewhere out on the East Coast now. Harlow's been talking to them again, trying to work past how they royally fucked her all those years ago. Why do you ask?"

Hearing that his opinion of her parents matches mine makes this much easier. "Have you ever been around Harlow after Jack called?"

He gives a nod.

"Have you ever noticed how she is after those phone calls?"

Fletch leans back in his chair. "Now that you say something, it is kind of strange."

I lean forward, crossing my arms on the tabletop. "Exactly. If they're really trying to repair their relationship, why is she always down and depressed afterward?"

"Fuck, man, I can't believe I didn't notice this sooner." Fletch runs a hand down his face. "With how much they screwed her, I just figured their conversations are on the heavy side. She never talked to them when I'm around."

If Fletch can see what I'm seeing, then I'm not losing my mind. Something isn't right with her parents. I have a gut feeling they aren't trying to rekindle shit on their end. "Can you investigate them? See what they're up to? Harlow said they're going through hard times right now but wouldn't elaborate."

"Yeah, sure. Grab a rocks glass. I just opened a bottle of bourbon. Together we might be able to get this figured out by the end of the day."

"I can't. Harlow's coming by. She wants me to... There's somewhere we need to go, or at least inquire about. I don't know how close or far away it is."

"Are you talking about the coordinates in that letter?"

I narrow my eyes. "You read it?" My voice comes out rougher than I intended, but I don't apologize.

He laughs and throws his hands up. "You're the one who left it out here on the table."

"That doesn't mean you can go through my shit."

He shrugs. "I was bored. Just like you happened to be on the plane ride to Ireland when you hacked into my computer. I think we're even now. You want me to pull up the coordinates?"

I don't know why I'm so pissed that he read my parents' letter. Maybe because the bomb they dropped had caught me so off guard, leaving me to wonder what I did know about my parents in their final days. I'd thought I would be taking over their business. Not that they'd shutter it and tell me to follow my dreams. Hell, did they even know what my dreams were?

"Do it. I gotta take a shower."

Chapter Thirteen

Harlow.

 I tap lightly on the front door of Marion's Suite and push it open to find Logan and Fletcher focused on the screen of Fletcher's laptop. Logan is freshly showered, his hair a little damp. I drop my bag, making both jerk their heads up. I move over to the seat next to Fletcher but don't lean over to see what they're working on.

 "What are you two up to?"

 "Trying to make sense of this," Logan says, frustration clear in his voice.

 A tight knot forms in my stomach. I hope they aren't looking into anything about my parents. After Logan's conversation with my dad earlier today, I feel as if I'm on pins and needles. I know I should tell them about my mom's cancer, but I know that would come with a flood of questions.

Questions that will lead right back to how the bill is being paid.

I lean back slowly in my chair, my nerves heightened. "Oh yeah?" My voice comes out a little too soft, but neither seems to notice.

"Yeah, the longitude and latitude coordinates. They're close," Fletcher says.

I wrinkle my brows. "What do you mean?"

"It means you two can take the Gator to this location."

That can't be right. I lean forward as Fletcher turns the screen toward me. Sure enough, it's a property that runs along the west side of my own.

"Oh my God." I cover my mouth and lean back into my chair. *There's no way.*

Logan stands and makes his way over to me, sitting on the opposite side. He grabs the hand that's covering my mouth and pulls it down. "What is it, wildcat?"

I shake my head, trying to recall my conversation with Marion all those years ago. This can't be right, though. She would've told me, wouldn't she? I turn to Logan, trying to get my thoughts in order. "It was a year before they passed away. Logan, oh my God." The more the memory filters through me, the clearer it becomes.

"You're killing me, woman. What are you talking about?"

"Marion—your mom—she came by one day and we took the Gator out for a cruise after we shot some rounds off at the target range." I shake my head and laugh. Logan and I may have kept our relationship a secret, but Marion knew better. "We noticed the property next to mine had gone up for sale. I was nervous, not knowing who was going to buy it and what they would do with it." I chew on my lip, the memory feeling like yesterday. "It sold two days later. I tried finding out who bought it, but I couldn't get any answers. After the years went by, I honestly forgot all about it."

Logan abruptly stands and starts pacing back and forth, tapping his finger to his lips. He stops suddenly, his eyes snapping to mine with an intensity that almost feels like a challenge. "You think they bought the property next to the Oasis?"

I nod. "I think so."

His eyes flicker with disbelief and he starts pacing the floor again, the tension in his steps palpable. He's all sharp angles, his body taut with urgency. The air around us grows thicker, his restlessness pressing down on me like a weight.

"Why would they do that?" Logan asks, more as a question to himself.

Because your mom was determined that we be together. That's my first thought, but I keep my mouth closed.

He stops pacing and faces me. "You ready?"

I smile. It might have taken a little push, but that was all he needed. I can see something in his eyes that I haven't seen for years. Hope. I just *hope* that we can understand why they bought this property for him.

I drive the Gator over to the same spot Marion and I did the day we came across the large For Sale sign. The sign is gone, of course, but an overgrown dirt trail is still noticeable. I hand my phone over to Logan.

"Pull up a map so we can pinpoint the exact spot of those coordinates."

While he works on that, I lead us down the uneven path, having to slow multiple times to get around fallen trees. It reminds me of how the Oasis looked when I was a little kid staying with my grandparents. At the time, there were only half a dozen cottages.

"Start veering to your right when you can."

I maneuver to the right slightly. The air is thick with the smell of wet wood, moss, and something faintly earthy, like the forest is still breathing in the last rain. The hum of the Gator's engine is constant, a low growl that vibrates through the seat.

Occasionally, the path clears just enough to let sunlight slip through the canopy, casting light on the dark soil below and illuminating patches of vibrant green moss and wild ferns. My heart pounds more wildly in my chest the deeper we travel down the path. About a mile in, a capacious brick complex with intricate cornices comes into view.

"Logan," I whisper. His eyes jump from my phone to me, following my line of sight to see the building sitting before us.

"What the hell?" Logan says, latching onto my thigh.

I maneuver the Gator around a couple of trees to reach the building. I put the Gator in park and he looks over at me, a wide grin across his face.

With lightness in my chest and energy soaring through me, I jump out of the Gator with Logan, eager to explore the mysterious building ahead. It's striking. Smooth gray—almost black—brick climbs halfway up the height of the two-story structure, creating a clean, modern foundation. The upper half, in stark contrast, boasts dark walnut with grain that's deep, almost luxurious in its richness. It's a beautiful combination of modernity and warmth, bringing luxury to the forest.

Our footsteps quicken as curiosity takes over. The building stands tall, almost imposing, but with a strange sense of forgotten beauty. The windows are covered in dirt. I press my palms against the glass, wiping at the grime, to peer inside, but blinds stop me.

I have no idea when this building went up, but I can tell it isn't that old. It's just been neglected... let's say for the last eight years. Marion and James must have had it built during the last year of their lives.

I surge with excitement, wanting to find out what the inside holds.

We make our way along the large building, taking in its sprawling presence. It must be nearly ten thousand square feet, maybe more. The structure seems to stretch on forever, the silence of the area amplifying the crunch of our footsteps on the gravel. Trees have been cleared away around the building that looms in front of us, both majestic and haunting in its isolation.

At the front, the entrance is framed by a wooden overhang, arching gracefully to a pointed tip above the large double doors, giving it a grand yet welcoming look. The design is elegant, understated but bold. Logan steps forward to try the front doors, but they don't budge. They're locked.

"What about the key in the envelope?" I ask, but he shakes his head.

"It's a key for a lockbox of some sort. It won't fit this one."

Crap.

He steps forward and wipes the dirt off the narrow window of one of the doors, pressing his face to the glass.

"Can you see anything?"

He continues to peer through the window, turning his head at different angles. "A-P."

"Huh?"

"A-P. That's all I can make out. Something is blocking the glass on the other side." He pushes off the door and takes a few steps back, with a look of frustration as he runs his hand through his hair.

"What if this building is someone else's?" he asks, his voice already sounding defeated.

I shake my head and make it to him just as he drops

down to the front steps. I kneel before him, wrapping my hands around his wrists. "It can't be. I would have known if someone else bought it. Maybe not right away, but eventually I would've come across someone or seen some activity. I got a feeling about this, chief. I think this was your parents' gift to you."

His sad hazel gaze reaches mine. "Wildcat." His voice is choked with heavy emotions. "You can't say that. If they bought this property and built this building, why wouldn't they have had the deed to the property in that safe—or the keys, for that matter?"

"Maybe it's somewhere else," I suggest. This can't be the end of their mystery gift to Logan. We're missing something. It's just a matter of figuring out what that is.

He shakes his head and swallows harshly, his Adam's apple bobbing. "I think we got too excited too quick. The key in the envelope isn't the key to open these doors. It's for something much smaller."

His back is hunched as he stares down at his feet, his eyes vacant. I hate seeing Logan like this. So vulnerable. So hurt. I scramble through my head, trying to figure out what our next move is, because if there's one thing I have learned over the years, it's that we don't give up when times get hard. Both his parents and my grandparents taught me that when something becomes too difficult, that's the most critical time to push through it.

I rise, straightening. I hold my hand out to him and wait. His gaze slowly rises to meet mine.

"The one thing that I've always admired about you is your strength to never give up and not give in. If you had backed down the moment you broke into my home, we wouldn't be standing here. Now get your ass up and let's search the perimeter." I keep my hand stretched out, waiting for him to make his decision. "Don't make me pull my .357 on you."

His eyes light up. He takes my hand and pulls himself off the step. Wrapping his arms around my waist, he tugs me against his body. "Are you teasing me with a good time, wildcat?"

I grin, the weight of this moment falling off my shoulders. "Maybe there's a reward in it for you. But..." I poke his chest. "Only if you keep going."

His eyebrow arches in bemusement.

I'm just as surprised as he is. All those walls that I carefully built around my heart continue to tumble down when it comes to him, and there's nothing I can do to stop it.

He's the cheese to my mac. The jam to my peanut butter. The heart to my soul.

"Is that so?" he asks, burrowing into my neck. I arch against his hard body and expose my neck to give him access. He peppers kisses up to my jaw, his fingers grabbing my chin, and pushes his lips to mine.

The kiss starts slow; we take our time with each other. The heat pouring off his chiseled body radiates through me, warming my body from head to toe. I want to get lost in this moment with him, but I can't. We still have work to do, and there's no way he's getting a reward before the work is done.

I push against his chest and our lips break apart. Breathing heavily, I stare into those hazel eyes that are filled with want.

He grabs my hand and pulls me down the steps. "Come on, wildcat. Let's get this over with."

We link our hands and make our way along the building. An hour later, we're back at the front entrance with no more laughs or knowledge than we had before. I don't know how I could be so off on my gut feeling that they built this with Logan in mind.

I know his patience is running thin and it's only a matter of time before he calls it quits on our little expedition. My phone pings from his pocket, causing me to immediately tense up.

Shit! I completely forgot he still has my phone from our drive over. I send a silent prayer to God above, begging Him to let it not be from my father. That's the last thing I need right now. Logan will be able to see a preview of a text, but he won't be able to unlock it. I never told him the passcode.

He pulls my phone out and unlocks it like he's done it a million times. Of course he's figured out the damn code to my phone.

"It's from Fletch. He wants to know how it's going." He hands the phone over to me and heads back up the front steps, trying to peer into the building.

I thank the heavens above that it's not my dad and send a quick response back to Fletcher.

Harlow: *We found a building, but nothing that would fit the key Logan has. We should be back shortly.*

Dots appear. A few seconds later, Fletcher's response comes in.

Fletcher: *Did you go to the exact coordinates?*

I start to respond, "Uh, hello? What do you think we've been doing the last couple of hours?" But I stop suddenly. I delete my draft and send a different one.

Harlow: *You are a genius!*

It doesn't take long for his response to come through.

Fletcher: *You're now just realizing that???*
Harlow: *I love you!*

"Logan!" I yell, not able to take my eyes off my phone. My hands shake from excitement as I close out the messaging app and pull back up the coordinates.

He's by my side within seconds. "What is it? Is Fletch alright?"

My eyes whip to his as my smile grows larger. Not only at the fact that Fletcher just pulled the blindfold off my eyes but also at the fact that Logan just showed concern about my best friend.

His nose crinkles and I love it. I keep beaming. "Aw, you're worried about Fletcher."

He scowls. "No, I was just wondering where I would have to pick his ass up from. I'm pretty sure that bourbon kept flowing after we left."

I smile at his denial. "Uh-huh."

"Enough, woman. What is it? Are we heading back yet?"

I flip my phone screen to face Logan, showing the pinpoint on the map of the exact location. "We were so focused on this building that we didn't check the exact location of the coordinates."

Logan grabs my phone and peers down at it. "Shit. I think it's right over here." He takes my phone and grabs my hand.

We track through the overgrown grass, heading away from the front of the building. We come upon a small clearing, but nothing unusual stands out.

"You have got to be kidding me," Logan says, a laugh vibrating from his chest.

"What?" I ask, my eyes jumping around for whatever I'm missing. There's literally nothing but weeds and boulders.

Logan drops to his knees in front of one boulder. It's different from the other ones. It's an orangish color with a white slash across it. I drop down next to him. He slams his fist into the large boulder, and I cringe, knowing how bad that must have hurt. He has officially lost his damn mind.

"Why the hell would you do that?"

"It's fake."

Fake? I lean forward and feel the boulder. Sure enough, it's made of hard plastic. With the overgrown grass, it blends perfectly into the landscape.

Logan lifts it from the ground. The long weedy grass tries to hold the boulder in place but eventually breaks away at his pull.

Lo and behold, a small box stares back up at us. It's a basic black box with a keyslot underneath the cover, sitting flush with the ground. A keyslot I have no doubt will take the key from the envelope.

Oh. My. God.

It takes everything not to scream at the top of my lungs. Instead, I shriek and plow into his body, wrapping my arms tightly around his neck and kissing him on the cheek.

He laughs, turning my head to kiss me on the lips hard, then pulls back and looks down at the little safe. "We had one of these on our property back at home. Once the underground safe went in, we never used it again."

He pulls the small key from his pocket, lifts the cover, and pushes the key into the slot, turning it slowly. The lock disengages.

I squeal in excitement, tackling Logan to the ground this time, before we even see what is inside. Smashing my lips to his, I revel in the excitement of this moment. It's almost too much for me to handle.

A low growl comes from his chest as he flips us over in the grass so he is lying on top of me. Brushing my hair off my forehead, he smiles down at me. His face is more relaxed than I've seen in a long time. I not only see his happiness but feel it inside him. This is the best day ever.

"Thank you, Harlow."

"Really we should be thanking Fletcher for leading—"

My words are cut off when his lips seal to mine for a quick but deep kiss. I don't argue.

Pulling away, he asks, "You ready?"

I nod enthusiastically. I'm ready for anything with this man. He pulls me up and we crawl back over to the unlocked box. I shake my hands to release all my built-up energy.

Logan pulls the box open. Inside sits a large envelope. He breaks the seal and pulls out the deed to this property. It's in Logan's name. I snatch it from his hands and scan it before hugging it to my chest.

"I knew it, I knew it, I freaking knew your parents were behind this!"

Logan reaches down into the safe and comes back up with a set of keys. This set is much larger.

"I think I know what these go to," Logan says, a devilish smile across his face.

Chapter Fourteen

Logan.

I can't believe it. When Harlow conned me into coming here after learning I hired a construction crew, I honestly thought it was going to be a dead end. Wasted time neither one of us had. I would've honestly rather sat with Fletch and hunted down more information on her parents than go on a wild-goose chase. But there was nothing wild about this chase.

Unless you count the way my wildcat attacked me to the ground in pure excitement. My wildcat is becoming a jungle kitten—one I can't wait to play with later tonight.

The set of keys is weighty in my hand as we make our way back to the main entrance. I look up at the building, seeing it in a new light. The mix of dark gray bricks and the rich wood screams my mother's doing all day long.

She could design anything, turning coal into diamonds with whatever she touched.

This building is one of her many masterpieces.

We take the steps leading to the double front door, my hand locked tightly around my wildcat's. I know without question that if she weren't here with me, my heavy legs wouldn't take me any further. This entire situation is so surreal that I'm afraid I might wake up at any second and it would be nothing but a dream.

The keys in my hand and the lock clicking open are very real, though.

I drag a deep breath into my lungs and let it out slowly. Harlow tightens her grip on my hand, smiling. This woman. This strong, independent woman with a heart of gold is too good for me, but that doesn't seem to matter. I don't care how selfish I am. She's been mine since the day I first laid eyes on her.

I push down on the latch and pull open the main door, the breeze causing a banner hanging on the inside to flutter. We both watch in silence as it settles back down.

HAPPY. That's what it reads in big bold metallic silver letters going down in a vertical line. I pull open the other door and read the other banner.

BIRTHDAY.

A gasp breaks from Harlow. I feel like I just took a gunshot to the gut. We both stand there, frozen in time, staring at a party decoration my father probably helped my mother hang for a birthday celebration that never happened.

My throat feels thick, my stomach sour. I brush my fingers along the banner, wondering if my parents touched the same spot.

"Logan," Harlow chokes out.

I turn to see a long hallway. The interior layout reminds me of a school. Along the wide hallway lie balloons. Deflated, lifeless.

I swallow the lump caught in my throat and pull Harlow forward as we walk down the hallway, following the balloons. There are several doorways on both sides, but after peeking through the first open door—which reveals a fully equipped gym—neither of us slows to look inside. I want to know what's at the end of this hallway, where the deflated balloons lead.

The farther in we go, the darker it gets, but we don't stop. We make our way through a large archway into a room filled with tables and chairs. I pull out my phone and turn on its flashlight. Each table is covered with cloth that reads "Happy Birthday" several times in small print.

Harlow attempts to pull her hand from my tight grip, but I don't let her. Not right now. I need every bit of strength she can give me.

Her smile is small. "Let's open these blinds so we can shed some sunlight in here."

I nod, my throat still too tight to make out words. We wander to the edges of the large room. Large windows, probably ten feet high, span across the entire wall. One by one, we lift the blinds and the sun beams through.

Turning around, I'm struck by the sheer beauty of this place. The building's stark white walls are accented with black, creating a striking contrast. Two spiral staircases ascend on both sides to the second floor, but only one has deflated balloons along the banister.

"You ready?" Harlow's voice is gentle and warm.

I find my voice. "More ready than I've ever been." Those words might be a lie, but nothing could stop me from climbing this staircase and seeing what's at the top.

My muscles loosen with each step we take as I soak in every detail of this moment. We pass a shut doorway and approach double frosted-glass doors with a name etched across them: Logan Keeyes.

With sweaty palms, I push the door open, revealing a meticulously arranged office. *My office.* Large windows adorn the back corner, flooding the room with natural light. The walls are covered with pictures, each framed in elegant black satin.

We step closer to inspect them. The photos vary in size, capturing different moments of my family's journey through life. As we linger over each one, it feels like traveling back in time to a place where nothing was too much to handle. Where every hurdle was a challenge I was determined to conquer.

Scattered among the pictures is Kali's artwork. Most of the paintings are of wildflowers, reminiscent of the Oasis. One catches my attention, and we stop in front of it. It isn't one of her paintings, but a photograph of her painting on a wooden wall. *Or maybe it's a ceiling.* I wonder where this was taken. I pull out my phone to snap a quick picture of it to send it to her later.

The photo next to it captures a day I will never forget. The day I fell in love with the woman standing beside me now. In it, my father and mother are wrapped in each other's arms, my mother's head resting gently on his shoulder. My sister Kali stands proudly beside our mother, leaning against her with a broad grin. I'm on the opposite side of my father, standing tall and confident with my arm tightly around Harlow. She's holding her .357, the very same gun she has with her now. The one on which I engraved our initials just hours before this photo was taken. We're all in the wildflower field, a place all of us loved.

None of us could have anticipated what lay before us. A tragedy that would rock our entire foundation.

"That was one of my favorite days," Harlow murmurs.

I look down at her. Her eyes glisten with tears she won't allow to fall. I hug her and kiss the top of her head. "It was one of my favorites too."

We continue down memory lane, absorbing each picture and painting until we reach the large desk positioned in the middle of the rear of the room. One picture hangs behind it, far larger than any other picture or painting in this room.

It's a picture of only me and Harlow. We're both

lying on a blanket in front of Diamond Lake. I didn't know this picture was taken, but I have no doubt my mother was behind it. Harlow's head is tipped back. She's laughing while I have one arm stretched out far, a mischievous grin on my face.

I always wondered if my mom knew Harlow and I were together. This finally answers the question I have long asked myself. Not only because she hung this photo, but because she witnessed this memory between me and Harlow when we thought no one was watching. Anyone can see the young love brewing between us. A memory frozen in place for a lifetime.

Harlow laughs lightly. "Your mom had no shame in her game."

I grin. She really did have no shame. Right before they passed away, I had been getting ready to tell my parents about Harlow and me... and show them the ring I had bought the week before. A ring that would remain in a small black velvet bag tucked safely away in a desk drawer for almost a decade with no one ever knowing about it. The same one I brought back to the Oasis over a week ago.

"I think she knew about us," I say.

"Oh, she knew, alright. She was probably wondering why we kept it under wraps."

I don't think she ever wondered why. I would bet everything I have that my mom knew exactly why we weren't coming out about being a couple. Harlow worked so hard for so many years to prove herself worthy of not only owning but running the Oasis. If word got out that we were together, everyone would have accused her of being a gold digger, something she's never been. Then add her parents to the equation; they would've done everything in their power to destroy what happiness she did have.

"What do you remember about that day?" I ask, curious as to what stuck out in her memory.

She smiles fondly at the photo. "That was the day you were convincing me why I needed our initials permanently marked on my .357. I think it took you a few more arguments before I caved."

She pulls her gun out of the harness and flips it to show the shaky engraving of simple letters: *SA + JW* and below that, *HR + LK*.

I'd carefully copied the typeface her grandparents had used to engrave the same gun decades ago with their initials.

"And it's still your favorite," I growl, grabbing her. I walk her over to my desk and lift her on top of it.

She laughs, sets her gun aside, and wraps her legs around my body. "I'm so fucking proud of you, Logan Michael Keeyes."

I trail my hands down her thighs and squeeze. "You're the most beautiful woman I've ever known, Miss Reece. Inside and out." I tuck a strand of her soft hair behind her ear. "Let's stop with all this shit and get back on track. It's as clear as that photo behind us that we're still head over heels for each other. Let me in, wildcat. Let me help you too. I know I was rough with your dad this morning, but I can go easy on him. I can support you guys in building a relationship. I can call him tomorrow and set up a time for them to come here. Or we can go there."

Harlow drops her head to my chest, hiding her face from mine. "Logan."

My name passes through her lips as if we have already been defeated. Like the thought of us isn't even an option for her future. She can try to push me away every day for the next hundred years, but it won't work. I will chase her until I take my last breath.

I lift her head to meet her gaze. "Just think on it, wildcat. You know how I feel. I'm all in. But remember, if you ever kick my ass to the curb, I won't be far. We're officially neighbors now," I say, leaning in closer. "And I'll give a whole other meaning to *Peeping Tom* by the time I'm done with you."

She shoves me back in a playful way and slides off the desk, laughing. "Alright, creepy Casanova, we're not done here yet." She nods to the right. I look over to see another door off to the side. This one is surrounded by deflated balloons as well.

"Maybe it's a bedroom with a large king-size bed for us to break in?"

"Since when have we needed one of those?" she retorts and struts off, her hips swaying seductively. I can't wait to tame this little wildcat later. I adjust myself and follow her as she opens the wooden door into the room next to it.

It isn't a bedroom.

It's a classroom with long heavy black metal desks lined up perfectly. A small laptop lies in front of each chair. I walk over to the closest one and peer down at the outdated computer. Technology changes every six months; none of these could do a quarter of what laptops can do today. I don't bother opening it. I'm sure the battery has been dead for years.

"May all your dreams come true." Harlow's voice is but a whisper, but she might as well be screaming these words. I look around the room, astonished by everything they did for me. I hadn't a clue any of this was happening.

I turn to Harlow. Her face is lit up like it's Christmas morning and she just got a new gun under the tree.

Something twists low in my gut. A dull ache that won't leave. "They got it all wrong." I wave my hand dismissively. "Maybe back then, but now..." *Shit.* I run my hand through my hair. "It's too late for this. I'm different. Hell, everything is different."

Harlow makes her way over to me, grabbing both my hands. "You're no different of a man than you were all those years ago."

I give her a deadpan look. "You know that's far from the truth. You know what I've seen... what I've done." There's no need to go into detail.

"So what? You took a side path off your journey, but that life wasn't meant for you."

I shake my head and drop her hands, needing to put some distance between us. She doesn't get it. "I can't go back to my life before or who I was then. When you're put in that situation, knowing that you're seeing your parents for the last time and not being able to do a fucking thing about it, it guts you, Harlow. It fucking cuts you so deep, you wonder how you're still breathing." My voice is rough and deep.

"It gutted all of us. Kali, you, me. We all felt the hit when it happened. I know your father put you in a fucked-up position, and it wasn't fair. But you can't change the past. Look around you, Logan." She pauses for a second. "This is what you were always meant to do. Do you think I've forgotten about all the visits we took to those schools with underprivileged kids? Everything you taught them? Everything you gave them?"

"I'm not a good man anymore."

"Bullshit! You did everything you could to get Kali safe and give each of you a fresh start in life. You've helped me out with repairs. You've helped Fletcher with his recovery. You did all that because you are a good man. You just need to open your damn eyes."

I killed all those men for vengeance, not for a fresh start for me and Kali. Hell, my sister might be living her happily ever after, but *is* she honestly happy deep down inside? I was lost—shit, I still am.

Fletch and I might have grown closer since I learned

he's no longer a threat, but I helped him for my own good. All I cared about was getting any competition out of my way. Shit, I pumped the guy full of drugs within seconds of seeing his ass in her bed.

And the Oasis. It always comes back to the Oasis. It's easy to see that she needs all the help she can get, but what's a little work when the prize is her? I would do anything to keep her by my side. What she doesn't realize is that it doesn't make me a good man. That makes me a selfish son of bitch who will do whatever it takes to get what I want.

Harlow is naïve to think she can twist me into something I'm not.

What the hell does she expect out of me? Out of everybody I know, I thought Harlow would realize there is no fairy-tale ending in our lives. We can only move on with the broken pieces of our souls.

"What do you want from me? Huh? You want me to sit back and play teacher while I fix up the Oasis for you? You want me to build you a little white picket fence and play house like I'm not some killer?"

As soon as the words leave my mouth, I regret them, but I push the remorse away. She wasn't there the day my dad told me to get the Double Eagle Very Rare bourbon. She wasn't there when I pleaded silently to my mother to come with me, only for her to refuse. She wasn't there when I went back and found both of them lifeless. She wasn't fucking there. Nobody was, and that's why I will always carry this burden alone.

"I don't need you or anyone else to build me a picket fence, you asshole," she snaps. "Because I already have one. It may not be white, but it's mine." Her chin is held high and her voice is low. "You want to throw away your dreams? Don't let me stand in your way. You seem to have everything figured out." A disturbing laugh breaks from her lips, her face reddening by the second. "Come on, chief, let's go. I'll help you pack your fucking bags right now."

Hearing her say this has my vision turning red. I grab the ancient laptop lying beside me and throw it across the room. It hits the farthest wall and breaks apart.

Harlow doesn't stop. She storms back into my office, and a second later, I hear my office door slam shut. But I'm not done yet. I grab another laptop and throw it across the room. It crashes right next to the first one. Turning around, I sweep my arms across the table, three laptops colliding with the table next to them. I pick up a chair and slam it to the floor multiple times. By the time I'm done, the chair is destroyed, and I feel like shit.

I scream into the empty space, letting my frustration, my hurt, my sorrow pour out of me.

I wish my parents had never done this for me.

Chapter Fifteen

Harlow.

Another sleepless night. I don't know how many more I can tolerate before they start to catch up to me. It's been a week since Logan and I went to those coordinates and all hell broke loose. I have no idea how it even got to that point. If he wants to be an ass, then he can be one on his own. Guilt eats at me for going off on him, but that guilt isn't for Logan.

My guilt stems from letting Marion down. Not only is the Oasis slipping through my fingers, but now I have officially turned my back on Logan instead of pushing him toward his dream of teaching. I can see in him exactly what Marion and James saw. He's made for something much bigger than blood on his hands, but getting him to see his own worth is a challenge.

It was clear when we walked into his office how much time, thought, and love they poured into that building. All the decorations and pictures hung on the wall took my breath away. I'm sure it did the same for him.

I know little about what happened the day his parents died. He's never gone into details about it with me or anyone else that I know of. He's done nothing but bottle up his feelings until they explode and pour over the rim like a powerful waterfall crashing hundreds of feet to the rocks below.

In the picture of him and me at the lake lying on the blanket, we were both so full of hope and dreams. Now those times feel far away. I don't know whether that's a place we could ever make it back to.

It's easy to get whisked away by Logan's charm and forget all the crap that surrounds our lives. When it happens, I feel like we are young again, with no challenge too large for us to take on.

I haven't heard from him since our fight, but I've seen Fletcher regularly. It's clear he knows that something went down between us, but he has steered clear of asking me any questions. Hopefully it will remain that way. I'm not sure what I would say right now.

The only good thing has been the call from my dad early this morning. My mom's body isn't rejecting the new trial medicine, so they're giving her another dose. To keep her progress moving forward, he needed another hundred thousand transferred. I didn't hesitate to send it, knowing that she's finally going to beat cancer once and for all. My dad told me the next round of medicine is going to be tough on her body, so I won't hear back from him over the next week and a half. He promised that if anything goes wrong, he will call me immediately.

A knock sounds at my door. It's a client I've been waiting on. I'm grateful for staying busy and keeping my mind off Logan and my mom while I get this client settled in for his two-week stay. He's new, so I'm on guard. I walk back to my bedroom and grab my Springfield Armory Hellcat. It's not my .357, but I left that one in Logan's office, and there's absolutely no way I'm going over there to get it. The Hellcat is my second-favorite to carry because it's great for concealing, easy to shoot, and fits perfectly in my small hands.

Another loud knock comes and I roll my eyes. Can people not wait a couple of seconds anymore? Ever since technology came along, everyone's patience has worn thin.

I tuck the Hellcat in my waistband and head for the door. Just as the next knock is coming, I swing it open, and with one look at the man standing on the other side, I almost swing it back shut. "What the hell are you doing here?"

"It is a pleasure seeing you again, Miss Reece." His strong Russian accent rumbles from his chest.

"You can't be here. I have a client showing up any minute now."

The arrogant asshole with the ridiculously square

chin smiles broadly. "Is this how you treat your clients? I can see why you're having such financial problems."

I prop my hand on my hip. "What are you talking about?"

He rests his arm against my doorjamb and leans in. "I'm checking in today." He must see the confusion on my face. "Fredrick Lyles, I believe, is the name you were given."

I narrow my eyes on Aleksei Morozov. "You made a reservation under a false name?"

"It seemed that would be the only way you would let me stay here."

I don't want Logan and him crossing paths. I was working on a plan for how Aleksei could come here while keeping him off Logan's radar. I guess he did warn me that he was a man of little patience.

I peel his arm off my doorjamb and push him farther onto my porch, closing the door behind me. "Why are you playing games with me, Mr. Morozov?"

"I should be asking you the same thing, Miss Reece. This deal we're working on isn't going to be cheap for me, and quite frankly"—he licks his full lips as his eyes travel down my body and back up—"I need to test the goods before I make any kind of purchase."

This is exactly why I wear jeans and T-shirts 90 percent of the time.

I don't know whether it's from lack of sleep or Logan ghosting me, but I whip my Hellcat out and press it firmly against his dick. "If you ever look at me like that again, I will not hesitate to blow your dick off and bury you in the back forty while you take your last breath. You want to do business? Fine. But you will show me some damn respect."

My grandma was the one who taught me to never take any shit. She was a hellcat in her own right and one to never cross. Running a business like this requires maintaining control over every situation and every person who steps onto this property.

Aleksei stands frozen. His stare is intense. I would find it frightening if I didn't work with this kind of person all the time. His smile breaks free again as he throws his arms up in surrender.

"My apologies. I'll do my best to keep my eyes under control, but it's a challenge with a beautiful woman such as yourself."

I pull the gun away and try to ignore the bulge forming in his pants. This guy is next-level weird. I slide the gun back in my waistband and shoulder past him. "Follow me."

His heavy footsteps follow, and he mutters, "More like the queen of the pitch black." I choose to ignore him as I make my way to my Gator.

"You can follow me out to your cottage." I put it in gear and head toward the Maserati parked in my driveway, leaving him to walk himself.

I wait for Aleksei to slide into his ride, drumming my fingers on the steering wheel. As soon as his door shuts, I take off toward the cottage I reserved for *Fredrick*. I take it as a lucky sign that the cottage I lined up is the Hidden Hedge. Not because of the intimate history it holds, but because Logan has completely renovated it. If I want this deal to go through, I'm going to need to impress him.

As much as I don't want to.

I find myself hoping to get a glimpse of Logan, even though Aleksei is following close behind me. It would only be another problem—something I don't want. But he's nowhere to be seen, almost as if he's living in the shadows.

I know he and a construction crew have been doing more work on the Oasis, but Fletcher doesn't know what exactly. All Fletcher has mentioned in casual talk is that Logan's been splitting his time between the Oasis and his property next door. I try not to allow hope to bloom in my chest at the thought that he's been going over there. For all I know, he could be burning the place to the ground and drinking his sorrows away.

But as much as Logan is very capable of doing that, I don't see him destroying what his parents built for him. Of course, from the noise of everything breaking in that classroom when I walked out, it's a sure bet he destroyed that room, but the entire building? I don't see it.

I can only pray that he breaks out of this rut he's put himself in before he destroys everything good left in his life.

As I approach the cottage Aleksei will be staying in for the next two weeks, I pull off to the side and hop out. I don't wait for him; I stroll to the front door and unlock it with a code. I walk in, leaving the door wide open behind me.

Everything looks as it should. I make my way into the kitchen and pause at the countertop where Logan and I were last week. My heart grows heavy. *I miss him so much.* I quickly dismiss the feeling and turn on my heel, heading over to a drawer. Pulling out some paper and a pen, I write down the access code for Aleksei to use during his stay.

Heavy footsteps tell me he followed me in. I can't help but think about how quiet Logan is when he walks. You never know when he's going to show up.

"Here's the code for this cottage," I say, pushing the piece of paper across the table. "The code changes at the end of everyone's stay, so if you plan to stay longer, you'll need to speak with me first."

Aleksei looks around, taking everything in. "This is nice. I can see why you charge so much."

I wrap my hands around the back of the dining table chair. "It takes a lot of work to maintain the cottages, plus a property of this size. Not to mention all the amenities."

He nods. He slides his black suit jacket off, lays it on the back of a chair, which he pulls out, and sits down. He loosens his tie and I notice the large red stain along the left side of his torso.

"You're bleeding."

He looks down and readjusts himself in the chair. "I'm sure this is nothing new for you to see, running a place like this."

Before I can stop myself, I make my way over to him. My hands automatically go to his shirt to unbutton it and get a better look, but I pull away at the last second. "Can you take your shirt off for me?"

A deep chuckle rumbles through his chest. "Are you going to shoot me if I do?"

"Stop being an asshole. Do you want me to look at it or not?"

He pauses briefly before doing what I ask. I head back over to a cabinet next to the fridge and pull out a bottle of vodka, thankful that I keep the cottages stocked with liquor. I pour him a glass. He's going to need it.

He cringes slightly when he tugs his shirttails from his waistband and pulls the shirt back. He has a two-headed eagle tattooed across his chest, with the wings wrapping toward his ribs.

I set the glass down in front of him and kneel to check his back. It has a slightly larger hole, but that's a good thing. "The bullet passed right through you. I have a medical team on staff 24/7. I'll give them a call." I begin to stand, but he catches my wrist.

"I don't want anyone else knowing about this." His words are hard and firm.

I peer down at him from under my lashes. "You need stitches."

He releases my wrist and grabs his glass of vodka.

"What I need is for no one to know about this. Why don't you take care of it?"

"That isn't necessary. All my staff have signed NDAs. They won't ever speak of what they see or do here."

His gravelly laugh rings out and he takes a sip of the liquor. "I'm sure you're not so naïve to believe they don't tell anyone."

I stand and cross my hands over my chest. "Well, Mr. Morozov—"

"Call me Aleksei."

This guy is already driving up the wall. I can only imagine what it will be like when he owns half of the Oasis. "Aleksei, I can tell you that my staff does take confidentiality seriously—and the NDAs they have signed. I have had the same staff since before I took over, and we have never had one issue to date."

"Until I know that, I can't take the risk. Are you going to stitch me up or leave me to it?"

I rock back on my heels and dig my fingernails into my skin. Why are men so damn stubborn? I look back down at the hole in his side and the blood seeping out of it. Dammit.

I walk out of the kitchen and head to the bathroom, where supplies for this exact situation are kept in every cottage. I drop them onto the table in the largest bedroom and return to the kitchen to wash my hands in the sink. It's been a long time since I've had to stitch anyone up.

I give one last warning to ensure he completely understands what he's getting. "I can promise you I won't do as clean a job as my staff would."

"I'm sure you'll do fine, Miss Reece."

"Harlow," I reply.

A small smirk forms at the corner of his mouth.

I lead him to the bedroom and lay out a couple of towels while I get everything ready. He's removed his shirt completely, and I keep my eyes off his rigid muscles. This man must shovel a shit ton of snow in Russia. He's built like he wrestles bears for breakfast. Even though he's an asshole, he's a beautiful one.

I begin to stitch him up. I'm tempted to botch the job just to prove a point but decide against it. I still need to make a deal with this man, and I have a feeling that wouldn't be the right way to go about it.

When I first saw the gunshot wound, I couldn't help but wonder if it was from Logan. I remember how pissed-off he was when Aleksei showed up unannounced in Ireland at his sister's wedding.

But I dismissed that idea. Logan wouldn't have missed. Not even an inch to the right and this bullet would have gone right past Aleksei. Besides, Logan likes his guns, but he loves nothing more than using the two *guns* attached to his body. He's built his body into a weapon itself. It's just another entry on my list of reasons I can't get enough of him.

"You aren't going to ask me how it happened?"

I poke the needle through his inked skin and pause, looking him in the eyes. He needs to understand exactly how we operate around here if he's going to become half owner.

"No. It's none of my business why this bullet went through you. My job is to give you a place to lie low and recover."

He nods and doesn't say anything more. I finish stitching the wound together and pull back to look at my work. *Not too bad. I still got it.* I clean everything up and am about to leave when Aleksei calls out my name.

"I want a tour of the property tomorrow."

I drop my head but don't turn around. The Oasis has been my life since I was a little girl, and the cold hard truth of losing half of it kills me inside. I think tonight will be a great night to crack open that bottle of red that's been calling my name all week.

"I'll be by tomorrow afternoon. Get some rest." I don't wait for a response. I walk out the front door like the walls are pressing in behind me.

Chapter Sixteen

Logan.

I lean back in my office chair. The space around me has become more comfortable over the last week. Fletch pours us both a shot of Double Eagle Very Rare bourbon, a bottle I picked up today. It seemed fitting to drink it here, the bourbon that told me my future all those years ago. The bourbon that changed my life forever.

I tap my plastic cup against his and we both shoot them. The lingering warm notes of oak, vanilla, and gentle spice on my tongue relax me further.

Fletch refills our drinks and pushes mine back to me. "I got something for you." He pulls his laptop from his bag and starts it.

I grab Harlow's .357 and trace the initials I engraved

into it back when life was perfect. I thought for sure that by holding it captive, I would've made her show up sooner to retrieve it. She hasn't.

I can't really blame her. I know I was a complete asshole when I lost my shit a week ago. It's on me to go to her and apologize. The problem is not knowing how the hell to do that. Every word I said to her about me teaching here and us running the Oasis together has played on repeat in my mind, and the more I think about it, the more I like the idea.

Then, I think about the last seven years with everything I've faced, everything I've done, and the dream fades away. I'm no longer the carefree, easygoing guy I was. The guy the kids looked up to, the one with so much hope and gratitude. I wouldn't know how to do that anymore, and I'm not willing to risk screwing up a single kid because of my demons.

Harlow's always seen me as a knight, but love can blind even the strongest person. I don't deserve her. I've known that since the day I met her. Yet I can't let her go.

Fletch slides his laptop in front of me, halting my thoughts. I look down at his screen and the pictures displayed in front of me. There are only two. I take my time examining each one in detail, hoping to figure out why Harlow's parents are going through a hard time.

The first shows Jack and Robin walking out of a clinic together, hand-in-hand. She has a large blue hat on that covers most of her face, but I know it's her without question. Harlow doesn't take after her mother much—except in her looks. Harlow has her grandparents' heart and drive.

"They live in New Jersey," Fletch says. "Not the best angle of Robin, but she's into oversized hats lately. I can't find a single candid shot of her without one."

"What's the clinic they're walking out of?"

He shrugs. "Supposedly outpatient care. The new private investigator I'm working with said he couldn't get inside. They have layered security, no directory, nothing online except some vague health language."

"Sketchy," I mutter, blowing up the image. It only blurs further. With Robin's face almost completely obscured, I zoom in on Jack. He's aged quite a bit since I last saw him; his face is tight, giving him a constipated look. His black hair looks fake. It must be a toupee.

The second photo is of them boarding a cruise ship, and it's worse than the first. This time, Robin's in yellow, with another huge hat and sunglasses. Jack has his back to the camera. It feels intentional, like they didn't want to be seen.

I push the laptop away and run my hand down my face. "They don't look like people going through a crisis. They look like people with money to burn."

"They must be. The address in the file is in a swanky neighborhood."

I crack my neck. "How long ago were these pictures taken?"

"Within the last week. They just embarked on the cruise earlier today."

I take a sip of bourbon, trying to figure out what the hell is going on. "What do they do for work? They never had it this good back in the day."

Fletch taps a few buttons on his keyboard. "Nothing. They haven't filed taxes in two years. They're living large off... something."

"Did they win the lottery?"

"Not that I could find. One thing's for sure: They've got to be gaslighting Harlow with some bullshit sad story. What I don't get is why."

"That's the million-dollar question." I tap my index finger against my lips. "Did the PI try running background checks?"

Fletch nods. "Yeah. Robin and Jack Reece come up clean. Too clean. No debt, not even medical records from the last five years. It's like someone scrubbed them."

That gives me pause. *Someone scrubbed them.*

"It doesn't make sense," Fletch adds. "Robin used to flaunt everything. She was flashy, too loud. Now she hides."

"Could be plastic surgery."

"Either way, they're not leaving a trail. Everything we're seeing? I think it's what they *want* us to see."

I was hoping to find some answers about whatever issues Harlow's parents are going through, but I'm left with more questions. "Can you try talking to Harlow to find out more about what's going on?" I ask.

Fletch closes his laptop and leans back in his chair. He takes a drink. "You two need to sit down and get your shit figured out."

I know we do, but every night when I watch her from the shadows, I can't seem to make my feet move. I told Fletch everything the night of our spat. He simply shook his head, a look of disappointment on his face, and went to bed. He loves and cares about Harlow as much as I do. "You're right. I'll fix it tonight."

Fletch doesn't respond. He packs his laptop away and stands. "What are you planning to do with this building?"

I look around at all the pictures and artwork on the office walls. This place has grown on me quickly over the last week. "I don't know yet." It isn't a good answer, but it's all I've got right now. I honestly have no idea which way to go.

"If you decide to open an academy, let me know. I might be interested in joining your team." He stands and grabs his bag. "I would be honored to work by your side."

It takes a lot to shock me, and Fletch's offer has done just that. "What about your business?"

He shrugs. "I don't know. Every time I go to get the ball moving on rebuilding my security firm, I stop myself." He picks up his plastic cup and finishes off his bourbon. "Staying at the Oasis has made me realize that the whole hustle and bustle of city life isn't something I crave anymore. I think this school your parents built for you is something I would want to be a part of."

I stand and walk around my desk. "You're really serious, aren't you?"

"Yeah. You inspired me to stop hiding who I really am behind closed doors. Now that I have a taste of that, I can't stop it. I want to live a more meaningful life. One with purpose."

"You have been doing that. You're at the top tier in security. You've helped keep so many families safe with your inventions."

He looks down at his booted leg for a long moment before his eyes find mine again. "I would've rather died than let anyone have insights into my inventions. It took over my entire life, and I didn't like where I was heading." He clears his throat. "But a life of teaching and watching others excel is what it's all about. I've kept my inventions a secret for so long. What better change of course could there be than teaching people how I created everything and watching what they do with that knowledge themselves?"

I smile. It's my first true smile since Harlow and I fought. Fletch is one hell of a man. "I'll keep your offer in mind."

He nods and leaves. We both purchased Gators for ourselves a few days ago. I should've known when Fletch bought one that he wasn't planning on leaving anytime soon.

I lean back in my leather chair and finish my drink. *Fletch would be honored to join my team.* Shit. I feel honored that he feels honored. I rub my hand across my chin. Not only do Harlow and Fletch believe I can do this, but so do Kali and Gage. When I sent my sister the picture of the painting on wood, she called me immediately. She'd thought that painting had been lost in the fire. When she asked where I found it, I told her about my birthday present from the heavens above.

She cried for at least twenty minutes, and within the first thirty seconds of her sobbing, Gage was on the phone demanding what the hell I just told her. They both want to come out to see the place. I was able to postpone their trip by telling them I wanted to get some work done on it first. It wasn't hard to convince them, being that the building has sat empty for so many years. I need to get my ass in gear and figure out what I'm going to do with this building before they arrive.

I always had a soft spot for kids who had a rough start or who walked around with chips on their shoulders like armor. Most of those kids were in their situations because of their parents' bad decisions. Kids are a breath of fresh air, not yet tainted by the evils our world throws at them as they age.

It all started after I helped a school board in Seattle recover from a nasty Russian ransomware attack. They asked me to speak at their district-wide STEM Week. I figured I'd show up, talk code, and leave. But the second I met those kids, everything changed.

They reminded me of me—restless and smart. I was hooked. There's this quiet satisfaction that comes with helping young people see their potential. Fletch is right.

I've wanted to have children with Harlow for as long as I can remember. We talked about it for a couple of months before everything went to shit. Harlow wasn't sure kids would fit into the Oasis, but between the two of us, I had—and still have—no doubt we could keep them safe. Just as her grandparents did for her.

I lock up the building and head over to Harlow's place, remaining in the shadows. She's outside on her patio tonight, drinking wine and cleaning a gun. I miss her laugh and playfulness. I miss her vanilla scent and pouty lips. I miss when her claws come out. I miss everything about her.

For an hour, I watch her polish every part of her gun while the radio plays on low next to her. Even with two bottles of wine next to her, I can tell her body is tense. She's stressed. I wonder what she would do if I walked up and gave her a massage. No words. No apologies. Just my hands on her, taking away the weight that sits heavily on her shoulders. Would she let me, or would I end up looking down the barrel of the gun she just polished?

It's worth the risk.

I take a step, ready to find out, but stop in my tracks when she stands. She looks up into the starry night sky and nibbles on her bottom lip. Slipping the gun in her waistband, she grabs the wine bottles and heads back inside her cabin. That's when I notice she must have drunk directly from the wine bottles because there isn't a wineglass in sight. I wait to hear the click of her lock and watch her disappear inside.

Tomorrow, after I finish the work I have planned at my place, I'll come for her.

You better be ready, wildcat. Your break from us is about to end.

Chapter Seventeen

Harlow.

Apparently, it takes more than two bottles of wine to get a full night's sleep, because I didn't get any. My mind raced all night with prayers for my mother and her new treatment.

All night, thoughts of Logan drifted in and out, some leaving me yearning for his touch, others leaving me pissed. He tells me I'm the stubborn one, but I don't have anything on him. Sometimes I swear his head must be as thick as concrete. I can't help but wonder how Marion dealt with him when he was growing up. She must've had to knock him upside the head multiple times. No wonder she loved wine so much.

One bonus of not sleeping a lot is that you can come up with a lot of game plans. By the time I got out of bed, I was forming one to help push Logan in the right direction regarding opening an academy. I made the call first thing this morning to set everything up for tomorrow.

"All these cottages are impressive," Aleksei says, pulling me from my thoughts.

"Thank you," I mutter as I lock up the last unoccupied cottage I was able to show him today.

That's another thing. I thought Logan had only finished the cottage Aleksei is staying in, but I was wrong. It seems Logan pulled out all the stops to bring multiple companies in while we were over in Ireland to manage the repairs.

It wasn't easy to hide from Aleksei the shock on my face over every cottage I showed him today. The renovations Logan has managed to set up have these cottages looking better than they ever have. And all in just three weeks!

That just pissed me off even more.

I hate that he dumped all his money into the Oasis. If all goes as planned, it'll be half Aleksei's. Logan is going to blow his top. I need to get with Fletcher and see if he can find out what kind of money Logan invested so I can pay him back in full. I might have to take out another loan to keep everything afloat and money flowing to my parents.

"What's the busy season here?"

We load into the Gator and I pull away from the cottage. "There really isn't a dead time. There's never a schedule for when people get shot or need a place to lie low. Sometimes we get slammed, and I have to turn people away from staying here. But I always offer the 24/7 medical staff we have. Other times we're slower. I can't ever remember a time when there weren't at least half of the cottages booked out."

"Who's we?"

"Huh?" I ask, turning my attention to Aleksei.

"You keep saying *we*. *We* have a medical staff here. *We* get slammed. Who's *we*?"

I didn't even realize I was doing that. I've never done that before. It's always been me and my staff, not we. There's never been a *we*. I guess with Fletcher and Logan here helping out as much as they have, I must subconsciously think of us as a team. "No one, sorry. It's just me as the owner and my staff."

He nods before asking, "Where are we going now?"

"Back to your cottage. All the others are occupied."

"I want to see more of the property. Isn't there a shooting range and a lake somewhere around here?"

"Yeah, sure." I turn the Gator around and head in the opposite direction. Fletcher told me he and Logan were going to be at Logan's property next door all day, which has me at ease. I have no idea what Logan would do if he caught me riding around with Aleksei Morozov all afternoon. This isn't something I normally do with clients.

I take him by the shooting range first. The wildflowers have been thick this year, but with the weather changing quickly, they won't last much longer. Kali would love to see it right now.

"We need to cut down most, if not all, of these flowers."

My jaw locks and I try to rein in my anger. "We're not cutting down the flowers."

He chuckles. "What man wants to be surrounded by a bunch of flowers while he shoots his guns?"

I stop the Gator and turn my full attention to him. "First of all, it's not only men who use this range. And the men who do are comfortable with their sexuality. Do you have a problem with yours that I need to know about?" If this arrogant asshole says anything, I'm kicking him out of the Oasis.

"Whoa," he laughs, his voice deep in my ears. "Believe me, sweetheart, I have no issues in that department."

I bet he doesn't, but I refuse to stroke any part of his oversized ego.

"I'm not your sweetheart." Only my dad calls me that.

His blinding smile appears. I really hate this guy. "Fair enough. My apologies. We'll keep the flowers. Now, how about that lake?"

I stare him down hard for another ten seconds. It may not seem like a long time, but I've learned that within a couple of seconds, it can get awkward. Not for me—for the other person.

I finally give a nod and drive us to Diamond Lake, the largest body of water on the property. It's really just a large pond, but *lake* sounds so much better. Sure, a few smaller ponds dot the area, and plenty of creeks wind throughout the property, but Diamond Lake is the most beautiful. Not just because of the history it holds for Logan and me.

I park in the grass and we both get out to walk near the water's edge. It's crystal clear. It doesn't matter whether you're on the shore or in the middle of the lake; you can always see down to the bottom. It's gotten too cold to swim in it now, but once it freezes over, I like to ice-skate on it.

"You really have something great here, Harlow."

I appreciate that he's finally learned how to use my first name. "It's been home for as long as I remember."

"You're very lucky to be able to say that. Not everyone is born into this type of beauty."

His response makes me itch to ask him what he means by that, but I bite my tongue. I can tell Aleksei is the type of man you keep at arm's length; otherwise, you better be packing some heat.

"How are your stitches holding up?"

"Sore. I might have ripped one out, but I can't tell."

I halt, and he does the same. "Can I take a look?"

"This isn't a ploy to get me to take my shirt off again, is it? I'll have you know, Harlow, you will respect me." His smile tells me he's joking, throwing my words back at me after our face-off yesterday.

"Don't flatter yourself. I've seen better." And that's no lie. Aleksei might be ripped, but so is Logan. With

Logan's eight-pack and divine V cut, it's enough to make any woman lose her damn mind. I would know.

Aleksei unbuttons his crisp white shirt and opens it. I lean down to take in the first set of stitches. They're red but look good. I peel his shirt back further to peer at the other side. He did pull a stitch loose, but it's still holding.

"What the fuck!"

I jerk at Logan's voice and turn to see him jumping off a Gator and storming right at us. Fletcher is with him, but with his leg still in a walking cast, it's going to take him a second to reach us.

I throw one hand in the air. "Stop right there, Logan Michael," I hiss. "This is Aleksei Morozov. He's staying here and is a client, so you will treat him with respect." I keep my voice firm, but that doesn't seem to matter.

Logan's murderous eyes land on Aleksei and take in his unbuttoned shirt and countless muscles. His glare makes it clear he doesn't give a shit about the gunshot wound I was checking.

"Why the fuck are you here?" Logan roars, a large vein pulsing hard on the side of his neck.

"Business," Aleksei responds casually as he starts to button up his shirt. "Why are you here?"

Oh fuck.

I'm all about keeping the peace, but if Aleksei wants to poke the bear, I'm sure not going to interfere.

Logan leans in, his fists clenched tightly. "You think I don't know about rich fucks like yourself? Harlow's off-limits. You don't fucking look at her and you damn sure keep your fucking shirt on around her."

Fletcher approaches, laying his hand on Logan's shoulder. "Weren't you in Ireland?"

Aleksei gives a tight nod. "Harlow and I are discussing business opportunities."

"What business opportunities?" Logan growls. He's about to explode.

I need to step in. "That's enough, Logan! You need to back off."

Aleksei turns to me. "You need to learn how to keep your little guard dog in check."

"Excuse me?" Logan asks, stepping forward.

I step between them before Logan gets any bright ideas. "Do you remember the way back to your cottage?" My question is directed to Aleksei, but I keep my eyes on Logan.

"I can show him," Fletcher offers.

I have never been so grateful. There's no way I can drive away with Aleksei right now without Logan beating the crap out of him. I need these two separated before all hell breaks loose. "Thank you, Fletcher." I turn back to Aleksei. "I'll see you tomorrow morning. We can talk further."

Aleksei looks over my shoulder. "Make it early afternoon. I have some business calls to make in the morning."

I nod, willing to agree to just about anything to get him to leave. Fletcher walks by, following Aleksei to my

Gator. As soon as they are out of earshot, I turn on my heel and jab a finger into Logan's hard chest. "What the hell was that?" My voice is filled with anger.

His hand clasps around my wrist, holding my hand tight to his chest. I try to pull it back, but it's pointless.

"What kind of business are you conducting with him?" Logan's voice is low and deep. It doesn't faze me one bit. I know Logan would never hurt me. What he needs to understand is that this alpha male bullshit has got to stop. Normally, I would find his caveman ways sexy, but not right now. He's going to blow my only chance at saving a piece of the Oasis.

"It's none of your damn business."

His eyebrow cocks upward and he leans in, bringing our faces only an inch apart. He smells amazing. "You *are* my business."

I yank my hand, and this time he lets go. "I think you're too afraid to face your own business, and that's why you have to meddle in mine."

He throws his head back and laughs. I really might shoot him one day. He takes a step closer to me, so close I can now feel his body heat radiating off him. "When are you going to learn that nothing in my life will ever come before you again? We may have taken a short break from each other, but that doesn't mean I haven't kept a close eye on you." His voice falls lower. "Apparently not close enough."

I swallow the lump forming in my throat, his words causing my heart to pump harder against my chest and a flutter to erupt in my stomach. He's going to kill me when he finds out why Aleksei is here. "I don't need a damn babysitter, Logan. I need you to figure out your shit and get your damn head on straight." I storm past him, walking to his new Gator. "And when the hell did you buy this?" I snap as I slide into the passenger seat.

I expect him to go to the driver's side, but instead his hand locks around the back of my seat, the other on the front windshield. I cannot deal with this today. I fold my arms across my chest and meet his eyes.

His hazel orbs are no longer steel. "You're right, wildcat. I do need to get my shit together, and I've been working on that all week." His eyes never leave mine. "I'm sorry about last week. I was an asshole when you were only trying to help."

I gape at him, completely caught off guard. I relax slightly, my fight draining. I'm so damn exhausted. "I'm sorry too." I break eye contact and look down at my fingers, fidgeting with the hem of my shirt. "I don't know what the hell we're doing."

His warm fingers press against my chin, bringing my face to his. "I don't either, but what I do know is that I can't walk away from you again. It's always been you, wildcat, since the day I first met you. I think as long as we're together, we'll figure everything else out. I'm losing my mind being this close to you, but not having you. Give us another shot and I promise I won't ever let you down again."

I close my eyes, trying to stop any tears from falling, but I fail. A warm drop leaks down my cheek.

Logan's thumb catches it while he rubs his finger back and forth across my cheek. His touch is comforting. He's the last person I should be taking comfort in. He may be able to make that promise to me, but I can't make that same promise back. When he learns about my debt, about me having to hand over half of the Oasis—a place his deceased mother poured her soul into, a place he poured his soul into—it's going to destroy him.

And in the end, us.

"Hey," he says softly.

I peel open my blurry eyes. I've been so hard on him to get his life back on track, but in reality, I'm the one who's crumbling apart.

"I'm in it for all the good and the bad. I don't know what you're going through, and I hope to God you'll open up to me about your troubles soon, but I promise I'll never leave your side again. I did it once and barely made it through. I won't make that mistake again."

A hiccup bounces out of me. "I don't think you know what you are saying, chief."

"With you, I always know what I'm saying. Because in the end, it's always about you." He leans in and presses his lips to mine, and I dissolve into a puddle of mush. He pulls back and looks down at me. "You on board with me?"

I choke on a sob caught deep in my throat. I don't know if I can ever understand the pull that Logan and I have for each other, but it's real and it's there. I want to be selfish for once in my life and throw my arms around him, making him and me an *us* again. But that isn't who I am.

When he discovers everything I'm hiding from him, there won't be another chance for us. When we broke apart all those years ago, it nearly destroyed me. As much as I want this, I know deep down that my secrets will shatter us to pieces. People always say that when times get rough, it only makes a couple stronger in the end. But not with Logan and me. We won't have a happily ever after.

"I can't. I'm sorry," I reply, my voice scratchy.

He rests his forehead against mine. "Please, Harlow, I'm begging you. I know I messed up leaving you hanging all those years ago. I should've trusted you when it came to you and Fletch. I wasn't thinking straight. I know that's a lame excuse, but it's the God's honest truth."

His raw candor hits me like a physical blow. My heart aches in the worst possible way with something I can't seem to give him back in return. "I understand, I do," I say, my voice thick. "Your parents were killed and you were lost. But that isn't why we can't do this again."

"Then tell me why." His voice is strained with desperation. "What do I have to do to show you I'm worth it? What's it going to take for you to believe I'll never let you down again?"

My chin trembles, and for a moment, the words I've

been holding back rise, begging to be released. The truth about everything. About my mother. About Aleksei. About selling half of the Oasis. But my throat closes. Everyone may think I'm strong, but with Logan, I'm weak. He's the crack in my armor. As much as I know we can't go back to what we were, I still can't seem to let him go. I can't lose him just yet.

My words come out in a shaky whisper. "I can't."

"Fuck," Logan curses, his forehead still pressed against mine.

I open my eyes, catching a glimpse of his face, his eyes squeezed shut, his features twisted in pain.

"How did we ever get to this point?" It's a low whisper of disbelief. "This wasn't how our story was supposed to end."

I shake my head, my voice tight with emotion. "I don't know. But I hate it too. More than you can imagine."

He pulls away and I feel the loss of his warm presence immediately. His eyes are red, staring at me with intensity. He doesn't have to say another word about how he's feeling. I can see it there.

I'm breaking his heart.

He turns away and stalks off a few feet, pacing back and forth. Something he's always done when he's deep in thought. He runs his hand through the thick blond hair on top of his head and looks up to the sky.

I lean my head against the headrest, drinking him in.

From the moment I first met him, I knew he was different from any other man I had ever dated. And just like him, I thought nothing would ever pull us apart. Our future growing old together was as clear as this lake.

He drops his head and turns back to me, his gaze burning with something deeper than just frustration. It's raw. His long strides bring him quickly to me. He kneels and grabs my hand.

"I can't accept you walking away. I'm not done yet. Hell, we're not done yet." His voice is strong yet vulnerable. "Let's step this back. We don't have to make any promises. Let's just test the waters and see what happens. Please, wildcat, just give me something... I'm fucking begging you. I can't breathe without you. I can't focus without you. I can't do anything without you."

I swallow hard, the lump in my throat threatening to choke me. I shouldn't agree to this. He doesn't know what I'm hiding from him, and when he finds out... It won't end well for either of us. I look into those eyes that are filled with hope and despair. I couldn't tell him no if I wanted to. I'm not ready to walk away from him either.

With a heavy heart, I whisper, "Okay." And just like that, I give in to the pull of everything my heart has been quietly aching for.

"Oh, thank fuck," Logan says as he pulls me tight into his arms while I hug him back just as tightly. "I'm coming home with you tonight."

I laugh but don't argue. I think we could both use a night together. A night to remember us and forget everything else. I can only pray that I don't break his heart for real this time.

Chapter Eighteen

Logan.

Harlow's soft body curled against my side feels like waking up in heaven. I never asked if I could stay the entire night, and she never stopped me. Finally, my little wildcat took a leap of faith, and I'll do everything I can to keep her happy. I will prove to her that we are meant for the long haul.

We wasted no time getting reacquainted between the bedsheets last night before she fell out hard against my chest. I could tell she hadn't been sleeping well lately by the dark circles under her eyes.

As much as I don't want to, I know I need to get up and head over to see Fletch. If I'm guessing right, he didn't offer to show Aleksei back to his cottage to keep things under control and play the nice guy. He did it to get as much information out of this prick as possible so we can dig into his background.

I pull out of bed slowly, careful not to wake her as I pull on my pants. I shut her bedroom door and walk into the living room, where my shirt and hoodie were yanked off me the second the alarm was set.

God, I swear sex with her only gets better. I readjust myself at the thought of her naked body laid out beneath me and slide my shirt over my head, choosing to leave my hoodie behind. I write her a quick note asking to meet at my office later today. It's time to stop playing games and show her I can be the man she needs.

I set the alarm and leave my new Gator with her to get around in today since Fletch drove hers yesterday. I jog back to my cottage. I need to release the built-up energy inside me. Twenty minutes later, I'm walking into the cottage.

Fletch is already up and on his laptop. "Fresh coffee is ready."

"Thanks." I head to the kitchen to pour a cup, first making sure he doesn't need a refill of his cream and sugar with a dash of coffee. Once back over, I pull up a chair next to him. "What do you got?" I ask.

"His name is Aleksei Morozov. He's the head of the most dominant Russian mob. Rumors have it that he killed off the last guy to take his place, though there's no definitive proof. He took the reins three days after the last guy's death by vote."

I whistle.

Fletch smirks. "Still disappointed he wasn't actually my date?"

"You can do better than a six-foot-something mob boss with murderous eyes."

His smile grows. "Thank you."

I tap my chest. "You're welcome. What else do you got?"

"This guy worked his way up the ranks, starting out as an errand boy in his younger years. He was their best assassin for close to a decade before coming second-in-command. From there, he became even more respected than the top guy he's rumored to have killed."

"Fuck, I knew this guy was bad news."

Fletch nods. "I looked into his contacts, and as usual, he has the police in his back pocket, but I'm not sure how."

"I'm sure it's money."

Fletch's eyebrows furrow before he releases them, his eyes scanning his computer screen. "That's the thing. I don't think he's been paying them off."

I sit up straight in my chair at this revelation. "You think he works for the police?"

He rubs his chin, shaking his head slowly. "No, I don't think so. But from what I can pull, he does have multiple contacts inside the FSB."

The Federal Security of the Russian Federation. It's equivalent to the US's CIA and DIA. They handle anything from counterintelligence and terrorism to border security and surveillance.

"Good work. I'm dropping by for a surprise visit this morning before we head over to my place. What cottage is he in?"

"You really do want to get shot by Harlow, don't you?"

I shrug. It's not like I haven't been shot before. It isn't something I aspire to go through again, but if she did put me in her crosshairs, she wouldn't shoot to kill. If anything, she would just give me a limp in my stride for a month or two. "I'll take my chances. Which one is he staying at?"

"The Hidden Hedge cottage."

I lean back in my chair, shocked. Harlow put this asshole up in our cottage? The cottage I first told her she was mine? The fucking cottage where we shared our first kiss?

Fletch must not notice the mental breakdown I'm having over this, because he continues blandly. "I've got one more thing I found on him. He's in town because he's looking to expand his footprint into the States. I think he might be wanting to take a piece of the Oasis."

"She would never sell this place. It was her life long before she even owned it. There's no way she would ever give it up. Besides, she's got us. She would come to one of us for help if she needed it."

Fletch cocks an eyebrow. "Are you sure about that? Harlow isn't exactly the type of person who asks for handouts."

Fuck, he's right. I push out of my chair, head to my

room, and grab my laptop. I set it down on the table next to Fletch and fire it up.

"She's going to lose her shit if she finds out you're digging," Fletch says quietly.

"I know," I mutter. "But I've waited too long already. She's stressed out, closed off, and barely sleeping. Something's wrong. Really wrong."

He hesitates, then leans back in his chair and folds his arms across his chest. "You're not the only one who's noticed."

"Exactly," I say, pulling up the firewall-bypass protocols. "And if she won't let us in, I'm kicking the damn door down."

Fletch clears his throat. "She trusts me, Logan. Always has. If she finds out…"

I stop typing and set my full attention on Fletch. "I get it. But if we do nothing and something happens to her, can you live with that?"

His jaw clenches. "You know I can't."

"Then help me help her. We need to find out what we're dealing with."

I honestly wanted to wait Harlow out. Let her open up to me in her own time. But what if she doesn't have much time left? She's been more stressed than I've ever seen her. I still don't know what's going on with her parents' situation, but there has to be more hitting her.

She's going to kill me if she finds out I've hacked into her bank accounts, but what other choice do I have? I guess it's going to be one of those situations where I do what I have to and beg for forgiveness later. If she's in any kind of trouble, I need to know. I'll burn this entire world down before I let anyone hurt her.

It takes me a good twenty minutes to hack into her accounts, and when I see just how bad her situation is, it knocks me back. How could I have not seen this before? When we did the walk-through of the cottages and talked about the repairs, she followed up with the most critical repairs she needed to do. Sure, the Oasis takes a lot of money to run, but what she puts in it should be way more than what goes out. Even accounting for the people who aren't well off she cuts a break to.

"She's almost broke," I growl, mad at myself for not doing this sooner.

"What? That's impossible."

I turn my laptop to Fletch and watch his eyes grow wide. "Fuck."

I get up and start to pace. *What have you gotten yourself into, wildcat?* None of this makes any sense. Is someone blackmailing her?

Fletch clicks away on my keyboard. "Recently, she's been transferring large amounts of cash, always sending it to the same account."

"Yeah, and her last withdrawal was yesterday for a hundred thousand." I stop in my tracks and turn to Fletch. "Didn't Aleksei arrive yesterday?"

Fletch's eyes widen. "He did. He told me himself."

This asshole isn't staying here to conduct light business. He's working on a much bigger deal. My pulse increases as anger over him taking advantage of Harlow begins to build.

"Can you dig into this deeper? Try and find out who she's sending this money to?"

"It won't be easy, but I can start looking into it."

I glance at my phone. *Shit. It's almost nine o'clock.* "Do that. I think it's time for Mr. Morozov and me to have a one-on-one chat." I head back to my room to change.

"Logan," Fletch calls out.

"Yeah?"

"I'm not trying to pry, but from what I'm seeing, you and Harlow seemed to work something out, considering you didn't come back last night."

"She's giving me another chance. We're taking it slow," I reply, walking out of my room.

A sad smile comes across his face. "I'm glad she's finally following her heart, but what you're doing right now... If she finds out, she might push you out of her life quicker than you can blink an eye."

But the alternative—letting her drown by herself—isn't an option I can agree to. "I just told her last night I was in it for the good and the bad. I can't sit back and watch her fall because she's too stubborn for her own good."

"I agree, but let's keep this knowledge on the down-low for now. If she finds out we're snooping around, we both might be out on our asses before the sun goes down."

"What are you thinking?"

"We don't tell her we know about her financial state. And we don't tip off Morozov so he lets it slip to her. We need more time to get answers. Why don't you try to get more from her about what she's hiding? I can work on these transfers."

I frown in consternation. "She has yet to open up to me about anything."

"Since when have you ever shied away from a good challenge?"

We smile at each other. Harlow may be in hot water, but she has two men in her life who won't allow her to get burned. May God help whoever is fucking with her. Their breathing days won't be long. Harlow thinks I was made to do more than have blood on my hands. I'm going to show her why the bloodstains will never leave.

I skid to a stop in the Gator and bang on the front door like I'm the motherfucking police. I hear heavy footsteps, and then the door is yanked open. This asshole is already dressed in a three-piece suit and has a phone to his ear.

"I'm going to need to call you back," he says. He hangs up and slides his phone into his pocket. Looking me dead in the eyes, he says, "I see Miss Reece needs to put a shorter leash on you."

Before he can even blink, I hit him with a hard right hook and send him tumbling back into the cottage. I pull my Beretta from my waistband and cock it. I'm not fucking around today. "Take a fucking seat, you piece of shit."

He wipes his lower lip, an evil smile forming on his bloody lips. "Fuck, if love isn't a beautiful thing."

"I said take a fucking seat, asshole."

He listens the second time. He stalks into the living room and sits down in a chair. I drop onto the couch across from him.

"Are you blackmailing Harlow?"

His eyebrows fly up into his hairline; my question clearly surprises him. "Blackmail the queen of darkness?" He chuckles. "I do not think anyone is that stupid."

I've heard people refer to Harlow as the queen of darkness before, so it doesn't surprise me that he does as well. They all might think they know the dark side of my wildcat, but I get to see the light, and no motherfucker is going to take that light out of her.

As much as I want to shoot him, I don't. His initial reaction makes it obvious he's telling the truth. I click the safety back on and slide the handgun back into my waistband. I lean forward, propping my elbows on my knees. "Did she give you a hundred thousand dollars when you arrived?"

A deep chuckle rocks his chest. "Give me? No, more like *I* gave *her* a hefty payment to stay, even though I'm here to do business with her."

"And what business is that?"

He leans back slowly, resting his foot on his knee. "My business is none of your business, Mr. Keeyes. You may be known as the world's best hacker, but that doesn't earn any respect from me."

He knows who I am. His words are nothing more than a power move. If he wants to show some of his cards, I'm all in. "I know you do work for the FSB." I don't technically know this—it's more of a leap of faith—but by the way his body tenses, I know I've hit the nail on the head.

"I see you have done your homework as well."

"When a snake is slithering around, I like to know what species I'm dealing with."

"Fair enough. Then you know why I'm here."

"Are you here to take over the Oasis?"

His arrogant smile makes another appearance. I should hit him dead on the mouth and knock a few of those pearlies loose. "Far from that. I'm here to invest. I like the concept of the Oasis and what Miss Reece has built."

"Then go run one of your own from Russia."

"If only it were that easy. What she has here... It's taken decades of hard work and loyalty. Something you can only build to this caliber with time."

"Don't bullshit me. You have the money and the

means to start one yourself. You're looking to expand into the States."

He gives an unperturbed wave. "Of course. Who wouldn't want to?"

"Then what's your endgame here? What the fuck do you want with Harlow?"

"I'm only here to do business with Miss Reece, but if I'm being honest, I originally wanted more. She made her point quite quickly with her Hellcat to my goods that she isn't interested."

My chest puffs out. My wildcat's claws are nothing to joke about. I love that she put his ass in place from the start. Hearing she used her Hellcat because I still have her .357 sparks shame in me. I should've brought her gun back sooner. "If her message wasn't clear enough, I can give you a better one."

Aleksei holds up his hands in a display of surrender. "I would never disrespect her."

"For your sake, you better hope not." I have no idea what time Harlow is getting together with this prick this morning, and the last thing I need is to be caught here. I stand and he follows suit.

"When you need your stitches removed, you come see me. You won't be feeling her touch ever again." I make my way to the front door, which is still partially open. I open it all the way and turn back to Aleksei. "The Oasis doesn't belong to anyone but Harlow. She's worked her ass off more than either of us could ever imagine. You would do right to remember that. Look to other investments. I don't want any trouble with you, but don't force my hand. I won't hesitate to take down anyone who threatens her or the Oasis."

    I don't wait for a response. I slam the door shut.

Chapter Nineteen

Harlow.

    Aleksei and I have been going over the financial reports on the Oasis for the last few hours, and I've never been more bored in my entire life. This is the part of running a business that I couldn't care less about. Hand me a shovel, a bullet-riddled client, or a hammer, and I'm all in. Give me a stack of paperwork and I can't seem to keep my eyes open. Maybe this is something that I can pawn off on Aleksei to handle if he decides to make a deal.

    I slept better than I have in a long time, and I know why. Being in Logan's arms does something to me. It's almost magical how he can drain all the worry and stress from my limbs, allowing me to take my guard down. Even if it's only temporary. The multiple orgasms could have something to do with it as well, I suppose.

Waking up alone to his side of the bed cold made my heart heavy. But when I walked into the kitchen and saw his note—plus his hoodie—I smiled. Grabbing the hoodie, I inhaled deeply, his spicy scent still strong on the soft fabric.

I need to tell Logan what's going on with my mother, but fear wraps around my throat and holds the words hostage. Because either he'll bolt, or he'll throw me a lifeline I never asked for. Either way, we won't survive it.

I put on his hoodie, of course. I'll be seeing him later today, but I knew having his scent surrounding me until then would relax my tight muscles.

Now, I study Aleksei. His focus on the numbers in front of him is deep. He's wearing a three-piece suit, which isn't unusual for my clients, but being in a hoodie makes this a little awkward. *No. What are you even thinking, Harlow?* It doesn't matter what I wear. I'm the one with the business, not him.

His lips turn down, and that's when I notice a small injury on the side of his chin. I really don't want to ask, but I have a gut feeling about how that might have happened. "What happened to you?"

His head jerks up. His eyes hold a questioning look.

I point to his chin. "You have a cut and a bruise."

He grunts. "I drank a little too much last night."

I utter to myself, "Thank God it wasn't from Logan." It doesn't take a rocket scientist to know my chief has a short fuse, especially when it comes to me.

"Why did you only charge the Willards a fraction of what you charged the Forresters?"

"Huh?" I ask, leaning forward to see what he's reviewing.

"Right here. The Forresters stayed in the Mossy Rock cottage for the same amount of time and were charged triple the amount that the Willards were."

"Oh, because the Willards are going through a rough patch right now. They just lost their home to a fire and needed a place to stay while they figured everything out."

Aleksei's expression says I'm the dumbest person on earth. "So what? They should be charged the same amount. It's none of our concern what their financial state is."

"They've been coming to the Oasis for well over twenty years. That's what you're supposed to do when people are struggling."

"Are they family of yours?"

I scrunch my nose up. I couldn't be more different from that family. "No."

"Well, again, it's not your problem. You're running a business here, Harlow, not a damn charity house. If people want to stay here, then they need to pay the price."

I cross my arms and lean back into my chair. This guy can be a jerk sometimes. "You're telling me you can turn away someone who's bleeding out and needs immediate medical treatment?"

"Were they?"

"No, but we had to treat second-degree burns on parts of their bodies."

He shakes his head and closes my laptop before turning to face me. "Harlow, I mean this with all due respect, because honestly, you have something amazing here. But don't you think that if you charged everyone the price they're supposed to be paying, you wouldn't need my help?"

If only it were that simple. "That has nothing to do with why I need you as a partner. Not only did my grandparents manage the Oasis that way, but so have I. It's never put us in a hole. If anything, it increases our business because everyone knows they always have a place to go. This might be hard for you to understand, but giving a small break to a long-standing client will pay dividends long into the future."

Aleksei studies me silently while his finger rubs back and forth across his chin. His gaze is intense. "Why *do* you need me as a partner, then?"

I was hoping he wouldn't ask this question... but had a feeling he would. I attempt to stay as vague as possible. "My family is going through a hard time right now, and I'm helping them out."

He grabs his glass of vodka and takes a slow sip. "I don't invest my money into anything without knowing the whole story."

Shit. I knew this was going to happen, and I can't say I blame him. It's not like I'm offering him the entire

Oasis—only 50 percent. But that means he needs to know I can hold up my side of the bargain too.

"My mother has cancer. She's on a new trial drug that insurance won't cover. I'm flipping the bill."

Aleksei's eyes go soft at my admission.

I tense, waiting for the pity to come out of him. That's the last thing I need or want from anyone.

"My mother passed away from cancer a few years back. We do not have medical insurance in the way you do in this country, but the toll was great." Instead of pity, he's just offered me a peek behind his mask. That isn't anything he had to share with me, but I'm grateful he did.

"I'm sorry for your loss."

He finishes his drink before leveling his dark eyes on me. "Thank you. I only tell you so you know I understand the situation you're in. Money didn't help my mother, but I hope it will save yours."

I give a curt nod, not trusting my voice not to crack at this moment.

"Does your man know about this?"

"No one else knows. I would prefer to keep it that way," I reply as my phone comes to life in my pocket. "Excuse me."

He waves his hand as I stand and walk into the next room. "Hey, you here?"

"Just pulled up to your place."

"Sit tight. I'll be there in ten." I hang up and turn

back to Aleksei. "I need to run. Is there anything else you need to see?"

He shakes his head. "I am good. I have to head out to handle some business for a couple of hours in Seattle. I will be in touch when I'm ready."

Nodding, I grab my laptop and let myself out. What I'm hoping will push Logan to open the academy has just arrived. I can't wait to take him over to what will one day become a school. I just hope this doesn't push him over the edge.

We pull up to Logan's building in my Gator and I park next to two others. We hop out and climb the stairs.

"Wow, this place is even better than I pictured," Riggs says.

"Wait until you see the inside." I push open the door. The birthday banners and deflated balloons are gone. I can only imagine how hard it had to have been to clean those up. I should have pushed our differences aside and handled that for him.

We walk down the hallway and enter the large room with tables. The decorations are gone, but the tables remain. Voices echo from upstairs, coming from the room next to Logan's office—the room designed as a computer classroom, the one Logan destroyed the last time I was here. To me, it's a great sign; Logan may very well be considering turning this place into an academy. And what better person to have on his team than Riggs?

Riggs owns and operates Elite Defense in Seattle. It offers a mixture of specialized physical training courses, along with a gym and spa. He and his wife Mimi just welcomed a baby, and since then, they've been talking about relocating out of the city.

I told Riggs about the building Logan's parents built as a surprise for his birthday, suggesting that it could be a great opportunity for his family and him. He could run the gym and teach his defensive classes here. I may have neglected to mention that I never discussed this with Logan, but I'm hopeful that Riggs's enthusiasm will encourage Logan to pursue his dream.

I hold my fingers to my lips. He smiles as we make our way up the stairs. I push open the door to find... not what I was expecting at all.

The tables that were in this room are gone, along with the large dry-erase board on the back wall. Instead, there's a large black desk with chairs around it. Fletcher is behind the desk and Logan is propped on the edge. Both sets of eyes meet mine and my surprise guest's.

"Riggs!" Logan calls out as he makes his way toward us, meeting halfway. They shake hands.

Fletcher approaches soon after. He's moving around better each day. Riggs and Fletcher shake hands.

"What brought you out this way?" Logan asks.

Riggs, dressed in his signature sweats and black shirt,

looks around. "Harlow told me about this place. I had to come check it out for myself."

"Did she now?" Logan says, giving me a sideways glance.

I give a large smile in return and flutter my eyelashes. "This is really something else."

Logan peers around the room, nodding in agreement. "It's growing on me. Have you gotten a tour yet?"

"Nope, just got here, but I would love to see the gym setup. I'm sure it won't take much to turn it into what I need to make it work."

Logan turns his attention to me, his eyes narrowing. I keep my innocent smile intact, thankful that Riggs isn't paying attention to our silent war.

Fletcher is, though, and steps in. Another reason I love this man so much. "I'll take you down there," he offers. They leave the room and Fletcher closes the door behind them.

Logan steps up to me, grabbing my hips and pulling me against him. "It seems my wildcat has been busy behind my back."

I giggle like a damn schoolgirl. If anyone else heard me do that, I would probably never be taken seriously again. "Just looking for some employees to get my chief's ass in gear," I purr back, just as Logan presses his lips to mine. A helpless moan breaks from my lips as I hopelessly fall apart in his arms. *God, this man can kiss.*

Our kiss isn't just a fleeting moment of passion. It's a promise. A silent vow that, despite all the past mistakes and heartaches, we have what it takes to make it through. I need to open up and tell him everything, but the thought of him walking away is keeping me silent.

He breaks the kiss sooner than I want and peers down at me. "I've missed this face."

I smile back. "I've missed you too." We stare silently at one another, but there's nothing awkward about it.

"You want to tell me what's going on?"

I attempt to back away, but he doesn't have it. His hands tighten around me.

"Riggs and Mimi are looking to relocate," I say. "They don't want their newborn son to grow up in the city."

"And what does this have to do with me?"

I shift back and forth, licking my lips with cautious hope. "He's the best on the West Coast. He knows almost every style of fighting. Did you know he's trained in sixteen different types of martial arts?"

"I'm well aware of his skill set, wildcat, but you're still not answering my question."

I lick my dry lips again. *Is it hot in here?* "I figured he would be a perfect candidate to join your team."

"I don't have a team."

"Well, not yet." I place my hands across his hard chest. "That's why I'm helping you build one."

He rewards me with his adorable lopsided grin. "What if I ask you to be a part of my team?"

A jolt of adrenaline spikes through my body. *Does that mean he's going to do this?* "What would I do?"

"Oh"—he chuckles—"I can think of plenty of things for you to do."

I slap his chest. "We're supposed to be taking this slow. I'm trying to be serious here."

Logan clears his throat. "All right. Well, for starters, I think *if* I decide to do this, I would like to pair up with the Oasis."

"How would we do that?"

"You have the connections. I'm sure all the people who come here have kids who could benefit from a specialty academy. I want to make this for college-age kids and offer something no other college provides: skills they can use in the lifestyle they are born into."

I rock back in his arms, picturing how it would look to combine the Oasis with Logan's school. It's actually a great idea. One that would further the amenities that I currently offer. But the fact that I will soon no longer be the only owner of the Oasis brings the reality of my situation crashing down on top of me.

Logan must see the doubt in my eyes. "I would pay for your services and connections."

I shake my head. "I couldn't charge you for that. If anything, you would increase my bottom line by adding an academy to my slate of offerings, and I should pay you."

"There's no way I could get this business off the ground if it wasn't connected to the Oasis. You don't have to make a decision right now. Just think about it. I'll get some numbers together and we can go from there."

"But—"

Logan interrupts my debate with another kiss before he releases me. "So, what do you think about the changes?"

This man can give me serious whiplash. I look around the empty room, noting that everything is in fact gone. "What did you do with the tables that were in here?"

"Fletch and I relocated everything to another room."

"Why would you do that?"

"Because he needs an office."

My jaw hits the floor.

Logan laughs and brings his finger underneath my chin to close my gaping mouth.

"Fletcher wants to join your team?" I never even considered Fletcher. He's at the top of his business, even with his building being destroyed. I've been dreading the day he tells me he's heading back.

"Hey, it wasn't my idea. He came to me and asked. He's in no hurry to get back to the city, so I told him I would set up an office in the meantime."

"What does that mean? Are you going to do this?" I try to keep my tone neutral, but I'm not sure how successful I am.

"Easy, wildcat. I'm not sure what I'm doing yet."

I nod and step back, but I only make it one step before his large, rough hand wraps around mine. "Come on," he says as he pulls me toward the door at the back of the room that connects this room with his office.

I walk through the doorway and am happy to see everything is still the same in his office. The only new item is a bottle of bourbon sitting on his desk.

He releases my hand and grabs a set of keys, unlocking his desk drawer. Pulling out my .357, he strides back over to me and holds it out.

I snatch it from him. I love the feel and weight of this gun. I rub my finger across the engraved initials. At the familiar roughness on the other side of the grip, I flip it to see the old engraving. But now there's a new addition.

SW + JW

HK + LK

My eyes jump to his, and I find him smiling softly. After my grandparents got married, my grandpa—Jon Walker—engraved my grandma Sally's new initials on the other side of the handle.

A laugh bubbles out of me. I shake my head at this man standing in front of me. "I think you might be getting a little ahead of yourself."

"Just waiting for you to catch up." He places his hand on my cheek and rubs his finger across my bottom lip.

My phone pings, breaking the silence. Logan steps back as I pull it out quickly, hoping by chance it's an update from my dad. He said he wouldn't be able to contact me for over a week, but maybe something has changed.

I glance at the screen. It's a text from a client currently staying here with her family. I quickly respond before sliding it back into my pants pocket.

"Was that your dad?"

"No, just one of the clients staying here."

His eyes hold mine. "You going to tell me what's going on with your parents?"

I let out a slow, deep breath, causing my cheeks to puff out like a blowfish's. I was hoping he wasn't going to push this issue so soon, but I should've known better when dealing with Logan. He never lets anything go for too long, and if he does, it only means he's hacking in and figuring it out on his own. The thought that he might do that sends a shiver down my spine.

My dad has enough weight on his shoulders right now and doesn't need Logan barging into their life.

"I don't want to talk about anything gloomy right now. I was thinking we should use this short break a little more wisely." It's not fair of me to distract Logan with sex, but if there's one thing I know will work, it's this. And after the night we had last night, I'm ready for more.

A growl rips from his chest as he grabs my hips and spins me to his desk, setting me gently on top. "Is that so?" he asks, his voice gravelly, shooting heat straight down to my core.

I bite my bottom lip and nod. I've never wanted anything more.

Logan's rough hands cup my face gently, and he claims me.

Chapter Twenty

Logan.

Harlow told me she wanted to take this slow, but I've refused to let her sleep alone for the last three days. The dark circles that once dominated the space under her eyes have disappeared. Our days are spent apart, tackling our own to-do lists, but we make up for the missed time late into the night.

I've officially taken over cooking dinner, and Fletch joins us every night. Regardless of whatever we take care of each day, we all agreed to meet at Harlow's at seven in the evening to sit down and rehash our days with one another. Our routine feels domesticated and perfect.

I'm running behind on meeting up with Fletch today at my place, so when I pull up in my Gator and see a Benz parked outside the school, I'm caught off guard. The car screams money; I don't recognize it. Neither

Harlow nor Fletch said anything about someone stopping by. I check my Beretta before tucking it away and jog up the stairs to the main entrance.

I push through the door, and by the time I make it to the stairs, I can hear arguing. I race up the stairs, skipping every couple. I slam the door to Fletch's new office open. I can tell there was a prior struggle because his laptop and paperwork are scattered across the floor. He's currently pushed up against the wall by a man I've never seen before.

The stranger whips his eyes to mine, a snarl across his face. I reach him in seconds just as Fletch yells, "He's got a gun." Before this guy can raise his gun, I'm tackling him to the ground and away from Fletch. This asshole is about to learn something about me.

We hit the floor and roll. His gun flies from his hand and across the room. He might be tall, but he has nothing on me. I roll on top of him and crash my fist against his nose. With a sickening crack, blood erupts all over his face. His nose is perfectly straight no longer.

The guy roars beneath me, trying to cup his nose as water pours from his eyes. I wrap my hand around his throat and tighten my grip. I lean inches away from his blood-soaked face. "You want to fuck with Fletch, then you are fucking with me, you punk-ass bitch."

"Get the fuck off me!" He chokes from the lack of oxygen. He's twisting and turning, trying to break my death grip, but he's no match for my strength.

An arm wraps around my bicep. I turn to see Fletch

holding the asshole's gun and attempting to pull me off him.

"You're going to kill him," Fletch yells as he tugs harder. I look back at the jackass to see his face turning beet red.

I loosen my grip around the guy's throat, stand tall, and give him a good kick to the ribs. He lets out a groan as he drags himself away from me. "How's it feel fighting a man who doesn't have a broken leg, you pathetic fuck?"

Fletch's hand goes to my chest and he backs me away. I'm so pissed at seeing this guy fucking with Fletch, it takes me a second to notice that Fletch's chest is shaking.

He's fucking laughing at me. What the fuck?

"Dude, you kicked my ass when I had a broken leg too."

Shit, I did. I let out a chuckle, dragging my hand down my face. "Yeah, but then you had your turn in Ireland."

"This is him? This is the guy you left me for?" Crooked Nose spits out, blood spraying out of his mouth. Thank God these are marble floors. I'll still need to keep Harlow away from this room until I can get it cleaned up. Who knows what sick disease this fuck could have?

I look to Fletch for some direction on what the hell is going on. "Who is this guy?"

"You remember when I was hooking up with someone in secret at the Oasis and Harlow pretended it was her?"

I nod. How could I ever forget? I thought Harlow was cheating on me with Fletch.

"This was the guy."

I look back at him with a pair of fresh eyes. This is the prick who caused so much turmoil for years straight? He's tall and skinny with short black hair. He's obviously loaded, judging by the car parked outside and the obnoxiously bright orange blazer he's wearing. Surely Fletch can do better. "Fuck, what were you thinking, wasting your time with this guy?"

"I have no idea."

We both stand back, arms across our chests, and watch the guy rise on his wobbly legs, still holding his nose. His eyes narrow on me before they move to Fletch. "You're nothing but a washed-up computer nerd. I can't believe I wasted a second of my time on you."

That's it.

I stalk across the room, done with him talking to Fletch like this. His eyes widen at the sight of me heading straight for him.

"Don't touch me! I'll sue!" he screeches.

I grab him by the shirt and drag him down the long flight of stairs, his legs slipping underneath him, unable to keep up. I push open the front door, pull him down the steps, and kick him in the ass. He stumbles into the grass below.

I'm going to have to have a talk with Fletch about his choice in men. This guy has nothing but bitch stamped across his forehead.

"Have a great day," I yell with a large smile.

The guy flips me off, storming toward his car. He peels out, kicking up a bowl of dust as he speeds away.

The clouds have thickened quite a bit since I arrived not long ago, and the sky is beginning to look greenish. A storm is rolling in.

By the time I walk back into Fletch's office, he's picking up the last of his scattered paperwork. He gives me a glance and shakes his head. "You're going to need to change your shirt before Harlow sees it."

I glance down to see a large amount of blood sprayed across my long-sleeved shirt. "This is why I never wear white." I walk over to a cabinet behind his desk and pull out a bottle of bourbon. "Drink?"

"Yeah."

I grab two plastic cups. We have yet to purchase any glassware. I pour us both a generous three-finger shot just as my phone dings with a text. I hand Fletch his drink and pull out my phone.

Wildcat: *Running behind at the Lavender Lodge. Won't be long. XO*
Logan: *Storm rolling in. Get your sweet little ass home.*
Wildcat: *I need 20.*

"Harlow?" Fletch asks as I tuck my phone away.
"Yeah, she's finishing up at the Lavender Lodge. Said

she'll be done in twenty minutes. You want to explain what that was all about?"

Fletch downs his drink in one go. "A big mistake. Jackass heard through the grapevine that I was staying here. He thought you and I were hooking up."

I choke on my bourbon. "Guess I need to work harder on getting the word out that Harlow is mine. I didn't realize you were still seeing that guy."

"I'm not. I haven't seen Naz in a long time."

I finish my drink and crush the plastic cup in my hand. "Let's head out. I don't feel like getting a wet ass."

"Hold up." He limps over to the bathroom door on the back wall. He's healing quickly. It won't be long before the walking cast comes off. A minute later, he emerges with a coral T-shirt and tosses it at me.

I catch it. "What the hell is this?" I ask, holding it away from me like it might bite.

"A shirt, dumbass."

I toss it back to him. "I'm not wearing that. I think Harlow has the same color dress hanging in her closet."

He throws it right back at me. "You want Harlow to see your bloodstained shirt?"

My shirt is ruined. Fuck. "Turn around."

"What?"

"Turn the fuck around, Fletch. I don't need you seeing my goods."

Fletch bursts into laughter, grabbing his stomach

and leaning forward. The dramatic asshole. "You think I like you like *that*?"

His laugh continues on and on, and now it's making me mad. "What? You don't think I'm good-looking?" I never thought I would care about what a gay guy would think about my looks, but here I am.

"Just because I'm gay doesn't mean I have the hots for every guy on the planet." When I stare at him, dumbfounded, because hello, I have an eight-pack, he continues. "Do you think every chick is hot?"

I crinkle my nose. None of them even come close to looking as hot as Harlow. Miss Universe couldn't even get a head turn out of me. "Hell no."

"Exactly. Now put the shirt on so Harlow doesn't kick your ass and hurry up. We wouldn't want your pretty hair messed up in the rain."

Fletch heads to the door as a grin slides across my face. "Aha! So, you *do* think my hair is pretty."

Fletch drops his head and shakes it. "Not at all. You don't use any gel."

And with that, he's gone. I run my hand through my hair, wondering if Harlow would like it if I put gel in it. I experimented with hair gels in my early teens, but I quickly realized how much I drag my hand through it.

I grab the hem of my bloody shirt, ready to take it off, when a piercingly loud alarm sounds from my phone. My phone only makes that particular sound when the emergency alert system goes off.

It only takes me a moment to realize what the alarm means.

A tornado has touched down nearby. I drop the girly shirt and run out the door. "Fletch!"

"Down here."

He's already made it down the stairs, thank God. I race down the steps and yell, "You need to get to the safe room."

"We've got to get Harlow. She's probably still at the Lavender Lodge."

I grab his arm, halting his forward progression. "I hate to tell you this, but you're only going to slow me down getting to her. I need your ass to get into the safe room now!"

I can see the internal battle he's having with himself, wanting to go to Harlow's rescue with me, but he knows I'm right. "All right man, go! Keep your phone on you."

I nod and run out of the building, my boots sliding a couple of steps from the heavy rain starting to pour from the sky.

I wish I had brought my truck. It's going to take me longer to reach Harlow in the Gator, but it's all I have to work with. The sky has a weird, unnatural glow. I peel out in the muddy gravel and head toward a new trail we made that connects to the Oasis.

With my foot pressed hard on the pedal, I try to shield my eyes from the rain and hail pelting my body from every angle. Several large tree branches have already snapped. Luckily, none block my path because I won't slow down. I finally come to the fore and get my first sight of the tornado.

It's heading straight for the Lavender Lodge.

Hold on, wildcat. I'm coming.

Chapter Twenty-One

Harlow.

I set my phone down on the bathroom sink after texting Logan. I'm running behind but need to finish cleaning the cottage for clients who are arriving tomorrow. The Lavender Lodge is one of my favorites. It got its name from my grandma when she decided to plant nothing but soft lavender around the perimeter of the cottage. It's the most remote cottage and has the most privacy. I think that's why it's one of the more popular units.

I finish scrubbing the toilet and head to the kitchen. The Lavender Lodge has a rustic charm. The living room is cozy, with mismatched furniture gathered around a stone fireplace. The windows all have white lace curtains, brightening the room. The old iron furnace holds a memory of Logan and me back in the early days. One I will cherish until my last breath.

The entertainment center stereo is playing in the living room, and I have an extra bounce in my step. I know it isn't from the music, or even from finally getting better sleep. It's from being wrapped in Logan's arms for the past three nights. He demanded that we sleep in the same bed, but I don't think I would have let him leave if he wanted to anyways.

As I wipe down the kitchen countertop with a soapy rag, my stomach rumbles. Logan is making ribs tonight and I can't wait. He's been managing dinner every night, and I think I've already gained five pounds from his seven-course meals. The man can cook. Fletcher and I have taken full advantage. I've never been great in the kitchen, and when money started getting tight, I had to let go of half of the Oasis chefs. Meaning I also had to let go of having meals cooked for me. Florence—the head chef—and her small remaining cooking staff have their hands full enough with all the clients.

Six clients checked out today, leaving me with six cottages to get cleaned before six more arrive over the next couple of days. The busy days are welcome, as they keep my mind off my mom and the worry that follows. I have yet to hear from my dad, but it's still earlier than he's supposed to call me with an update. I'm sure I've kept God up late every night, praying for a miracle.

Aleksei hasn't contacted me since we went through the Oasis's finances. I'm hoping this doesn't mean he isn't interested in becoming partners. I did a drive-by on the Hidden Hedge cottage early this morning to make sure his car was there. Thankfully it was. Aleksei might be an arrogant asshole, but he's also a businessperson. I can't see him up and disappearing on me without letting me know his decision.

If anything, surely he would tell me how much of a disaster the Oasis is and laugh in my face before driving off into the sunset with his money held tight in his hand.

A strange, loud noise comes out of the east, drowning out the music, almost as if a freight train is running along nonexistent tracks right outside the cottage. That makes no sense. The nearest set of train tracks must be a good fifty miles out.

I wring out the kitchen rag, lay it across the divider in the sink, and dry my hands off. Rain starts to hit the kitchen windows, coming down fast. The music cuts off. I'm going to have to wait it out before I head home. I walk out to the porch to text Logan I'm going to be a little longer, but don't feel my phone in my back pocket. Where the heck did I leave it?

Ever since I was a little girl, I've always loved to watch a good storm roll in. It was something my grandpa and I loved to do together. The rain is coming down in sheets. Hail the size of golf balls pings off the ground at a rapid pace.

Shit, this one's going to cause some hail damage. I hope the guys have already made it to my cabin. A strong wind whips my hair around wildly. I take a hair tie off my wrist and bunch up my hair, pulling it back as well as I can.

That freight train–like sound is overwhelming. *What is that noise?* I walk to the far side of the porch and peek around the corner.

Lightning strikes down in three large bolts as I come face-to-face with a roaring tornado heading straight my way.

Oh. My. God.

Fear slices through my body in an instant. I turn and run back to the front door, push it open, and slam it shut. My heart beats so hard against my chest, I'm afraid it's going to crack a rib. I race around the cottage, looking for my damn cell phone. I finally spot it on the bathroom sink next to the toilet and rush to it. I have to warn Logan and Fletcher so they can take cover.

My shaking hands are trembling, causing it to slip through my fingers and drop to the floor. I reach for it again, my grip firmer as I flip it over—and discover that my screen is cracked. I hit the button and the screen lights up. I punch in the code to unlock it.

I try calling Logan, but it only rings once before going to voicemail. *Shit!* I hang up and call Fletcher's phone, but it doesn't ring at all; it goes straight to his voicemail. *Please be okay.* I run across the living room and slip on the rug. I stumble backward and fall on my ass. My .357 slides out of my waistband and under the couch.

I dive toward the couch, reaching underneath. My fingertips barely graze the tip of the barrel. Tears fill my eyes as I extend my hand again, except this time I push it farther away.

Hail is beating against the windows loudly like a drummer with rage slamming their sticks into a set of drums. A cracking noise fills my ears. I sit up just in time to watch the window blow apart into pieces and come flying right at me. Screaming, I curl up on the floor and cover my head as glass covers my shaking body. I scurry to my feet but keep low as I rush toward the front door. The entrance to a secret tunnel is right outside the porch and to the left. If I can get to it, I should be safe. I open the door and am greeted with winds far stronger than I am.

I latch onto the doorframe, hugging it as closely as possible. A sob rips from my chest as my mind turns to Logan with his sweet hazel eyes and smile that melts me on the spot. I should've told him the truth when I had the chance. I should've confessed how every moment we spent apart has felt like a lifetime of pain. How his absence left an aching void in my heart that only he can fill.

I should have told him how I never stopped loving him. How he's haunted me in all my dreams. How, despite our tribulations, he always remained the center of my universe. How there was only ever him for me.

But now it's too late.

As the wind beats my body and my arms grow weaker by the second, I know I don't have any time left to do that. The regret is overwhelming. He'll never truly know the depth of my love for him. I can only hope that somehow, my love will reach him from the heavens above.

My cries have become uncontrollable as a numbness settles over me. An accepting numbness. I loosen my grip, ready to throw in the towel one last time. I've missed my grandparents and Marion and James so much. It will be good to finally see them again. And if my mom doesn't pull through, I can wait there with open arms.

With that thought, I open my arms and let the wind carry me away.

It's a free feeling to just let go. To give in and stop fighting. To no longer resist the inevitable. To accept defeat head-on and with your chin held high. Just as I close my eyes, I slam into something hard and hear an "Oomph" behind me.

Large arms that I would know in the complete dark wrap around my waist.

"I got you, wildcat," Logan's husky voice breaks through as he pulls us back into the cottage and slams the door shut.

He picks me up in an instant and carries me toward the back of the house, opening a closet door. Without delay, he tosses out the mop and broom, pushes us into it, and shuts us into complete darkness. I slide to the floor with him, wrapping my arms and legs around his body.

"Why, Logan? Why would you come here?" I cry into his soaked shirt as he rocks me back and forth, rubbing my back.

"Because I'm nothing without you."

My choked sobs rock my chest as I grip his shirt tighter and the cottage trembles around us. "I'm scared, chief."

His arms tighten around my body. "Shh, it's going to be okay, baby. I got you."

The rain and hail have picked up. More glass cracks and breaks around us. I never thought this little closet would keep us safe one day. I pray it can.

"Where's Fletcher?"

"He's okay. He's in the safe room back at my place."

I nod against his neck, thankful that one of us is safe. If my clients hadn't left this cottage earlier today, it would have been a disaster.

It still might be.

"My gun, I lost it," I say. The tornado screams its arrival, piercing our ears. The wall starts to shake and shift violently around us. I curl into a ball on Logan's lap, his body wrapping around mine in a protective form.

Light pierces the darkness of the closet, and we both snap our heads up, eyes wide, trying to understand how that's possible. The roof is gone. Completely gone. Irretrievable. A wave of terror crashes over me. There's absolutely nothing I can do to stop this tornado. The rain, hail, and wind assault us instantly, battering our bodies relentlessly.

One glance into his eyes and I see my uncertainty mirrored there. "You shouldn't have come here," I say, my voice strained.

His gaze softens for a split second before snapping upward, then back at me. "Head down, wildcat."

I bury myself back against Logan, his body a shield over mine. A massive crash erupts as something large slams into the cottage. The world shifts and collapses around us. I scream as we're thrown backward, my back slamming into something solid. At this point, I'm not sure what's what. Up, down, it all blurs. Splintered wood rains down on us and the air vibrates with the force. I pray desperately, clutching Logan tighter, begging God to keep him safe.

Time seems to slow to a crawl. It's as if everything pauses, giving me too much time to reflect on my life, on every choice I've ever made. It all narrows down to the essentials, highlighting what really matters.

It's then, in the midst of chaos, that I realize how much time I've wasted on things that don't matter. The small irritations, the petty distractions. None of it holds weight in the face of annihilation.

My grip on Logan tightens; I'm overwhelmed by the thought that he threw himself into the path of destruction to protect me. Are our souls bound, so that even when death stares us in the face, we'll face it together?

And then, just as suddenly as it began, it stops.

An eerie silence settles around us, our labored breathing the only noise left to be heard.

"It's over," he says, his voice hoarse as he attempts to rise. But he doesn't get far. I have no idea how much debris he's holding up with his body or how we ended up like this, with his body sprawled on top of me, sheltering me beneath him. But I know one thing for certain. I could not be more grateful for the fact that I'm not lying in this rubble alone.

"Fuck, I'm not sure if I can lift this off us. Do you have your phone?"

I start feeling around the best that I can in these tight quarters, but every pocket comes up empty. "No, do you have—"

I'm cut off by Logan's ringtone. Oh thank God!

"It's in my back pocket. Can you reach it?"

I reach around with shaky fingers until I feel the hard case and pull it free. "It's Fletcher." I answer the call before it reaches his voicemail. "Fletcher, oh my God, are you okay?"

"Oh, thank fuck, Harlow. I tried calling your phone, but it's going straight to voicemail. Is Logan all right?"

I nod, which is stupid because he can't see me. "Yeah, we're okay, but we're stuck. Can you run by Aleksei's cottage and check on him first?"

"What the hell, woman?" Logan mutters.

"Yeah, I'm probably going to need his help getting you two out anyways. I'm already on my way."

I end the call, and the call screen drops away to show

his wallpaper. It's a picture of me asleep in his arms. I can tell he took this a couple of days ago because of the silky gray top I'm wearing. I flip the screen to show him. "Care to elaborate?"

"I plead the Fifth."

My smile is short-lived when I notice all the blood on his shirt from the light of the phone.

"Oh my God, you're bleeding." My free hand tugs at his shirt, frantically trying to raise it so I can check his injuries.

"It's not mine."

My hand freezes. I have never been happier to hear him say those words. "What do you mean it's not yours?"

"It's nothing... It's just ketchup." Logan can barely hold his lame excuse together. His chest vibrates from holding back a laugh.

"You are so full of shit." I cackle, making him release his own. God, it feels good to be able to laugh. To be alive.

Logan peers down at me, amusement dancing in his eyes. "We were having a hot dog eating contest. It got a little out of control."

"You do realize that Fletcher will tell me what really happened the second he gets here."

Logan leans down and gives my nose a quick kiss. "Tornado hair looks good on you."

I roll my eyes, noticing his change in subject. "Yeah, it gives a whole new meaning to *blowout*." I reach up, pressing my fingers in his hair and ruffling it. "There. Now we match."

"Would you like it if I put gel in my hair?"

My nose crinkles. "What?"

He shifts slightly, readjusting himself. "I was thinking maybe you would like it if I gelled my hair."

I have no clue as to why he would ever think something like that, especially at a time like this. "If you put gel in your hair, then I can't run my fingers through it."

He grunts appreciatively. Something hard jabs me in my thigh.

I attempt to adjust myself, but we are in such a small space, it's a challenge to do. "Something's jabbing me."

Logan snorts.

I hit his shoulder. "I'm serious, chief."

"I'm trying not to."

I still, realization hitting me. "You're hard right now?"

"Fuck, wildcat, anytime I'm around you, I'm hard. Do you think we can pull off a quickie before they get here?"

I laugh as Logan peppers my neck, sending goosebumps across my body.

"Just follow the giggles." Aleksei's voice carries over to us.

"We're over here," I yell just as Logan mutters under his breath about cockblockers, and I can't help it—I laugh more. I have never felt so happy to be here, be alive, and have everyone be okay.

Boards shift above us and flashlights beam through the cracks. Logan starts to strain his body as the sounds of debris being tossed rain around us. The twilit sky shows itself as another panel is taken from above us.

Logan wraps his large hands around mine and pulls us both up. We both glance around to see the destruction of the Lavender Lodge. Nothing is left standing. It's a sobering moment to witness that God is the only reason Logan and I are still alive and without major injury.

Aleksei and Fletcher stand off to the side, helping us climb out of the damage.

As soon as my feet touch even ground, I reach for Aleksei's flashlight. "Can I use that really quick?"

"What do you need that for?" Logan asks as Aleksei hands it over to me.

"To find my gun. It was in the living room and slid under the couch," I say, moving the light beam across the pile of rubble. *Where* was *the living room?* The entire cottage is leveled. I can only hope that my gun still lies within this pile and wasn't swept away in the strong wind.

If the wind did take it, I won't ever see it again. I'm already losing half the Oasis, half of my grandparents' legacy. I cannot afford to lose their gun too. *No!* Panic grows and my chest tightens painfully, feeling like it is about to collapse. I whip the beam of light from left to right, my motions jerky. I can't breathe.

Logan's hand presses against the flashlight, lowering

it to my side. "We can come back tomorrow when it's daylight," he says, his voice gentle.

I shake my head, tears flowing down my face. "You don't understand! It was my .357. I can't lose that gun. I have to find it. I can't fail my grandparents more than I already have." My chest is twisting tighter. I can't get any oxygen into my lungs.

His hands cup my face. He leans down in front of me, bringing our faces an inch apart. My tears come so fast, he can't catch them all. He fixes his eyes on me intently. "Easy, wildcat. You're having an anxiety attack. I need you to breathe, baby. Take a deep breath. Can you do that?"

My body shakes as I keep my eyes locked on him and attempt to take a deep breath, but I can't. I can't breathe! I can't move. I feel as if my lungs have been filled with concrete.

"Follow my lead, wildcat." He takes a deep breath and slowly lets it out. I follow his lead, a small burst of air hitting my lungs.

"That's good, baby. Keep going." He takes another breath in and releases it. My breaths are jerky. I try to follow along with him. Eventually, oxygen starts pouring into my lungs. He smiles warmly at me, gradually calming the storm brewing inside me. After a couple of minutes—or is it hours?—the tightness in my chest fades.

"I'll come out here as soon as the sun rises tomorrow and find that gun. Even if it takes me all day. Okay?"

I hiccup; my breaths are jumpy and uneven. I look about. Fletcher and Aleksei are watching me closely. I don't cry in front of *anyone*. Ever. Logan's the only person alive to have witnessed it, and recently, it seems to have become a common occurrence.

I bet Aleksei won't ever think of me as the queen of darkness again after watching my breakdown. I can kiss our deal goodbye, having shown weakness. It's the one thing you can never do in this type of work.

Logan lifts me bridal-style in his arms. I bury my head against his neck, letting him shield me from watching eyes. He's the only place where I feel safe.

Chapter Twenty-Two

Logan.

I slow to a stop. Four glowing eyes stare back at me. Two does cautiously cross my headlights. I watch with fascination as they walk right in my path, refusing to let their fear of me detour them from their journey.

That's exactly the way I see Harlow. She's always faced any problem, big or small, with unshakable resolve. Her breaking down in front of Aleksei and Fletch splintered the armor she never lets anyone see past.

You would think that surviving a tornado after it levels the house you were hunkered down in would break you. But that isn't what did it. What broke her was the loss of her beloved gun, which can never be replaced. Her .357 Magnum revolver is more than just a gun. Her grandparents gave it to her shortly before their untimely deaths. It's the gun that I carefully engraved our initials into, right underneath her grandparents' initials.

I want that gun back in her hands as much as she does.

The sight of my wildcat holding on to the doorframe with everything she had ripped a terror through my body like I'd never felt. I yelled out to her, but my words were swept away in the strong wind and rain. I've never run faster in my entire life.

The moment she let go and opened her arms, my heart stopped beating. Terror shot through me like everything I feared most had just stepped into the room. Images of what could have been flashed in front of my eyes. If I had been a second later, I would be looking for something other than the gun right now.

When her body slammed into mine, I wrapped my arms around her and held her tighter than I have ever held on to anything before. There was no way I was allowing God to take her from me yet. He would have to wait.

After I carried her inside her home last night, I checked her carefully. Thankfully, no damage was present. We ran a hot bath. We dropped into the steaming water, and I looked over every inch of her body. We were both lucky yesterday evening, only ending up with a handful of scrapes and bruises.

I dried us both off and carried her to bed, expecting to hold her until her breathing evened out. One simple kiss and nibble from my wildcat to my chest transformed into a slow, passionate dance between the sheets. I soaked in every pleasurable touch, whether I was giving or receiving. If there was ever any doubt that we were made for one another, we washed it away with every kiss, lick, thrust, and moan.

Sometimes it takes a certain event, one that makes you see how suddenly everything around you can be ripped away at the snap of a finger, to show you what really matters. I wasn't uncertain about Harlow and me, but my nebulous feelings about opening the academy have become crystal clear.

Once she was fast asleep, I got moving. Tornadoes are rare in this area because of all the mountains. As I approach what used to be the Lavender Lodge, I know without a doubt God protected us last night. The entire cottage was leveled and everything lies in disarray. We shouldn't have survived to see another day.

As the sun starts to rise, I start pulling large pieces of wood aside. With the amount of debris here, I need to contact a company to come out and help. This is going to take some time to go through. Finding her gun is going to be like finding a needle in a fucking haystack.

A pair of headlights creeps up, pulling next to my truck.

I stop my progress and watch Aleksei fold himself out of his Maserati, wondering why the hell he's here. Instead of his normal three-piece suit, he's in dark faded jeans and a sweatshirt. He has something in his hands. His attire changes his look completely, making me second-guess whether he really does run the most dangerous mob in Russia. But he's built and holds himself with so much power in everything he does, so I believe he does—and has seen more than most people.

"No suit? I figured you slept in one."

His lips twitch as he tosses me a pair of work gloves. "Do you even own a suit?"

I think back to the days when my father and I conducted business in our Armani suits. At the time, I thought that was what made a man a man. When I wore one, I felt powerful, in control. I only wore a suit to the Oasis one time, and that was the first time I came here to help Harlow.

Every time I returned, I dressed casually, ready to work on the cottages and assist Harlow in any way she needed. The way she peered up at me through her long lashes, I knew in that moment that no suit could ever make me feel as powerful as her bluish-gray eyes did.

"Not anymore." Though that might change when I open this academy. "What are you doing here?"

Aleksei pulls another set of gloves from his pocket. "Helping find her gun."

My eyebrows shoot up in disbelief that he would help anyone else. "Why?"

He pulls a glove on one hand and then the other. "I think it's pretty clear how much that gun means to her."

I narrow my eyes. He still hasn't told me exactly what his business dealings are with Harlow, only that he is looking to invest. I can respect a man who keeps his business to himself. Hell, I do the same thing. But everything changes when Harlow is involved. I meant what I said: She is my business. "So you decided to help find her revolver out of the goodness of your heart?"

He studies me silently for a minute, and I hold my strong stance in place. "She has a lot on her plate right now, and that is something I can relate to. If finding this gun will help her in any way, I want to do it."

What the fuck?

"What do you know about what's on her plate?"

"More than you know, and before you start throwing punches, I don't mean that in a disrespectful way."

"I know she's having money problems, and I'll be helping her with that," I say, my jaw tightening. He can't possibly believe that he knows more than I do. I know Harlow better than I know myself. She may not have told me herself, and I may have had to hack into her bank accounts to learn that tidbit, but I sure as hell won't be telling this asshole that.

"It's not the fact that she is going broke. It's the why."

It's a bullet to the chest. It takes everything not to show my shock. My wildcat trusted this man with her deepest secret but not me. I'm a man with a lot of pride, but when it comes to Harlow, I find it easy to ask the next question and show my cards. "Why's she broke?"

Instead of the cocky look I expect from him, his mouth turns downward. Sadness lurks within his eyes. "She asked me to keep that confidential."

A fire grows inside me as anger and hurt make an appearance. "And she thought she could share something confidential with you?"

He shakes his head, running his gloved hand across the top of his head. "She didn't have a choice. I left her no other option but to tell me."

Not even realizing it, I take a step toward him, preparing to show him what the corner of my elbow to his face is going to feel like.

He quickly steps back and holds up his hand. "But what you told me about Harlow and the Oasis has changed a few things for me. Then I take everything she told me…" He drops his hands. "How she reacted last night… Now I'm just not sure how to handle it."

I stop in my tracks, my fists still clenched tightly. I can read between the lines. "You're here to buy the Oasis after all."

"Not exactly. I came here to discuss becoming a partner with her. We would both own equal shares of the Oasis. I can help pull her from her debt, and she can help me expand into the States."

Fletch was right. Harlow would rather give up half of the Oasis than ask for a handout. If anybody becomes partners with my wildcat, it's going to be me. "Where's her money going?"

"I can't tell you. I'm a man of my word and I gave that when she told me. But from the way she latched onto you last night, I have no doubt she'll tell you herself."

I nod. I know I need to hear Harlow herself tell me

about whatever is causing her to be stressed out. I pull on the gloves and we get to work separating the pile piece by piece. It's the only thing I can do to not lose my shit.

The work is long and tedious, and by early afternoon, we've both stripped down to our T-shirts, the abnormally warm weather taking a toll on us.

Aleksei and I sit on the pile of wood that we have already gone through, munching on apples.

"I hear you're starting an academy," he says. I can see why this man is so powerful in Russia. He never takes his eyes off anyone.

"You're too old to be a student, so don't ask."

He chuckles and leans back on our makeshift bench. "What kind of academy will it be?"

I take a bite of my apple and crunch on it while I debate my answer. It won't be a normal academy, like thousands throughout the US. Instead, I want it to be a different type of education. "It'll be one of a kind, like the Oasis. I want to help build skills that can actually be useful in students' lives."

He nods, taking the last bite of his apple before chucking it into the woods. "What kind of skills?"

"Self-defense courses, weaponry safety and practice, business management, software, and security systems." I toss my apple into the same tree line and wipe my hands on my jeans before standing.

Aleksei stands next to me, sliding his work gloves back on. "It sounds like a perfect fit for the Oasis."

"It will be, and I plan on partnering with Harlow."

He gives a knowing nod. "And that's how you're going to help her financially without her feeling like you're giving her charity."

"She doesn't need you to keep the Oasis going forward. I'll never let the Oasis fail."

Aleksei's stare hardens. No doubt he dislikes the fact that I'm standing in the way of his expansion into the States.

I turn to head back to the pile of debris, ready to find the gun, when his next words stop me in my tracks.

"Let me know when you open your academy. I have a couple of nephews who could excel in a program like that one." He walks by, not giving me a passing glance as he grabs what could be a door and throws it on top of the pile.

I force my legs forward and begin working alongside him, not showing the effect his words have on me. As much as this dream scares me, everything keeps leading me in the same direction. First Harlow and Fletch, then Gage and Kali, and now Riggs and even Aleksei believe in the academy.

I force those thoughts from my mind and focus on the task in front of me. Fletch hung back today, setting up a new phone for Harlow and helping her with the new clients arriving throughout the day. One major issue is that one of the families was booked to stay at this cottage.

I was already spending every night with Harlow, so it didn't take much for Fletch and her to move our things back over to her place to free up Marion's Suite. I'm grateful Harlow's hectic schedule has been keeping her away. She needed distraction, and she has plenty.

By the end of the day, we're beat... and without the gun. Aleksei and I head back to Harlow's for dinner—a goulash dish, I think, that she and Fletch have attempted to make. It's horrible, but I don't care. I know dessert is going to be great.

Chapter Twenty-Three

Harlow.

I'm not sure what changed between Logan and Aleksei, but when they both showed up for dinner a few nights ago, anxiety snaked through my limbs. After the initial shock of seeing that Aleksei was still here after my meltdown, my second thought was that I wouldn't be able to face him after he witnessed it. It was as if I were hanging on by a string and it could snap at any moment.

To my relief, nothing was brought up, apart from the dismaying news that they hadn't found my gun yet.

The good thing is that I'm busier than a worker bee. I've been getting the newly arriving families all settled. After the Lavender Lodge was demolished by Mother Nature, I appreciated that the family who'd originally booked it was okay with taking Marion's Suite.

I helped Fletcher move his belongings—and those of

Logan's that hadn't migrated to my cabin or his academy—back to my place and did a quick clean job. It was ready to go an hour before the family arrived. I offered them a discount for the change-up, but they dismissed the offer quickly. I wasn't going to argue. I need every dime I can get.

An advantage of settling everyone in was that I got to inspect the majority of the property. Except for the back quarter, everything was intact, showing no sign that a tornado was so close mere days ago. The only cottage that was damaged was the one Logan and I were trapped in.

Surviving the tornado was one of the scariest moments of my life. Losing my grandparents' .357 Magnum revolver in the chaos was even worse. I have no idea if it remains buried under the rubble, but I pray it's still there.

"The couple staying in the Ivy Hollow cottage just left," Fletcher says as he walks up to me. He's been helping me out the past few days, not only as an extra set of hands but also as a way of keeping my mind off things. I don't think there's a better best friend.

"Thanks. I'll hit that one next after I stop by the clinic to check on Johnny Kapps." Mr. Kapps is a long-standing client who's had his hands on military-grade weapons for the past four decades. I'm not sure how he ended up with a bullet to the kneecap, but I'm relieved to see he's okay. He just received a knee replacement from my medical staff. He's scheduled to stay here while he recovers with assistance from one of the nurses on staff. That's six weeks of steady income for the Grecian Wildflower cottage, the one closest to the wildflower gun range.

"Do you have a second?" I ask Fletcher.

"Sure," he says, leaning against the counter. His walk is almost back to normal and he's heading to the clinic today to see if he can finally get the walking cast removed. With the way he has been getting around, I would bet money it's coming off. Well, if I had any money to bet on, that is.

"The night of the tornado, Logan's shirt was covered in blood. You wouldn't happen to know anything about that, would you?"

Fletcher chews on his lower lip, assessing me. "It wasn't blood. It was paint."

"Paint?"

"Yeah, we were doing work at his place, and it got out of control."

I cross my arms and bite my inner cheek to not laugh. Logan and Fletcher have become fast friends. I couldn't be happier, but seriously? "Really. Because Logan told me you two were having a hot dog eating contest and it was ketchup."

Fletcher drops his head and chuckles, shaking his head. "You remember Naz?"

How could I ever forget that asshole? He crushed Fletcher's heart after playing him like a fiddle. I'm not sure what Naz has to do with anything, though. "Yeah..."

"Well, he stopped by the academy. He heard I was staying here and thought Logan and I were a couple."

My eyes widen in surprise. "No!" I say in a rush. That is the funniest thing I've heard in a while.

"Yep. The asshole had me pinned against the wall, being a complete jerk, when Logan showed up. Your man broke his nose with the first punch he threw." Fletcher is smiling largely, clearly feeling good having had Logan on his side.

Logan defended Fletcher. I don't know why Logan would hide that from me, but he didn't need to. I love the idea of Logan having Fletcher's back. It wasn't too long ago that these two were always going at it.

"Good. I'm glad Naz won't have a straight nose for the rest of his life. Serves him right."

"Ah, well, I'm sure he already has an appointment with his surgeon, but this will definitely put a cramp in his schedule for a couple of months."

My new phone pings, and I check my messages, hoping to hear something from my dad, but it's from Mr. Kapps, wanting to know if his room is ready.

"Logan?" Fletcher asks.

I shake my head. "No, Mr. Kapps. I need to head to the clinic and take him to his cottage."

"Let's ride together. I have to be there shortly to see the doctor anyways. You can take my Gator and just stop to pick me up."

"Are you sure?" My Gator has been MIA since the

tornado came barreling through. Logan's Gator, by some miracle, was still there with only a couple of dents and scratches.

If we have yet to find my big Gator, I'm not sure how lucky we'll be at finding my gun. The thought alone depresses me. I push the negativity away. It's not like I have any other choice. "Yeah, of course."

We hop in and head to the clinic. Once there, Fletcher heads one way, while I head to Mr. Kapps's room. The doctor informs me that his surgery went great and he'll be back up and walking in no time at all. You can't get better news when you are talking about a man in his eighties.

I drive Mr. Kapps over to the Grecian Wildflower cottage. I get him settled in on a chair, pull a footstool over, and prop his leg up.

"Where's that young man been lately?"

"Who? Fletcher?"

He chuckles and it turns into a fit of coughs. The man loved his cigars in his earlier years. I head to the kitchen, grab a bottle of water, and pass it to him.

He takes a drink before resting the bottle on his thigh. "No, the other one. The one back from the dead."

That's one thing I like about this man. He never beats around the bush or sugarcoats anything. "How do you know about him?"

He snorts. "Everyone on your staff has been talking about him, especially the women." He bounces his eyebrows. I roll my eyes. "He sounds good for you, kid."

I take a seat across from him. "I don't know what I would have done if he hadn't been here." Admitting the truth out loud feels like unloading a truck full of masonry bricks, leaving a refreshing feeling throughout my body.

He nods, taking another drink. "Your grandparents would have approved."

Johnny Kapps started coming here thirty years before I took over. I have several memories of his wife and him when I was a little girl, running around picking wildflowers and catching bugs. He was close with both my grandparents, so hearing that he believes they would approve of Logan and me together tugs at my heart.

I just don't know how much they would approve of losing half of the Oasis. I swallow down that thought, not wanting to bring it to light. No clients will ever know that Aleksei will be half owner. If the deal goes through, we've agreed to make him a silent partner.

"Thank you. That means a lot coming from you."

"When are you going to get off your ass and make it official?"

I laugh and shake my head. "If only it were that simple."

"It is, my dear," he says firmly. "Our minds can be a dangerous thing. We can complicate things that are made to be simple. Take my late wife Gloria. She made me work my ass off for her. It took me almost a year before that stubborn woman would let me in. After she did, everything fell into place as it was meant to be."

I lean back in my chair. I remember his wife well. She was beautiful, with bright red hair and a sassiness I envied. "What wouldn't she open up about?"

"Money. Of all the things it could have been, it was money." He shakes his head in disappointment. "She'd been struggling to take care of her younger siblings because her mother passed away when she was sixteen and her father was developing alcoholism. Instead of telling me what was causing her so much stress, she carried the burden alone when all she needed to do was ask me for help."

Her situation sounds eerily close to my own. "Maybe she wanted to prove she could do it by herself."

"That's exactly why she kept it secret from me. What she didn't understand was that's what couples are meant to do. They help each other out. They have each other's backs and support one another through thick and thin."

My mind goes to Logan. I know that Logan would jump into action without hesitation the second he learned my mother has cancer. He would move mountains to help not only me but also both my parents. But Logan is in a different situation from that of Mr. Kapps. He's still trying to find his footing, his place in life. If I were to unload all this onto him, he would put his own dreams of teaching on the back burner for me.

"You can't blame her for not wanting to disrupt your life and everything you had going."

"Let me ask you this, my dear." He leans against the armrest. "If the shoe were on the other foot and someone you loved and cared about was hiding something from you, something you could help them with, would you want to know?"

I open my mouth to retort, but no words form. He's right. I would be pissed if Logan didn't come to me for help. Hell, I was pissed when his parents were murdered and he shut me out. Everything after that became chaotic between us and, in turn, planted a wedge that lasted for seven years.

So, the question becomes clear. Why *don't* I open up to Logan or even Fletcher about this? I was so upset with Logan for years when he wouldn't let me in to help him, and yet I'm doing the same thing to him.

I have to break the pattern. I have to tell Logan about my mother before this breaks us apart again—this time for good.

"Does it ever get old being right all the time?" I ask.

He smiles warmly.

I head out after leaving Mr. Kapps with Old Man Joe's contact information—in case he needs a discreet courier for sensitive documents or to relay word to some of his off-the-grid contacts. I hop back in the Gator and send a quick text to Fletcher asking how long he has left. He responds that he still has another twenty minutes, which will give me enough time to swing by and talk to Florence. If I am going to do this, then I'm going to need help making a kickass dinner. I need my head chef's advice. It's the least I can do for what I am about to tell him.

I call my dad next, wanting to inform him that I plan on telling Logan and Fletcher about my mother's cancer. He's been adamant about no one knowing, but my guys aren't *no one*. He doesn't answer, so I text him about the tornado and say not to worry, that I'm okay, and to call when he gets a chance. I don't mention anything else.

I can see that he reads my text immediately but doesn't respond. I can't say it doesn't sting a little bit. I know if I ever have a kid and they messaged me something like that, I would be blowing their phone up. But I guess my dad does have a lot on his plate. I'm probably being selfish.

I drop my shades to shield my eyes from the sun and head out. I have a lot to do before Logan gets home tonight.

Chapter Twenty-Four

Logan.

Aleksei and I are still working on clearing away what was left of the Lavender Lodge. I could've had the construction crew I have working on other cottage repairs help, but I don't want to stop their progress. Besides, I don't want to take the chance of someone overlooking the gun.

Aleksei brought in a couple of his men to help search the surrounding property, and they found Harlow's Gator this morning. It was all the way over on the lot on the east side. The property is vacant and almost as large as the Oasis. They snapped a picture and sent it to Aleksei. Twisted and ruined, but it was nonetheless found.

At the end of the day, I invite Aleksei and his men to join us for dinner, but they all decline. I don't think Aleksei can stomach another night of Harlow's cooking.

I can't say I blame him. After all, he doesn't get the dessert I do. Instead, they offer to pick up her Gator and drop it off by the shed near Harlow's house.

It's almost seven in the evening by the time I make it home. Rich aromas hit my nose and the heavenly smell carries me into the kitchen. Harlow stands with her back to me, studying handwritten notes. I sneak up behind her, wrapping my arms around her waist and inhaling her chestnut hair.

She squeals in surprise. Laughing, she turns around and locks lips with me for a quick kiss. We break apart and she smiles. "You're early."

She's in a great mood, so telling her I have yet to find her gun is not high on my to-do list. I lean in and nibble her neck as she giggles, goosebumps pop up across her tan skin. "I have to clean up first. How long do I have?"

"Thirty minutes and not a second longer." She begins to pull away, but I yank her back to my chest.

"Come with me," I growl, her sweet vanilla scent making my cock twitch.

"I've worked too hard on this meal to let it get burned."

"It would be worth it," I reply, taking her mouth again. She's velvet and fire on my lips, the kind of taste that makes you forget your name. I release her and walk backward out of the room, getting my fill of my beautiful woman as her cheeks flush red.

Twenty-eight minutes later, I'm clean and starving. Harlow has set up the table outside on the patio, with a campfire roaring off to the side. Fletcher is here now and already seated, wearing that stupid coral-colored shirt he tried to make me wear the other day. He takes a sip from his rocks glass. He looks good and refreshed. It takes me a second to realize what's missing.

"They took it off," I say as I walk out onto the patio. It's getting cooler at night and perfect for outside dinners.

"Yep, a week sooner than they planned. I guess you do know something about physical therapy after all."

"Of course I do." I grin and slap his back. "Now that the boot's off, I plan on working your ass ten times harder now."

Harlow struts out and uncovers the dish to reveal a chicken that has been baked to perfection. I about fall over with how good it looks and smells. "You made this?"

Popping a hand on her hip, she looks me dead in the eyes and says, "Kind of."

I throw my head back, laughing. She's too damn cute for her own good. Pulling her to me, I kiss the tip of her nose. "You want to elaborate on *kind of*?"

She sucks on her bottom lip, making it very difficult to concentrate on anything else. "Well, Florence tossed it all together and gave me notes on how to cook it or bake it." She waves her hand. "You know what I mean."

I grin down at her. She may be amazing at everything she does, but cooking isn't one of them. Baking either. Her asking for help saved me from having to admit her dinners suck. But hey, since I won't have to, I might as well try and get some extra brownie points. "C'mon, that goulash you made wasn't too bad."

Fletch chokes on his drink behind her.

My wildcat rolls her eyes. "That was spaghetti, Logan, not goulash."

"That's what I said."

"Are you always going to be difficult?"

I grab my chest as if her question caused physical pain to me. "You think I'm difficult? Look at Fletch." I point to him. "He doesn't even know how to dress."

Fletch's eyes narrow on me and I smile widely in response.

Harlow looks over to Fletch as he adjusts himself in the chair, his chest puffing out slightly. "Actually, I love that shirt. The coral really brings out your complexion and highlights your cheekbones. I think I even have a dress that color. Where'd you get it?" she asks.

Fletch leans his head to the side to get a good look at my scowl, then fills her in on his stores of choice.

She says, "You should go with Fletcher next time he goes."

Now it's my turn to roll my eyes. I would rather take another bullet than wear anything coral, but I seal my lips.

We all settle in and eat the baked chicken. It's covered with a made-from-scratch light white cream sauce and sun-dried tomatoes. Aleksei is going to kick himself in the ass when I tell him what she *kind of* made.

After dinner, I help Harlow clear the dishes. Fletch

comes inside and announces, "I'm taking off for the night."

Harlow wipes her hands on the towel. "Where you going?"

"I have a date."

I chuckle before saying, "You better change that ugly fucking shirt first."

Fletch shrugs like my opinion means nothing and heads out while we finish cleaning the kitchen.

Once we're done, we head back to the patio. Harlow pulls out a couple of chairs while I stoke the fire. The nights are getting cooler, but nothing but warmth runs through me when it comes to alone time with her. It's rare for us, so when it happens, I want to take full advantage. I run back into the house to grab her a bottle of wine and myself a bottle of bourbon. I also grab one of my hoodies for Harlow to put on; her arms are covered in goosebumps.

I pour our glasses. We lean back into our chairs and watch the flames dance under the darkened sky. I debate how to bring up her money issues without revealing that I hacked into her accounts. Who knows when we're going to get another night alone again?

"Can I see your drink?" Harlow asks, eyeing my bourbon on the rocks. Not sure where this is going, I learned a long time ago not to ask questions. I hold it out to her, and with her free hand, the one not holding her glass of wine, she slams it back in one go.

I cock my head to the side.

She gives me a silly smile. "Liquid courage," she says.

That's all it takes for me to grab my glass and refill it. I don't put as much in it, not wanting her to get too much liquid courage. Maybe Aleksei called it right and she will finally open up to me about what's going on.

I hold it out to her and without hesitation, she downs the second glass. I refill it.

"No more. I'm good."

"This one's for me," I reply and she nods, taking a small sip of her wine.

I adjust myself in the chair for a better view of Harlow. She notices this and squirms in her seat. I love that after all these years, I can still make her squirm. She sets her wine on the table next to her and wipes her hands across her jean-covered thighs. "I'm sorry. This shouldn't be this hard, yet it is."

"Take your time, wildcat," I say.

She nods but doesn't make eye contact. She's clearly uneasy by the way she keeps shifting in her chair and tugging on the hoodie that's too large for her small frame. I want to blurt that she has nothing to worry about when it comes to her finances, but I remain quiet.

She shakes out her hands, grabs her glass of wine, and takes a large gulp. Then she slams it back down and turns to face me.

"My mother has cancer."

As if my hearing has stopped working, I question whether I heard her correctly. That can't be right. Fletch just confirmed that they were on a cruise last week.

My nonresponse must take her by surprise because she starts babbling. "I should have told you sooner, and I'm so sorry I didn't. It's just been a lot to take in and I didn't want you to worry. You have enough on your plate with the academy, and you've already put that on the back burner to help me with the cleanup from the tornado."

I place my hand on her leg. "Breathe, wildcat."

She nods and takes a couple of deep breaths.

"Good girl," I praise her as she attempts to calm down. I reach over and hand her my drink. This time, she takes a small sip. "How's your mom doing?" I ask, not knowing if this is something new or something she's been battling for a while now. Maybe she hasn't started treatment yet and they were taking one last trip before it all began.

"I don't know. She's hanging in there, I guess. I haven't been able to talk to her yet." Harlow drops her head.

Hanging in there, she guesses? "You haven't seen her." I don't pose it as a question, because it's clear she hasn't, but she doesn't take it as a statement.

She shakes her head. "No, but I've tried." She exhales slowly and looks up at the moon, partially hidden by the clouds rolling in. "My dad told me he's working on it, so I'm hoping I'll see her soon. She was getting worse, to the point that even he wasn't able to see her for some time."

The hair on my arms stands straight at her soft-spoken words. Something is off with this entire situation.

Since when can't you see a cancer patient? With technology and protocols nowadays, if that were the case, which I highly doubt, why couldn't she make a FaceTime call?

Robin Reece isn't in bad shape right now. She might have had her face covered with the large hat in that photo Fletcher obtained, but she didn't appear to be having any trouble climbing those tall stairs onto the ship.

Now it's my turn to take a sip of my drink, but it isn't for liquid courage. It's to try and calm the rage that is slowly building inside me. "Have you talked with the doctor about her condition?"

"Dr. Montgomery? No. My dad has had a hard time meeting with him as well. He's one of the best on the East Coast and has a lot of patients."

I try not to show the tension in my neck, shoulders, and arms. Hell, at this point, my damn pinky toe feels tense. "Is she getting treatment?"

Her nod is jerky as she licks her lips. "Yeah, for the last couple of years. Nothing worked, and it kept spreading. That's when it got so bad my father couldn't even see her." She swallows hard as if she has a lump in her throat from picturing the condition of her mother. "She started this new trial drug over a week ago, and so far, her body hasn't rejected it."

The last couple of *years*? That answers the question of where all her money has been going. Those motherfucking scumbags. I crack my neck, the tension becoming too much to handle. Harlow takes notice, but quite frankly, I don't give a damn.

"I've been covering the medical bills for my mom since this all started. This new trial drug isn't covered and costs five hundred thousand dollars."

I grind my teeth at the amount of money she's giving these people who left her to fend for herself because she wouldn't sell her grandparents' business. She worked her ass off to keep her grandparents' dream—her love and dream—alive, and now she's losing it over her parents' greed.

This must be how they paid for the cruise and how they can afford the obnoxious home they now reside in. They never had it like that and were always bitter toward Harlow when she inherited the Oasis. That's why I never cared for either one of them. They felt they should've received the inheritance, not her.

She gulps audibly, her forehead glistening from a thin layer of sweat. "That's why Aleksei is here. He's willing to become a silent partner to the Oasis, and in return, I'll give him half ownership."

I rub my forehead, trying to ward off the headache that has begun pounding in my skull, but it's worthless. If there's one thing I can't stand in life, it's when someone I love is being taken advantage of.

"Say something. Please."

My gaze slowly lifts to meet hers. She wants me to say something. I don't think she realizes what she's asking for, but if she wants my honest-to-God truth, I'll give it to her. "When did you become so naïve?"

Her lips pinch together, clearly not appreciative of

my question. "Excuse me?" she hisses, her body locking up.

I plant my legs wide, bringing my elbows to rest on my knees, my face closer to hers. "You've been giving away all your hard-earned money to someone you haven't seen or spoken to."

"It's for my mother, Logan. Not some stranger off the streets looking for a handout."

I slam the remaining shot from my glass and throw it into the fire. The glass explodes and the flames burn higher. She jerks back. What did she expect me to do? Tell her I'm proud that she has been manipulated? Excuse me, *is* being manipulated.

"Your parents have never been good people, Harlow, so stop kidding yourself. They're as much of a stranger to you as someone you pass on the street."

We both rise from our seats, anger and frustration soaring between us. "Don't give me that shit. You would've given away everything you have to save your parents."

I clench my fists at the mention of my parents. "They weren't pieces of shit like yours."

The sharp slap that rings out against my cheek is the only noise around the crackling fire. "How dare you say that? We might have had our differences, but that doesn't mean I can sit back and watch her die."

I throw my arms wide. "And that's exactly why they're playing you out of all your damn money!" I roar. "You've never questioned anything when it comes to them. You just keep your little pocketbook wide open for them to stick their greedy-ass hands into."

"Fuck you, Logan! You have no idea what you're talking about."

"I wish I didn't." And I mean it. I wish I were wrong about this, but I know I'm not. She can't see this because of her large heart, which she wears on her sleeve for the people she loves. "And you won't be signing over any part of the Oasis to Aleksei Fucking Morozov."

Her eyes turn to slits as she props her hands on her hips. "You don't get to tell me what I'm going to do."

I shake my head at her ignorance. I feel like I am about to fall off a cliff at any given moment, so I do the only thing I can. I walk away. Slamming the door open, I stalk to our bedroom and grab my truck keys.

When I come back out of the cottage, I find her standing in the same spot. Her chest rises and falls in hard bursts.

"Did you know your parents have been on a cruise all week long?"

Her face shows shock for only a brief moment before she conceals it. If I didn't know her as well as I do, I would've missed it.

"I can't stand back and watch you destroy everything." I give her one last look before I turn my back and head to my truck. This wasn't how I expected the night to end, but one thing's for certain.

I can't get out of here fast enough.

Chapter Twenty-Five

Harlow.

I did it. I finally told Logan about my mom's cancer, and it turned into a complete disaster, just like I feared. I had hoped Logan would understand, especially since he lost both his parents. But I was wrong.

Logan never cared for my parents, and I get it. I truly do. But everything has changed with my mother's diagnosis. It's brought my dad and me closer over the last two years, and soon, I'll be closer to my mom.

Logan's major trust issues are getting in the way. He needs to learn to step back and not let his past experiences color everything. Ever since his parents were murdered, he hasn't been able to bring himself to trust anyone.

Except for Fletcher. I shake those thoughts from my head. There's no room for ignorance any longer.

I'm literally walking in circles in my home. My mind

feels like it's about to explode, replaying everything he spat out last night. He called me naïve. That word alone is enough to bring my blood to a boil. And the icing on the cake is that he never came back home last night.

In true Logan fashion, he just up and disappeared, leaving me high and dry once again. He has proven to be great at that. At sunrise, shrouded in fog, I take Fletcher's Gator and hit the trail to the academy. There's no sign of him. I head to Aleksei's cottage next, but once again, Logan's truck is nowhere in sight. Now I'm heading to what was once the Lavender Lodge. I don't care who is there. Logan and I are having it out.

Then I'm going to escort his ass off my property for good.

If he has a problem with me helping my dying mother, then he can kiss my ass. I don't care that my parents aren't perfect. Who is? They're still my parents, and I would do anything in the world to help them. They might not have earned top marks in parenting, but they would never con me out of so much money—a sum that, thanks to this latest treatment, has now climbed to well over a million dollars.

My phone vibrates in my pocket. I slow the Gator and pull it out. Aleksei's name flashes across my screen, and disappointment punches me hard in the chest. I wanted it to be Logan. After all the shit he pulled, I still wanted it to be his fucking name on my phone. I drop my head in pure disgust. I wanted to hear Logan beg for my forgiveness.

Jesus. I'm desperate to believe he didn't leave me high and dry.

I shake my head. Maybe he's right. Maybe I am naïve, but it seems I'm only that way when it comes to him. I lean my head back on the headrest, tempted to turn this Gator around and climb into my bed to hide from the world today.

A bed that still smells like him.

I shoot a text to Aleksei telling him I'll be there shortly and turn the Gator around. I make it back to my place in no time flat. Stomping up the porch, I enter my code to unlock my door and head straight for my bedroom.

I rip off the comforter, the sheets, the pillows, and even the bed skirt and haul them outside. I head back in and grab my mattress. I tug it through my house, knocking over several things before getting through my back door. I toss it on top of everything and head back for the box spring.

By the time I find gasoline and a box of matches, I'm breathing heavily and sweating. I waste no time splashing gasoline over everything and take a step back. It takes me five matches before I can get one to light. My hands are shaking too badly. I toss it on and a blast of hot air blows across my face. Even with everything burning, I can still smell him. That's when I take notice of the hoodie I am wearing.

Logan's hoodie.

Not giving two shits, I peel the hoodie off my body,

leaving me heaving in only my bra and jeans. My hair is a wild mess, but I don't care.

This is why you never go backward in life. Logan was an ex for a reason. He should have stayed in my past, but like a *naïve* woman, I let him walk right back in and ruin me once and for all.

This is all on me. I have no one to blame but myself. A deranged laugh spills from my lips. I swear I'll never fall victim to Logan's charms again. I don't care if he opens that academy. I'll make damn sure we never coexist again.

"Um, Miss Reece?"

I turn to see Mrs. Carter standing back about ten feet from me, twisting her hands. She and her husband just arrived a couple of nights ago. I know what I must look like to her. My bed is now turning to ashes in my driveway and I'm standing half naked outside, panting like a damn dog. "There was a spider in my bed."

Her eyes go wide at my lame excuse, but how else can I explain my meltdown? If my clients see that I am losing my mind, how can they trust me to keep them safe? I take a deep breath and let calmness flow through me. Some type of box-breathing crap that my grandma taught me many years ago. I'm not sure it even works, but what else do I have to lose?

"What can I do for you, Mrs. Carter?"

"Oh well." Her eyes glance at my burning mattress before they land back on me. "I just stopped by to see if you could come and look at my husband's stitches. They're still red, and I wanted to make sure it wasn't infected, but I can see you're busy, so—"

"Nonsense, I'm available. I'll be over in a few minutes," I reply, straining to keep my tone in line with how it needs to be. Her husband was cut badly and waited too long before coming here. He hadn't been cleaning it and arrived with it already infected. The doctors told me they had removed the infection, but I can understand her concern for her husband.

I'm sure he never left her high and dry.

I look down at Logan's hoodie, which is gripped tightly in my hands. I toss it into the fire and turn to head back inside to get a shirt. Mrs. Carter is still standing there, but now her lips twitch from holding back a grin.

"Another spider?"

I smile. "Something like that."

It ends up being another hour before I make it to the remains of the Lavender Lodge. A couple of men are hard at work clearing debris. I don't recognize any of them. One thing missing is a black truck, confirming that Logan did leave and hasn't come back.

I look at where the cottage once sat and take it all in.

I guess it makes sense that it's nothing but rubble now. The Lavender Lodge is where it really got started for Logan and me, and in a bittersweet way, where it all ended for us too. It feels as if it were years ago that Logan came to this very spot and saved my life.

And now that I've told him about my mother, whatever we had is a pile of rubble as well. It's fitting.

"Harlow."

I turn my attention to the side to see Aleksei walking up to me with a smile. He's wearing dark jeans and a black sweatshirt, throwing me off for a second.

"I didn't know you owned anything outside of a suit."

His deep chuckle rumbles through his chest. "That's exactly what Logan said."

My shoulders tense at his name. "Is he here?"

Aleksei eyes me warily. "No, I have not seen him today. Should he be?"

I really don't want to open this Pandora's box. "No, not at all." I turn my eyes back to where the cottage once was, not able to take his stare. "You guys have really knocked this out." His eyes don't leave me, but I refuse to look at him.

Eventually he turns his attention to what is left, and I thank the heavens above. "Yeah, we should be done today."

"I see that. Thank you. You didn't have to get involved."

"Considering I'm going to be part owner..."

He leaves his Russian accent–laced words hanging in the light breeze. It was never supposed to end up like this. It was only supposed to be me owning the Oasis… and whoever I married. Then maybe we would have a couple of kids to pass the Oasis down to.

Oh God, how is that even going to look down the road? If Aleksei gets married and has a family, is he going to want his heirs to take over his half? What if his kids and my kids don't get along? What if their visions are too different and his kids refuse to be silent partners?

"You're not changing your mind, are you?"

This time, I do make eye contact with him. "No, of course not. I'm just wondering how this is going to go after we're gone and our kids are running this place."

His eyebrows shoot up and a wicked smile comes across his face. "Our kids? I didn't know we would be creating any children together with this agreement, but I can most definitely add that into the contract."

I roll my eyes. I swear men only have a one-track mind. "I meant my kids and your kids." I shake my head. I'm getting way ahead of myself. "Never mind me. I'm just having an off day."

Thankfully he doesn't question further and changes the subject. "I have something for you." He jerks his head, and I follow him over to his Maserati. He unlocks the door and leans in, grabbing something out of the glovebox. "I think you've been missing this."

I take my grandparents' gun and clasp my trembling fingers around it. My eyes burn as I try to hold back sudden tears that want to escape. It doesn't even have one scratch on it. I don't know how that's even possible.

"Mr. Morozov," one of the guys yells. Before Aleksei can retreat, I rise on my toes and wrap my arms around his large frame.

"Thank you so much," I choke out as his grip tightens around me.

"It was my pleasure."

Aleksei backs away to go talk with his team of workers. I look down at one of my most prized possessions and rub my fingers across the initials engraved into it. I wish I could be mad that Logan put our initials permanently on it *again*, but I'm not. When Marion first showed up like an angel sent from God, it changed my life, and meeting her son changed it again. I'm not sure where I would have ended up if I'd never had all the Keeyeses' support.

"Low!" Fletcher shouts as he pulls up next to me in Logan's Gator. I'm assuming he took Logan's since I took his. "What the hell is going on?"

"Aleksei found my gun." I hold it up and give a weak smile. I hope Fletcher isn't in the know regarding what went down last night, but by the concerned look on his face, I realize it's only wishful thinking.

He wastes no time jumping out and walking over to me. He engulfs me in a large hug, then pulls away.

"Before you even start," I say, "where is he?"

"I was hoping you knew. He called me late last night, hollering about bloodsucking scum and how he's sick and tired of watching people getting taken advantage of." He looks over my shoulder, then meets my gaze. He jerks his head at Aleksei. "Is this over that asshole?"

"My mother has cancer." The words tumble out of me so easily that it shocks me.

Fletcher takes a step back, raising his hand to his chest. "Oh my God. Did you just find out last night?"

I look down at the pebbled ground and kick a rock. "No. She's been battling it for two years now." My eyes lift to his green ones.

His face pales.

The cat seems to have caught his tongue, so I elaborate. "Logan told me that my parents were on a cruise last week and how they're horrible people who are taking advantage of my naïve ass with all the money I've given them so far."

I expect Fletcher to throw his arms around me again and insist that we drink all the wine in the house and eat chocolate all night long. That's what we did when Naz shredded his heart. Instead, I get a silent Fletcher, who's now having problems looking me in the eyes.

"I think it's time for me to ask you what the hell is going on."

His shoulders slump forward. "That's probably my fault."

It's my turn to step back. "What do you mean?" I remain as frozen as a statue.

He plants his hands on his hips and tips his head back to the sky, dragging in a breath like he's bracing for impact. "I hired a private investigator to check into your parents. He sent me a picture of them boarding a cruise ship last week... and I showed it to Logan."

"You went behind my back and hired a private investigator to stalk my parents?" I whisper-yell. How could he do that? *Maybe because I refused to talk to anyone about it*, my conscience sneers in the back of my head. I rightly choose to ignore her.

"We were worried about you, Low. You've been so stressed and we wanted to help."

I dig my nails into my palms, my chest tightening. Both of the men in my life who I love and trust went behind my back. Whatever happened to sitting down and talking with someone? I'm sure if they had tag-teamed me, I would have eventually caved... Maybe.

Knowing these two, they probably hacked into my bank accounts and already know my financial state. I'm going to eliminate anyone in my life who knows how to make a pie chart in Excel. They're too dangerous.

"I want to see it." I hold out my hand.

Fletcher groans but wisely decides to comply. He unlocks his phone and scrolls through it. He turns the screen toward me.

I yank it from his hands and almost immediately drop it. It's hard to see either of their faces, but there's no doubt that it's my parents. My mom's face is mostly covered by a large yellow hat, and my father's back is completely turned to the camera.

The thing I stay locked on is her stride up the stairs

to board this ship. My father isn't even helping her. In fact, he's a few steps in front of her. I'm at a complete loss. Yes, he told me her first treatment went well and her body didn't reject it, but he also said it was a touch-and-go situation.

I push Fletcher's phone back into his hand. "Don't bother stopping by tonight. I need some time to myself." I turn on my heel and stomp back to the Gator.

Turning the key, I glance over to where Aleksei was standing earlier and meet his intense stare. I don't know if he heard any of that conversation, but I'm not waiting to find out. Everyone can kiss my ass right now.

Chapter Twenty-Six

Harlow.

I lean forward in my chair, my elbows resting on the dining room table. I've lost track of how many times I've pulled up his phone number, only to close it back out. I know I won't be able to get anything done until I talk to him, but the lump in my throat is only getting larger by the minute.

Sure, the things I need to get done consist of drinking chilled red wine and finishing off a bag of chocolate. I need to suck it up and hit the call button before I don't.

Before I lose my nerve, I do it. It rings a couple of times before connecting. I'm not sure whether I'm happy he answered or not.

"Sweetheart."

"How was the cruise?"

Silence greets me and my eyes fall closed. I wait for

his answer with bated breath. If Logan is right about them taking advantage of me... I can't even fathom what that will mean.

"It was what your mother needed, though she couldn't enjoy the entire trip. I was getting ready to call and tell you about it, but it seems someone beat me to the punch."

"You have me on the phone now. I'm listening." My tone is low but firm. I won't allow anyone to get in my head until I gather knowledge from every angle. I know Logan believes what he's claiming, but I also know he's hotheaded and is quick to jump to conclusions. Case in point: Logan would have bet his life that Fletcher and I were hooking up.

My dad clears his throat before speaking. "Oh, sweetheart, it was nice. Dr. Montgomery was the one who tossed the idea out to me. He thought if she could get away somewhere to give her mind a mental break from all the anguish she's been living in, the second dose might have an even greater effect."

I chew on the inside of my lip, mentally weighing his words. *Why wouldn't he bring her here?*

I'm not sure how he takes my silence. He continues. "I hope that doesn't upset you. Your mother has been through so much. This trip was a breath of fresh air for her. She spent about 80 percent of the time in bed, but she loved gazing out the little window when she wasn't sleeping."

Guilt claws at my throat, but I have to say it. I've

never been the type to hold back, and I can't now. "She boarded the cruise on her own. She looked fine to me."

"If only the entire trip had been like that," he says, his voice calm and steady. "You know how your mom is about the public seeing her like this. By the time we got to our room, she collapsed into my arms. I had to carry her to the bed."

Frowning, my shoulders drop in pure disappointment at myself. I do know exactly how my mom is about public appearances, and I'm sure that's why she was wearing that oversized hat. She's always cared way too much about what everyone felt about her. I tried telling her that everyone else was only a distraction to her own dreams, but she would always laugh in response.

"I need to come see her. And you."

"I already have it in the works."

"You do?" I ask, now feeling like a bigger piece of shit for even thinking they were taking advantage of me.

"Absolutely, sweetheart. I talked with Dr. Montgomery, and he wants to meet you as well. His schedule is booked tight, but he had a cancellation and can see us all."

I sit up straight in my chair. Not only will I see my mom and dad, but I'll also get to meet with the doctor. "That's great. When?"

"Monday morning. We'll be the first appointment."

Today is Thursday. That should give me time to arrange travel and make sure things are set with the Oasis while I'm gone. It doesn't matter. I would move mountains to be there. "I'll see you both in a couple of days. Should I book a hotel room?"

"No, we have room for you here. I'll text you the address. Safe travels, sweetheart."

We say our goodbyes and I end the call. An unexpected release of tension sweeps my body. I pop another piece of chocolate into my mouth. I knew there was no way Logan was right about my parents, but I would be lying if I said he didn't get me thinking.

Come Monday morning, I'll have all the answers I need. Maybe after her treatment is done, she can come out to the Oasis and stay for the holiday season. She's never been much for the countryside, more a city slicker, but it's worth a shot. She might want to step away like she did when she took the cruise.

I uncork the bottle of wine and pour myself a hefty glass. I think after the day I have had, a little unwinding is long overdue. I head over to the couch, but just as I am setting down my glass, a loud knock comes at my front door.

Seriously?

I pull my gun from my waistband and head to the front door. It isn't unusual to have clients stop by unexpectedly, but that doesn't mean I can ever take my guard down. I peer through the glass and see the last person I thought would be on the other side of the door.

Tucking away my gun, I enter the code to the alarm system, disengage the lock, and pull it open. "Well, this is a surprise."

Aric leans against the door jam, his pitch-black hair tousled and his bright emerald eyes blazing. His usual cocky smile is on full display. "I noticed you didn't say it was a pleasant surprise."

I pop my hand on my hip and tilt my head. "Didn't I?" I respond with a smile.

"You most definitely did not." He jabs his finger, pointing toward my driveway. "Is that a burned-up mattress in your driveway?"

I completely forgot to clean that mess up. "It was time for a new one," I say. He's in his normal attire, a Brunello Cucinelli suit, but it's slightly crinkled and stiff, the jacket sleeve darkened by liquid.

"The great Aric Hemmington has finally been shot. Or is this a knifing I'm working with?" I step aside and motion for Aric to come in.

He strolls in as if everything is fine, grabbing my glass of wine and slamming it down in one go. Well, maybe not as fine as I thought, but he sure knows how to hide it well. "Damn. You always have the best wine," he says, turning to face me. "And it's a bullet hole to my bicep. Should be an easy patch."

I grab the empty wineglass from his hand and jerk my head for him to follow. I refill it and hand it back to him, then pour one for myself.

"Take your shirt off. I'll grab the materials." I head to the bathroom to grab everything I'll need to stitch him up. Aric has stayed at the Oasis plenty of times and has used the amenities I offer, but never once has he been shot. At least not to my knowledge.

I return to the kitchen to find Aric shirtless, leaning against my counter, sipping wine, and smirking. He's cut; a distinct V disappears into the waistband of his slacks. His chest and abs are completely covered in tattoos.

"Who's the lucky bastard to be the first one to shoot you?" I ask as I drop everything onto the table. I take a sip of wine and head to the sink to wash my hands.

A husky laugh fills my ears. "It was a lucky lady, if you can believe it. A miscalculation I won't be making again."

Drying my hands and smiling largely, I snap on a pair of gloves. "She sounds like a keeper. Probably the only woman who could handle you."

Aric grunts in response as I begin to clean his wound.

"I need to pull the bullet out. Are you going to need something stronger than wine?"

A cocked brow is all I get for an answer, and that's enough for me. I remove the bullet and watch his expression. It's almost as if he gets off on the pain. It should terrify me, but it doesn't. I've known Aric for many years. He may be one of the most dangerous men in the world, but only to the people who deserve it.

"I hear Victor is still alive." I mention his father in an

attempt to spike conversation before I start dragging a needle through his skin.

"The game isn't over yet. My wildflower unknowingly helped me prolong his miserable death."

I push the needle through his skin. "Kali's not your wildflower."

He ignores my statement. "How's she been?"

I push the needle through his skin again. "She's doing better than I've seen since her parents passed. She and Gage will be visiting soon." At least that's what Logan said. She wants to see his building.

Aric nods. "How've you been? I hear you've had your hands full lately."

I pierce his skin a little too deeply, unsure exactly what he knows. Aric's always a wildcard, knowing things he shouldn't.

He chuckles at my reaction.

"Mmm," I say. "The tornado caught me off guard."

"More than Logan has?"

"You know how he is. He's more like a hurricane, plowing through everything before you even know what hit you."

"No one can ever say he sits on the sidelines waiting for someone else to make their move. He's always looking at the big picture." Aric shakes his head. "Shit, if I could get your man to work for me—"

I interrupt him. "Never going to happen," I pull the needle through his skin one last time and cut it, tying a knot. I slap his arm across the stitches, and he grins, the devil that he is. "He's not my man, and you know damn well he would never do any work for you." I snap the gloves off and dispose of them.

"Come on, Harlow, even a blind man can see you and Logan were made for each other."

Before I can respond, a sudden force hits my front door and it flies open. Shit, I forgot to engage the security system when I let Aric in. Aric and I have our guns pulled and trained our unexpected guest before he can even blink.

"Shit, Aleksei, you can't just walk in here like that," I say. I lower my gun and press my hand on Aric's to get him to drop his.

"Hey, it's not my fault you didn't have your security system set."

He walks in, a file folder in his hands. His eyes reach Aric. "Mr. Hemmington, it is a pleasure to meet you."

Aric puts his shirt back on, then walks around the table and reaches his hand out to shake his. "Mr. Morozov, call me Aric. I heard you were thinking of doing business in the States. I just didn't realize it was with Miss Reece."

They shake hands. "Aleksei. And only if Miss Reece will grant me the honor of working together."

Aric drops his hand. "You're selling the Oasis?"

"No, of course not. I'm merely looking at partners."

"You can't get a better partner than Logan."

I deadpan, "Do you see Logan anywhere, asking to be a partner?"

Aric shrugs, evincing boredom. "His loss." He grabs his belongings and addresses Aleksei. "You screw Harlow over in any way, you better be prepared to go to war with not only me but everyone in the States. If you fuck with her or the Oasis, start counting your breaths. You won't have many left."

My jaw falls open and my heart soars as Aric heads for the door. "Wait, you're not staying here to recover?"

Aric faces me. "I have a little minx to catch." And with that, he disappears out the door like a damn ghost.

Wondering how well a mob boss takes a threat like that one, I turn my attention to Aleksei.

"And *that* is exactly why I need this partnership with you."

"Because Aric Hemmington just threatened your life if you screw me over?"

He smiles. "Because every single guest here would do the same thing Aric just did. That's how much they all respect you."

I lean back onto the counter, glancing at the folder in his hand. "What's that?"

He walks forward, dropping it on the kitchen table. "That is the contract, Miss Reece. I've made adjustments, so I would recommend reading it through in its entirety. I'm heading back to Seattle for a couple of days, then to New Jersey Sunday, but you will find instructions on how to contact me in there."

I can't believe it. What are the odds that he has business in the same state I need to go to? "Wait, can I catch a ride with you?"

His brows crease. "To Seattle or New Jersey?"

"New Jersey. I can take an Uber once we get there to take me the rest of the way."

"You have yourself a date."

Chapter Twenty-Seven

Harlow.

Instead of being a responsible adult, I drink not just one bottle of wine but two. I sit in a chair on my patio and stare at the folder in front of me. I told myself on Thursday that after I finished my first glass of wine, I would read the contract.

It's Saturday night, and I come close, I really do. My fingers dance across the folder, but I can't make myself open it. Aric's words keep replaying in my mind.

You can't get a better partner than Logan.

The day Logan walked into my life, I was a goner. His blond hair, hazel eyes, and body had me at first sight. Then he opened his mouth and was unlike any other guy I'd ever talked to. I quickly learned he was different.

He was smart and motivated. He wasn't afraid of hard work and long hours. Sure, he plays hard, but he works even harder. He's just like me, and together we were truly a powerhouse.

I remember sitting back and thinking about the future of the Oasis when I was younger. In every picture that came to mind, Logan was right next to me. Aric was right when he said that.

But Logan destroyed my heart seven years ago when he left me high and dry. And the cherry on top was when he accused me of hooking up with Fletcher. It was as if he didn't know me at all. The cold shoulder he gave me when he visited his sister while she was staying with me... It still pisses me off. And seven years after we exploded, he sucked me right back into his orbit, and like a naïve, lovestruck teenager, I fell for his charming ways once again.

I won't be making that mistake ever again. Logan may be my soulmate, but we can never seem to land the plane. Instead, we fly straight toward the sun, only to switch off the engines and plummet hard to the ground, leaving my heart busted into a million pieces.

I've tried to find love with someone else, but with all my time devoted to the Oasis, I've never had a chance to explore anything further. Maybe once the ink is dry on the contract, I'll have more time for me.

But I know deep down it's a lie. No other man has ever come close to sparking any interest in me. I hate that I miss my chief as much as I do, but like every other obstacle that falls in front of me, I'll make it through because that's what I do and that's who I am.

By Sunday morning, I have everything sorted for my short getaway from the Oasis. I haven't read a page of the contract, and my body aches in areas I didn't even realize could ache. That couch has been unforgiving. After taking some aspirin and a long hot shower, I feel better. I message Fletcher, telling him I'm going out of town to visit my mother and will be back in a couple of days. He knows the code, so he can stay here if he wants. I'm still mad at him for sending a PI to stalk my parents. I can't wait to send him pictures of the truth.

Aleksei and I board his own personal jet from Seattle late in the day. His plane is stunning, all cream leather seats and gold accents. It has not only a bathroom but a bedroom as well. I would be lying if I said it didn't tempt me to climb in and sleep the entire flight, but I made myself a promise to read the contract, so once we are finally cleared to fly, I do.

After reading the last page, a tear rolls down my cheek and splashes down onto the paper clutched tightly in my hands. My eyes are pooled, making the words I just read blurry. I think I have cried more over the last few weeks than I have in my entire life. Crying seems to have become the norm for me. Just when I think everything is moving in one direction, I get turned in another. Before, I never had a problem. I could roll with whatever came my way. But lately, it seems like everything is only breaking me down.

A click of a pen is the only noise in the cabin as I lift my eyes to Aleksei's, who's sitting across from me. He leans forward, his large arms resting on the small gilded table between us, and holds out the pen. When I don't move, he sets the pen down and gently pulls the contract from my fingers.

I watch as he flips it around, taking the same pen he tried to give me, and signs his name at the bottom. Turning the contract back around, he slides it in front of me and rests the pen on top.

I drop my gaze to the pen and study it. It's also gold and sleek and looks like it cost a fortune. Who would have ever thought that my life would change after using such a simple object? I wonder if the person who made this pen knew that it would change someone's life after using it only once.

With sweaty hands, I pick up the pen before meeting Aleksei's eyes again. Another tear drops, this time falling into my lap. I roll my shoulders, trying to calm my nerves. "This isn't what we agreed upon."

Aleksei leans back in his chair and grabs his glass of vodka. His eyes never leave mine as he takes a slow sip and sets it back down. "I'm well aware of that."

I shake my head, trying to grasp everything I just read. "I don't understand."

"The way I see it, you don't really have a choice. Sign the contract, Harlow. It wouldn't be smart to pass on a deal like this."

I swallow the lump in my throat and dry my eyes. I lock my shoulders, because I'm the granddaughter of the late Sally and Jon Walker, and that's how our family represents. Pulling the contract closer, I sign my name at the bottom and push it back to the center of the table. Clicking the pen closed, I look up at Aleksei Morozov.

"I'm keeping the pen."

By the time we land at Newark Liberty, it's later than planned. The moon hangs high in the sky. With all the city lights, you can't see a single star, even though I know they're up there. I miss the Oasis already.

Wrapping my arms tightly around my body, I follow Aleksei down the airstairs and onto the tarmac. The ground is damp. It must have rained here earlier. I reach for my luggage, which he's pulling alongside him, but he simply swivels it out of my reach. I give a questioning look.

"Come. I have a ride ready and waiting to take you where you need to go."

"You didn't have to..." I start to respond, but he's already turned his back and is walking away. I huff and wrap my arms around my body again, following him. He better not get used to walking off when I am talking to him. If we were at the Oasis, my .357 would have made its presence known to teach him some damn manners.

We approach a stretch limo. An older man promptly climbs out of the driver's door. "Mr. Morozov, Miss

Reece," he says, tipping his hat to me as he walks to the trunk and unlocks it. Aleksei sets my bag inside and shuts it before looking back at the driver.

"Isaak, please take Miss Reece to her destination for the evening and remain with her until she's ready to take my plane back home."

"Oh no. That's not necessary. I can take a commercial flight back."

"I wasn't asking you, Harlow. I'll see you soon."

See me soon?

"When?" I call out, but he doesn't respond. He disappears into the dark shadows. Turning to the driver, I say, "He really needs to learn some manners."

Isaak chuckles. "Indeed. Now, Miss Reece, let's get you on your way."

"Please, call me Harlow. Do you need me to enter the address into your GPS or something? I can just sit up front with you on the drive to the hotel. There's no need for a limo."

He lets out a light chuckle. "I have everything under control. There's a bottle of chilled wine waiting in the back for you. Why don't you unwind with a glass? I'm sure you could use it after your long flight."

Well. I can't argue with that kind of logic. "How far away are we?"

"Just over an hour, Miss Reece."

I almost ask him again to call me Harlow again, but I think it will be a never-ending battle. He has the appearance of an older Bruce Willis with a sly smile. I like him already.

As soon as I slide onto the warm leather seats, the door closes and the locks engage.

What the hell?

I check the door handle, but it doesn't budge. There aren't even locks on the door for me to unlock.

"Have you missed me, wildcat?"

I changed my mind. I no longer like Isaak... or Aleksei, for that matter.

Chapter Twenty-Eight

Logan.

My obsession with this woman truly knows no bounds. I will move heaven and hell for her without question. And just as I have promised, I will eliminate anyone who tries to fuck with her, regardless of who they are.

When I talked with Fletch and Aleksei earlier today and learned that my wildcat was taking an unexpected trip to the East Coast, I had to change my plans. After getting everything prepared for Harlow's arrival, I contacted Aleksei while they were en route, letting him know everything was in place and to make sure her luggage was put in the trunk of the limo.

Harlow presses her body against the door, trying to keep as much distance as possible. Her bluish-gray eyes burn with fury. I can read right through them. She's debating how she wants to kill me.

With the partition window still down from our chat earlier, Isaak gets in next to my friend, who sits in the passenger seat, though he doesn't turn around. Isaak knows who's in charge and is under strict instructions.

"Isaak," Harlow says, "I need to get something out of my bag, please."

He looks at us through the rearview mirror, jumping between Harlow and me. He's not sure what to do. Harlow's good at throwing a person off track without them even realizing it's happening. If it isn't her beauty, it's her nonchalant tone or unconcerned manner. Either her .357 is in her bag, or she wants out of this car. And if she gets out of this car, it won't be easy getting her back in.

I shake my head and add, "We'll need some privacy, Isaak."

"Of course, Mr. Keeyes."

Harlow whips her head toward me as the partition closes and the car begins to move.

"What the fuck, Logan? You think you can just up and disappear on me again and all will be good?" she spits out, anger deep in her eyes. "And who the hell is up front with Isaak?"

I have no idea if she has her .357 on her or in her bag—surely Aleksei doesn't observe TSA protocols—but I need to eliminate any chance of her changing my plans tonight. Without warning, I lunge at her, and a shocked squeal flies from her sweet lips.

I flip her away from the door and around, her back hitting the seat as I press myself against her body. She squirms beneath me, trying to reach for something. It doesn't take a genius to figure out what it is. I lock my fingers around the wrist of the hand that's going for one of her weapons—her .357. I can't take the risk of the gun going off and hitting Isaak. I have a feeling that won't go well with Aleksei. I bring her arm up where I can grab hold of the gun.

The bullet leaving the chamber is loud, almost deafening, but thankfully the gun is pointed toward the roof. She freezes. I'm not sure she's shocked that it went off, but I don't waste time thinking about it. I rip the gun from her hand.

One down, one to go.

Harlow lets out a frustrated scream as my hand drifts down her body. I pull her cell phone from her back pocket and toss it to the floor before my hand continues down the path of her leg. She usually keeps a knife in an ankle holster. I press my full weight into her chest as my hand tugs on her blue jeans, raising her pant leg away from her ankle. True to my wildcat, I feel the warmth of the handle across my fingers. I remove it from the holster.

Her fight drains as I take her last weapon, leaving rage in her eyes. I give her a quick kiss on the tip of her nose.

"Much better," I say, rising off her. Both weapons

are now in my possession. I tuck them safely away. I've known my wildcat for too long to give her a chance to take them back.

"You're an asshole." She sits up, her hair disheveled from our wrestling.

"And you're beautiful."

She shakes her head at my compliment. "Where are we going?"

I lean back in the seat and adjust myself. My cock doesn't seem to get the memo that now is not the time to be making an appearance. "We're going to visit your parents."

Crossing her arms, she narrows her eyes at me. "No. I'm going to see my parents. You're not taking one step inside their home."

My lips tip up at the confidence she holds. "Being that you're supporting their lavish lifestyle, I think it's only fair that they support us as a couple."

"Ha." She reaches for the wine that's chilling on ice and pours two glasses. She leans forward, offering me one. "There is no *us*."

I smile and ignore her words, taking the glass from her. "Thank you."

"Don't thank me. Just take a sip so I know you haven't tainted this bottle with God knows what."

I laugh and tip the glass back, making sure to take a big gulp. She's got me all wrong. I want her well aware of everything that's about to go down. Letting out a dramatic "Ah," I lean back in the black leather seat, spreading my legs wide as I watch her take a small sip. I don't want her to get drunk, but I know she's going to need something to get her through this. "I heard we need to go bed shopping again."

Her eyes dart to mine, clearly not expecting me to know about her playing a card from my bag of tricks. She adjusts her body, locking in her shoulders and crossing her sexy jean-covered legs. "I figured if you didn't want to share my old bed with anyone else, then why should my next man have to share a bed that we fucked in?"

She's poking a red-hot poker to a bear by saying that to me, and it's working. My smile drops from my face. I lean forward and speak low, with precision. "Careful, wildcat. We wouldn't want anyone to get hurt thinking that's acceptable." I know she's talking out of her ass, intentionally trying to piss me off. But I still feel the need to make it perfectly clear that she's mine and only mine.

She glares back, then turns her head to look out the window. Then she whispers words I hate. "Don't you think it's time we go our separate ways?"

I slide across the bench seat, closing the distance between us. She takes another drink, not looking my way, though I know she's aware that I'm sitting right next to her now. "How do you separate your heart from your soul?"

She gulps audibly. I put my fingers under her chin, turning her to face me, but her eyes are cast downward.

"Do you know how to do that, Harlow? Because I sure as hell don't. I went seven years. Seven fucking years thinking that you moved on from me with Fletch without blinking an eye. Seven years of trying to get you out of my mind. Seven years of trying to get underneath another woman just to get a break from the mindfuck that I was in. And you know what happened every single time?" When she refuses to say anything, I continue. "I couldn't do it. I couldn't fucking go through with it, Harlow. Not one damn time."

Disbelief reflects on her face.

"You've always been it for me. There's no other wildcat who could ever take your place. When are you ever going to accept our fate?" I plead.

"You expect me to believe that you haven't been with anybody else since me?" she asks, a slight tremble in her voice.

"Yes, I expect you to, because that's the truth. Don't ever forget my confessions, because I mean every word I've ever said. You're a part of me as much as I'm a part of you. I've never betrayed you, even when I thought you were betraying me. I know I messed up by shutting you out, but I can promise I will spend the rest of my life making that up to you."

I drop my hand, giving her space to absorb my confession. Her shaky hands raise her glass to her lips and she takes another small drink. My heart pounds in my chest. Everything I just admitted has left me feeling vulnerable.

I don't have to wait long before she composes herself, in true Harlow fashion. "It's too much, chief. I have no choice but to forget." She twists the stem of the wineglass between her fingers, watching the red liquid swirl around in her glass. "I have to focus on my mom's health and keeping the Oasis afloat. We're not young kids in love anymore. Life has taken a toll on both of us... Everything is different now."

I reach out to grab her hand, but she pulls away swiftly. Frustration and anger surge through me. *What will it take for her to realize I won't leave her again?* I drain the rest of my wine in one gulp, then toss the glass to the side. The only way to get her to understand comes in the form of teaching her parents a tough lesson in life. Determined, I slide back across the bench and reach under the seat. Harlow watches intently as I pull out a black duffel bag. With a steady hand, I drag the zipper across the leather and pull out a black hardcase.

Setting the case across my thighs, I lean back and flip the two clips, opening the case. Harlow takes in my black Beretta M9 as I pull it out. This is my only other love besides my sister and the wildcat sitting next to me. My pride and joy, and it's perfect for the show we're heading to. With the option of a single or double shot, what really sold me was the threaded barrel.

I grab the silencer and slowly thread it onto the barrel, then load one in the chamber. I turn to my wildcat and watch as the color drains from her face.

"You're right, Harlow. Everything has changed... And more is about to."

Chapter Twenty-Nine

Harlow.

My glass slips from my fingers, hitting the floorboard and splashing across the white carpet, staining like blood. Blood that Logan is clearly ready to spill. I need to get a handle on this before he does something that he can't come back from. He slides the empty case back underneath the seat.

It's my turn to reach out. I put my hand on his knee. His gaze drops to where my hand rests, then slowly reaches my face. He doesn't utter a word, but his eyes are doing all the speaking for him.

He's going to kill my parents.

"Listen, chief. I think we both need to relax and figure everything out. Let's go to a hotel room tonight. My parents weren't expecting me until morning anyways."

He cocks his head, studying me like he always does. "A hotel room?"

I nod quickly. "Yes. Let's let Isaak know we want to go to the hotel I booked. We can go see my parents first thing tomorrow morning before her doctor's appointment."

"You're on board with going to see your parents together? I'm done hiding us, wildcat. It's time everyone knows who you belong to."

I nod frantically. "They already know you've been staying with me. I'm sure they assume you never left." I'm pulling at strings. Anything to keep him away from my parents, so I can keep them out of harm's way.

"Kiss me." His words come out deep and rough.

"What?"

"I've missed your sweet lips on mine. I need to feel us again. These past few days have been pure torture for me."

I know he's testing me, seeing if I'm being honest about the hotel room for tonight. Without a second thought, I lunge at him, throwing everything to the wind. This is how it's always been between us. When we're hot, we're on fire, but when we're cold… I refuse to think about that. All that matters is showing him my soul. Because if I'm honest with myself, I've missed him more than I'll ever admit. And if this buys me time to get this whole fucked-up situation under control, then it's a win-win for me.

Our kiss is frantic and intense, just like always. Like

we both cannot wait another second to become one. Straddling his body, I drag my fingers through his thick hair as his large hands encase my body. He hugs me tight to his strong chest and our tongues tangle together in the most beautiful dance.

Logan will always be it for me. Even if we don't make it through our second go-around, it's always been and will always be Logan Michael Keeyes. I probably know more people than most, but where my heart lies, only one stands out.

I purr as he squeezes my ass and groans into my mouth. I rock forward and feel his hard shaft between my legs, turning our heat into an inferno. All that separates us from Isaak and the other man up front is a simple plane of tinted glass, and it doesn't even bother me. All I care about in this moment is us. That is what this man makes me feel.

Before I can undo his belt, he pulls away, breaking our kiss. Our breathing is heavy. He grabs my hips and pulls me off his lap. I miss his heat instantly. At least one of us is in the right state of mind to know we need to wait until we make it to the hotel room before anything goes further.

"How do you drop this partition down so we can let Isaak know?"

He licks his lips, almost as if he's trying to get every last taste of me off his lips. His lust-filled hazel eyes locked onto mine. "We don't want to keep your parents waiting. We'll go there first."

My lips break apart. "I know you think you're doing the right thing for me, but you're wrong. I flew out here not only to see my parents but to meet with the doctor. My parents have gone through hell the last couple of years, and if you stress them out any further…"

I leave my words hanging in the air, the rest of the words too hard to get out. Neither of my parents can handle this level of stress on top of what they've been dealing with. A cold smirk runs across his beautiful, chiseled face. Goosebumps skitter across my skin.

"I think the doctor is going to be the most exciting part."

I have no idea what Logan means by that, but I don't ask. I lean into the warm leather and cross my arms. This isn't going to end well for him. I'll make damn sure of that.

When we pull into the driveway, I know Isaak must have the wrong address, because there's no way that my parents live in a house this size. It looks more like a castle than a home, very different from the one they had on the West Coast.

Logan leans down and grabs my phone from the carpet between his feet. He slips it into his pocket. Asshole. I regret not plugging in the address that my father gave me before my flight took off. I was too worried about reading the contract Aleksei gave me.

I refuse to believe Logan when he says that my parents have been manipulating me the entire time. No one in their right mind would ever do that to their own child. And how could they get a doctor to meet with me and discuss my mother's treatment? No medical practitioner would agree to fabricate something like this. Nothing is making sense at this point, but one thing's for sure: They don't live in this castle. They're barely making it.

Isaak opens the door for us. I climb out first, the wind catching my hair and tossing it across my face. A large form exits from the front passenger seat of the limo.

"Conner?" I ask, surprised. I didn't realize he was the man sitting up front with Isaak. I assumed it was another employee of Alexsei's.

His lips tip up slightly, but all I get is a grunt. Moonlight glints off the thick scar that runs down the side of his face. Anxiety builds as each second ticks by. The outside of the house has lights shining on it from the lawn, but the inside is completely dark. I'm praying that whoever lives here is already fast asleep, and we'll have no other choice but to wait until morning.

"Isaak, you can wait in the car. We won't be long," Logan says as he wraps his arm around my shoulders.

I shrug him off and head up the path. The house looms ahead, all gleaming windows and architectural ego. I've never seen the point of a mansion. It's just more square footage for dust to gather.

I can feel Logan right on my heels as I climb the brick stairs. "You realize this isn't my parents' house," I snap, my anger building deep into my bones.

Logan ignores me, walks ahead, and enters a code at the front door.

"How the hell do you know the code?"

He turns his head back toward me and cocks a brow. *Alright, stupid question.* He did manage to break into my alarm system in under ten minutes, and that was a system created by the best in the country.

The light turns green, and the lock disengages. He swings the door open and motions for me to walk in. My knees lock into place, not allowing my feet to take a step closer. I can't do this. I take a step back.

He cocks his head at me in question. "Don't you want to see your parents?"

I shake my head, my throat closing shut. Maybe this is the house of the doctor who's treating my mom. I take another step backward, getting ready to bolt. To where, I don't know. But I know if I run, Logan will chase me.

I start to turn on my heel right as a steely arm wraps around my waist and lifts me off my feet. A large hand covers my mouth. Because my back is to Conner's front, I can't hit him with my fists, so instead I start to kick my legs. I scream, hoping to wake someone in this neighborhood, but his hand muffles my attempts.

My fight is pointless against this brute. This is exactly why I always carry two weapons on me, but Logan has left me in a situation I've never been in before. I'm not so naïve as to believe I can overpower the men I have to deal with without a little help from a blade or gunpowder. As soon as we enter the warm home, I stop my struggles, and Conner sets me back on my feet.

Logan closes the door behind us and turns the alarm system off, then turns to face me.

I narrow my eyes on the man I love, my hate for him growing by the minute. "You're seriously going to wake whoever lives here?"

"Oh, wildcat, I promise you they're already awake."

I scrunch my nose as he hits the lights and the inside of the house comes to life around us. This home is even grander on the inside. Real hardwood floors with expensive Oriental rugs lie under a chandelier that looks dipped in gold. A large double staircase leading up to the second floor is the center of attraction.

This must be the doctor's house.

Logan stalks toward me, grabs my hand, and pulls me toward the closed French doors off to the left. I try to dig my heels in, but I'm no match for his strength.

As we approach the doors, he stops abruptly, turning to peer down at me. "I made a very clear promise to your father that if he ever did anything to hurt you, he would have to answer to me. Your parents made this decision. Remember that."

I try to yank my hand from his, but it doesn't work. He turns the handle and opens the door to my new nightmare.

I take in the sight and feel my blood drain from my face. This is worse than a nightmare. My mom, my dad, and someone else are all very much wide awake. My mom's chestnut hair, the same as mine, is knotted up like she's put up a good struggle. My dad looks like Logan spent more time with him. His left eye is almost swollen shut, and blood leaks from his ear. The last guy—I have no idea who he is—sits in the worst condition. His clothing is bloodstained over his entire body.

"Who the hell is that?" I demand, jerking my chin toward the third man.

Logan doesn't answer. His jaw flexes once.

All three are gagged with cloth and tied to chairs, with a plastic sheet underneath them. Without a second thought, I take one step toward my mom. Logan's large hand wraps around my arm as he yanks me back to him.

I whip around, my fists hitting his large chest. Tears stream down my face at allowing my parents to ever be in this position because of the decisions I've made. "You son of a bitch, untie them now!" I scream, my nerves shot. I wish nothing more than to have my trusty .357 on me right now. But he knew I would use it, and that's why he made sure I didn't have any weapons.

He grabs hold of my wrists and wraps them around my back, bringing my struggle to a halt as he peers down on me. His hazel eyes bore into me. "I did this for you. I may have walked away for a few years, but I never took my eyes off you that entire time. My only regret is not figuring out your parents' game sooner."

"Have you completely lost your mind?" I hiss, my heart pounding hard against my chest.

"Only for you." He leans down and kisses the tip of my nose, which I'm unable to stop him from doing, and looks over me. "Conner."

I feel Conner's hands wrap around my forearms, holding me in place. My entire body begins to tremble as Conner turns my body so I can watch as Logan approaches my parents. He removes the gag from my father first, who instantly starts coughing.

Oh. My. God. I'm going to kill Logan the first chance I get.

"Jack," Logan says, slapping my dad's back hard. "Would you like to do the honors of telling your gorgeous daughter what you and your lovely wife have been up to?"

"I will end you, you worthless piece of shit!" my dad roars. His eyes crinkle at the corners as they narrow on me. "I told you he was no good, but you never listen! Now look what you've done to us—"

My dad is cut off by the blow of Logan hitting him with his Beretta. I scream and struggle to break away from Conner, but it's useless. I know that, but watching him hurt my dad is too much to take.

The hit was hard enough to put my dad in a dazed state. He groans, his head hanging downward. Logan makes his way to my mother as my heavy heartbeat reaches my ears. There's absolutely nothing I can do to stop him. I've never felt as vulnerable as I do right now.

"Logan, please don't do this to me," I croak, my throat dry from the rushed breathing.

He rips the gag from my mom's mouth.

Her attention turns straight to me. "Baby, honey, he made me do it. I didn't want to, but your dad insisted—"

"Cut the bullshit, Robin," my dad yells, blood now pouring down his temple. "This was as much your idea as it was mine." Defeat fills each word he says.

My mom whips her head toward my dad, the whites of her eyes large. "My fault?"

An evil laugh comes from my dad's chest. "If your damn parents had left us with the Oasis, we wouldn't be in this situation."

"If you had taken her money sooner, we could've disappeared before Logan showed up!"

"She didn't have the money, Robin!"

A sharp pain strikes my chest at both of their confessions. I watch them go at each other like starving coyotes. Their betrayal leaves my heart heavy in my chest. I look around the room, my eyes landing on multiple gold-framed photos of my parents.

This *is* their home.

My eyes flutter shut, the last of my tears falling down my cheeks. My struggle to get away from Conner stops. I used to think there were lines parents wouldn't cross. I was wrong.

Growing up, my grandparents never had much to do with my parents, and now I understand why. They knew the evil that lived deep inside each of them. I can't help but wonder... If my grandparents hadn't raised me, would I have ended up just like them?

The weight in my chest shifts, and I slowly open my eyes. Logan has put the gags back in my parents' mouths, silencing their heated argument. I look over to him, expecting to see a cocky gleam. Instead, I see sorrow.

My chief never wanted this for me; it's clear in his hurt-filled eyes. He didn't leave me high and dry like he did in the past. He took the reins into his own hands since I was too blind to see what was really happening.

Logan walks around the chairs and makes it to me in a few long strides. I don't even realize that Conner has already dropped my hands and backed off until Logan pulls me to his chest. "I need you to breathe, wildcat. Can you do that for me?"

I give a jerky nod and try to calm my heart from thundering in my chest. I didn't even realize I had stopped breathing. It's harder than it should be, taking in oxygen. My chest feels like it is caving in. I take in Logan's warm embrace and focus on his steady heartbeat until my breathing returns to normal.

I glance over to my parents. My dad is shaking his head at me in disgust. My mom is now sobbing uncontrollably, snot running into her cloth gag.

Logan's rough hands cup my face gently. He turns me away from them so I fall under his gaze. "Don't give them another second of your time. They took advantage of you, knowing they could because of your strong loyalty and incredible heart. But that doesn't make you weak. I promise you I'll make sure they live the rest of their lives repaying their debt to you."

I nod again, not able to speak yet. I drop my head to his chest and close my eyes again. I think about all the times they weren't there for me growing up. I think about their anger when my grandparents passed and left me the Oasis. How they ultimately disowned me. Then I think about how they came back into my life two years ago and how grateful I was to have another chance with them. A second chance.

I guess not all second-chance love can happen. But I know one that can.

Swallowing to rein in my emotions so I can speak, I lift my head and look up at my chief. "I love you." My words are barely a whisper, my voice still struggling to fall from my lips.

His eyes soften as he brushes my hair away from my face. "It's about damn time." He seals his lips to mine.

I wrap my arms around his neck, pulling him as close as possible, while he deepens our kiss. Tingles race up and down my body, and everything around us disappears.

His kiss eases the tension from my body. My chest swells with gratitude that Marion introduced me to her son all those years ago. Logan holds my heart and soul. He's my everything. My world.

We break the kiss and press our foreheads together, breathing each other in. The front door opens and closes, causing us to both look up.

Aleksei walks in and assesses the situation. *He knew.* This entire time, Aleksei knew what I was walking into. "Oh good, I didn't miss the fun part," he says as he strolls in, his hands in his pockets, looking between my parents and the mystery man.

"Fun part?" I question, my eyebrows creasing in confusion.

Logan answers for Aleksei. "Do you know who that third guy is?"

I turn my attention to the man strapped to the chair next to my mom. He must be in his early fifties, with jet-black hair and a fairly good-sized build, though nowhere near the hulk of the other men here tonight. "No. Who is he?"

"This is Martin Giles, otherwise known as Graves."

Graves. Where have I heard that name before? His real name doesn't ring a bell, but his alias does. My thoughts run wild until it hits me with such force, I snap my head over to Martin. "You're a contract killer. One of the best. Haven't you stayed at the Oasis before?" I pause, pulling hard from my memory bank. "Yes, you have. My team had to patch you up years ago. You had a bullet wound in your shoulder. But your hair... It was long and light brown."

I turn to Logan, not understanding why a well-known assassin would be sitting in my parents' house.

"Tonight, Mr. Giles would have been introduced to you as Dr. Montgomery."

I gape at my parents, my father's head hung down and my mom's eyes refusing to meet mine.

"You were going to have me killed?" I shout, astonished that they would stoop to this level.

I've had to deal with some of the most dangerous people in the world, but they all look like child's play when you compare them to what my parents were going to have done to me. Was it not enough that they were draining my bank accounts? I was barely scraping by to make ends meet at the Oasis.

My heart, which moments ago shattered at learning they were manipulating me, has now turned to steel. "What happens now?" I ask, turning to face Logan.

He smiles. "Mr. Giles won't be leaving this home breathing, and as for your parents, Aleksei and I have made special arrangements for them."

Aleksei's face, staring down my parents, is harder than stone. "You make me sick. You're a disgrace to all mothers. You're lucky I can't gut you like the pigs you are." He spits at my mom and it lands on her face. He's probably thinking about his own mother's cancer battle.

Aleksei turns to me. "I have a camp back in Russia for people like your parents."

"You knew about this, didn't you?" I ask. "You knew what Logan was doing."

He steps away from my parents. "I did. When Logan told me what they were doing to you, I wanted to kill them myself. Instead, they will fly out tonight in one of my cargo planes. They'll live out the rest of their pathetic years working in the Pits for me."

"What's the Pits?"

Logan's finger goes under my chin as he directs my attention back to him. "Believe me, you don't want to know. Would you like the honor of ending Mr. Giles?"

I have lived my entire life around men most people would fear to even pass on the sidewalk. I have seen countless injuries, from gunshot wounds and stabbings to severe burns and missing limbs. But one thing that I haven't ever seen was the death of another human being, by my hand or anyone else's.

I can guarantee Logan knows this, but Aleksei probably doesn't, especially because he's heard me called the queen of darkness. In this world, you can never show weakness, so I need to tread lightly. Aleksei and I may have signed a contract together, but that doesn't change the fact that he can't know that I've never killed another person. If anyone knew that, all my threats would hold no teeth.

I look back at Graves, his dark eyes burning into my skin. If this guy walks out of this house alive, he wouldn't squander time putting any of us six feet under.

And that's enough for me.

I take Logan's Beretta and close the distance. I press the barrel to the top of his right knee and pull the trigger. Graves tosses his head back, the gag muffling his screams. I do the same to his left knee.

"Enjoy hell, you piece of shit," I hiss, angry that my team helped this man. Refusing to acknowledge him any longer, I turn back to my chief and pass back his Beretta. "You can handle the rest."

Understanding crosses his handsome face. "Conner, take my wildcat to the car. I'll be right there."

He kisses my nose and takes a step back, his right hand gripping his Beretta. I turn on my heel, refusing to look at my parents one last time, and walk out the front door with my head held high.

Chapter Thirty

Logan.

I have a great deal of respect for Harlow, and last night only tipped the scales more. With her, it honestly doesn't surprise me. She's spent the last two years of her life believing her mother was dying of cancer while draining her bank accounts and dreams in the process.

Last night, she ended it.

I may have found all the missing puzzle pieces, but how everything would end was up to her. I can't imagine being in her shoes. Having to face her parents, the two people who should love her more than anything in the world, only to learn they have been manipulating her from the start... It must have been agony.

When I called Aleksei while they were en route, I didn't know how to handle her parents. He wanted to kill them, slowly and painfully. Even with everything wrong they did to Harlow, she would never have accepted Aleksei or me ending their inadequate lives. I might not have had the opportunity to be the reason for their last breath, but that didn't mean I was out of options.

Aleksei told me about a place he runs out in Russia called the Pits. A place darker than hell itself. After one day there, I have no doubt that Jack and Robin Reece will wish I had taken their miserable lives.

My wildcat had her world rocked, but she left with her head held high. She's the type of woman who anyone would be proud to stand beside. I thank God every day that I get to be that man next to her.

When she uttered those three words to me, I wanted nothing more than to bang on my chest and scream to the world that she was mine. Once and for all. Seven years ago, I went in the direction of my own ill-conceived idea to leave Harlow out of the war that hit my family. I only grew to regret it.

To royally screw up the opportunity of a lifetime and get a second chance is more than I'll ever deserve. But I did learn two valuable lessons I will never forget.

One: I will never underestimate my wildcat again. She's strong, independent, and one badass woman. She's been able to successfully run a business that has nothing but danger knocking on her door daily. What's most impressive is how she's never lost control of any situation. Most people could never achieve that in her shoes.

And two: I will never need another chance with Harlow because I will burn this world to ash before I ever walk away from her again.

I sit next to her on Aleksei's airplane. His aircraft is absurd, with posh cream leather seats and gold accents highlighting all the money he has. Five minutes after boarding, I already know how I want to have my own personal plane built. It will make Aleksei's look like a child's toy.

I slide a folder across the table and in front of her.

She stares down at the folder silently, not making a move to open it. I'm not sure what she thinks is inside, but by the way her face hardens, I'm sure she knows it has something to do with her parents.

"I wasn't able to recoup all your money, but this is a detailed report of what I was able to do these past few days. There's more to come once I sell all their assets."

Her eyes drag upward to meet mine. "There's more besides that massive house?"

As much as I want to hide what they have done to her, I won't. "They have a yacht, quite the car collection, and another home in Wales."

She peels open the folder. I watch her mystic eyes scan the documents and take in everything her parents have been doing since day one. Her breathing starts to pick up, her chest rising and falling faster with each word she reads. I place my hand on her leg, hoping to give her my strength and remind her she isn't alone anymore.

It works. By the time she's done, her breathing is

back to normal as if she just read the morning paper, and her muscles are more relaxed underneath my fingers.

"Don't sell the house in Wales."

I tilt my head, unsure where she's going with this. She clears her throat, sitting taller. "With Kali and Gage living in Ireland, it would be nice to have a place close to them when we go to visit."

The fact that she wants to keep a place that her parents bought from manipulating her to have a place while we visit my sister says everything about our future. But that isn't what makes my heart skip a beat. It was her making plans for when *we* go to visit my sister and Gage. She's making plans for our future. Together.

"Done. I'll liquidate everything else as soon as I can. From what Fletch and I have worked up, you won't need to worry about losing the Oasis."

She closes the folder and turns in her seat, facing me straight on. "I signed a contract with Aleksei already." Her tone is low, and she's probably wondering how I'm going to take the news.

"A revised contract, correct?" If that motherfucker changed anything we spoke about, he and I are going to have issues.

She crosses her arms, fury flashing in her mesmerizing eyes. "I take it you hacked into something and found that out?"

"That he's buying the property next to you and will be building an airstrip for people to be able to fly directly into the Oasis?" I respond.

"Along with building additional cottages there for his people to stay while they're in the States," she adds.

I smile. I found out who owned the property on the opposite side of the Oasis. Aleksei gave them an offer they couldn't refuse. "He's also looking at putting additional dorms on his property for the academy. I didn't have to hack into anything, wildcat. Aleksei came to me."

Shock registers on her face. "You're the reason he changed the original contract?"

"No. He didn't want to take any part of the Oasis from you, but he wanted to be a part of it. He just didn't know what that looked like. I sent him an option to consider."

Her light laugh fills the cabin before she audibly gulps, her face turning serious again. "Thank you." Her voice is but a whisper. "Thank you for bringing the truth to me. You were right. I was being naïve, something I swore I would never be. It's just that when you think your parents are in trouble..."

I place my finger on her soft lips, stopping her from going any further. "I was wrong to call you naïve. You were right that day. If I were in your shoes, I would've given the moon to get my parents back, even if it meant only having them for one more day."

"I would give everything up to have your parents back too."

Her words slam into me and I pull her to my chest. She loved my mother and father with all her heart—not only because they helped her with the Oasis, but also because of the strong bond that grew quickly between them. Harlow was always meant to become a Keeyes.

Her hands wrap around my neck. She pulls herself onto my lap and presses her lips to mine. Our kiss starts light and sweet, but eventually the need grows too strong and a growl erupts from my chest. I thread my fingers through her chestnut hair, missing the way she feels.

She breaks the kiss but doesn't pull away. Her forehead rests against mine.

"Logan... I meant what I said. I forgive you. But you can't ever do something like that again without talking to me first."

I go still.

"You left without a word, all while you were digging through my life behind my back." Her voice stays calm, but there's iron underneath it. "What you did helped me, yes. But next time, if there ever is a next time, we need to figure it out together."

I nod once, firmly. "You're right. I shouldn't have gone about it the way I did. I'm sorry." I squeeze her hips. "No more solo missions, wildcat. Ever."

"Good." She brushes her lips against mine. "Because I'm not going anywhere and neither are you."

She pulls just far enough back to meet my eyes. A small smile tugs at her mouth. "So... You're going to move forward with the academy?"

"I am."

She sinks her teeth into her bottom lip, a small smile

playing across her lips. "You know, there's a bedroom in the back—"

That's all she can get out. I shift us and rise, lifting her in my arms as she squeals in surprise.

"I thought you would never ask," I say.

Her legs wrap around my waist and I walk us to the back of the plane, kicking the bedroom door shut with my foot.

I hope the pilot takes the long way home.

Epilogue

Ten months later, July

Harlow.

"I still can't believe it," Kali says, stepping beside me as the light breeze moves through the evergreens. Her pink dress flutters at her knees, a soft mirror to my sage green one, as we take in the air of barely contained anticipation before the academy comes to life.

The hot sun beats down on us, but I couldn't care less. This day has been a long time coming. Even though we have a long way to go and much work ahead of us, it's a huge step forward.

"I think your brother and I were just as surprised as you were to find this building next to the Oasis."

She slaps my arm, laughing. "No, I mean yes, that was a huge surprise. But I wasn't talking about that." She has a grin on her face. "I can't believe you and Logan are together. You've always been like a big sister to me, and now we're really going to be sisters."

I smile, her excitement infectious. There's no ring on my finger, but that doesn't seem to concern her. She's more like the Kali I remember before the fire, and we owe that to her husband Gage. And as much as Gage has helped Kali, she's done the same for him. Gage was lost for years, taken over by his need for revenge. One look at Gage today and I can tell he's finally at peace. Unless another man tries approaching Kali, that is. As far as I'm concerned, any man with balls that big is on his own.

My mind filters back to my parents, and I have to stop myself from wondering how they're coping working in the Pits for Aleksei. He hasn't told me much, just that they are alive and learning new lessons daily.

Watching Kali and Logan move on from the loss of her parents has given me the strength to move on from the loss of my manipulative parents. It's a hard pill to swallow, but it's getting easier as the days go on.

Today is the grand preopening of Logan's academy. There are a couple hundred people here to see what lies behind the large wooden doors.

Fletcher has taken it upon himself to design the sign for the academy. No one has seen it yet, and we couldn't be more excited. Logan stands at the top of the stairs, a mischievous smile playing at the corners of his mouth as he watches the ruckus unfold. The black Armani suit fits him like it was made for this moment—sharp and striking, just a touch too polished against the weathered stone steps beneath him. He crooks his finger at me to join him. I shake my head. They want me to help reveal the new sign, but this moment doesn't belong to me. It belongs to them.

Kali nudges me in the ribs. "You better get up there. You know he isn't going to do a thing until you do."

Gage walks up to Kali and wraps an arm around her shoulders, pulling her to his side. He smiles largely, his adorable dimples on full display. "Yeah, Harlow, get your ass up there so we can all get the hell out of this furnace. You don't want to see what this little lion turns into when she's overheated."

"Wildcat," Logan yells. Everyone looks around to figure out who he's talking to.

I roll my eyes but climb the stairs to stand with my two favorite men in the world. Logan reaches out a hand. I take it and close the distance.

"This is all you guys. I don't want to take away from your day," I whisper to him.

He pulls me close and tucks a loose strand of hair behind my ear. "If not for you, I wouldn't be standing here right now." He kisses the tip of my nose, places a hand on the small of my back, and leads me underneath the covered sign overhead. Aleksei, Riggs, and his wife Mimi—holding their infant boy—all stand off to the side.

Fletcher takes the mic and clears his throat, drawing

everyone's attention. "Ladies and gentlemen, on behalf of Logan, Harlow, and myself, I want to thank you all for coming today. This journey has not been easy. We faced numerous late nights and made more sacrifices than we can count, but it has all come together as it was always meant to."

Cheers erupt from the crowd. Fletcher smiles, his gaze on a particular person among the guests. Greg, the new man in his life, became a part of our family immediately. If I can keep my chief and Aleksei from threatening him on a weekly basis, all should be good. They call it initiation. I call it testosterone tag.

Fletcher turns to Logan. "You've become more than my best friend's partner. To me, you've become a brother. You've shown me how to be true to myself, live without shame, and embrace life to the fullest. You've taught me more over the past year than most people have in a lifetime. It's my honor to work alongside you."

The crowd cries out in unison with heartfelt "Aw!" as Logan and Fletcher shake hands, sealing their bond.

"All right, everyone." Fletcher claps his hands together. "I know you're all cooking out here like shish kebabs, so how about we get this moving?" He looks at Logan and me. "Ready?"

We both nod, grabbing the gray ropes that hang from the canvas above us, and tear them away. The crowd goes wild as I step back and look up to see the sign. My hands cover my mouth, blown away by its brilliance.

The large black sign sits in the center of the high arch. It looks almost like a black mirror with large silver lettering. Simple yet bold, the design is perfect. Across its surface, the words LINKED KEEYES ACADEMY shine clearly.

I turn to Logan and find him watching me. "Aren't you going to look at it?"

His mischievous smile returns. Wrapping an arm around my shoulder, he tugs me close and brings his mouth to my ear. "I hacked into Fletch's plan and saw it already."

I push him back, laughing and not the least bit surprised.

"The fucker hacked into my plans, didn't he?" Fletcher says as he walks over to us.

These two *are* just like brothers. They've come a long way. When Logan and I first started dating, they only seemed to tolerate each other. Then add to the equation the period when Logan thought I was sleeping with Fletcher, and it was all-out war between these two. Now I stand back and watch them shake hands and smile at one another like old friends. Sometimes, I admit, I get jealous of their bromance, but in the end, I wouldn't have it any other way.

We're all a family... including our newest member, Aleksei.

He's already installed a small landing strip and started construction on his property. The first batch of cottages that went up was for him and the staff of Linked Keeyes

Academy. He's now working on adding additional cottages for his people when they come to the States, plus a couple of dormitories for students.

Riggs and Aleksei open the front doors, and everyone flows into the academy. We follow the crowd inside and I beeline to the champagne. Logan and Gage head off with Fletcher to separate the throng into smaller groups and lead them on tours of the building.

Kali comes up behind me. "So, there was never a *you and Fletcher*?"

I grab another glass of champagne and hand it to her. "Only best friends."

She nibbles on her lower lip. "I'm sorry I said anything to Logan. I swear I had no idea that you and Logan were ever together."

I place my hand on her shoulder. "Hey, it's all good. We should have told you." I raise my flute to hers in a toast. "To finally getting the sister I've always wanted." I tip my glass back, taking a large sip of bubbly deliciousness. When I bring it down, I notice Kali hasn't taken a sip.

Oh. My. God.

"You're not drinking."

Her eyes quickly go to the flute of champagne before they reach mine. "Oh, this? No, it's not what you think." Her thumbnail goes straight to her teeth, a telltale sign. "I hate champagne."

I snort at her blatant lie. She was never good at it. "Since when?"

Her eyes go wide. "Since I learned that champagne kills twice as many brain cells as any other drink. I drink beer now, so don't be surprised when you start noticing a belly on me soon. They aren't lying when they say people who drink beer like mother's milk get beer guts." She lets out a kooky little laugh.

I smile. I've missed her elaborate stories.

She must take my nonresponse as a cue for her to continue because that's just what she does. "Anyways, yeah, I *so* can't wait to get back to our cottage tonight. I have a full case of beer in the fridge just for me. I already told Gage he's on his own tonight."

"Really? Well, in that case"—I look around the room—"I'm sure the men have some beer around here somewhere." I know damn well there isn't any, but I love watching her panic.

"Oh no, none for me. After one beer, I don't know how to stop, and that's when the clothes start disappearing. Next thing you know, I'm butt naked and passed out on the front steps."

I smile, happy for her. Kali is going to make a great mother. "Congratulations."

Her cheeks turn red. "Thank you. We're excited and nervous and so freaking happy. Please don't say anything to Logan. We're planning on announcing it tomorrow." She hands me the flute and I set it back on the table.

It takes everything in my power not to scream in pure excitement. Logan is going to be an uncle.

Logan.

The preopening of Linked Keeyes Academy today couldn't have gone better. The sky had been overcast until twenty minutes before we opened the doors. I could feel my parents with me. It was them shining down on us. It may have taken several more years than they anticipated, but I finally did it. I took the words from their letter and the birthday present they left me and made them smile from above.

What I'm about to do would send my mom to tears. I've never been more nervous in my entire life. I wish she were here with me tonight to calm the nerves firing throughout my body. My father would shake my hand and tell me how proud he was.

I stand in the shadows, waiting for my guest of honor to arrive while I take in my favorite place in the world. The lake where it all began. With the help of a few of Aleksei's guys, it looks perfect. The wind is calm, so the fake lily pads bearing small lit candles stay in place on the water's surface. The dock is wrapped in fairy lights, reminding me of the best night of my life.

The night that changed my life forever.

Thirteen years before, August

Logan.

Her kisses are the sweetest thing in the world. I can't get enough. We just finished work on the Lavender

Lodge, which took twice as long because we can't keep our hands to ourselves. I finish tightening the last clamp on the new drainpipes under the kitchen sink.

I've just set the wrench on the counter when she suddenly tackles me. She wraps her legs around my waist as I walk us back to the table, but her legs kick out and she directs me to the wall, so I perch her atop the old iron furnace.

I don't hesitate to take anything she's willing to give. Harlow Reece is like no other woman I've ever met before. She doesn't care about the latest fashion or getting her nails done. She's all about the hard work she's putting into the Oasis, and thank God she needs me. It's pretty damn clear she doesn't need many people in her life.

Her beauty is natural and her curves are perfect. I can't count how many times I've spent in the shower thinking about every inch of her skin that I've been lucky enough to see. She's every man's dream, and for some messed-up reason, she only wants me.

What's more is her love for kids. She's adjusted her schedule to accompany me to schools with less fortunate student populations. I'm not the greatest social person out there; I've always stayed behind my computer screen most of my life. But Harlow brings everyone out of their shells and allows them to shine like they were always supposed to. Including me.

I'm not sure how I'm going to pull off taking over my parents' business *and* starting an academy, but I know one thing for sure. I want Harlow right next to me the entire time.

My hands make their way down the sides of her body until I reach her hips. I dig my fingers into her soft skin. I pull her body closer to show her the effect she has on me.

She breaks the kiss and pulls back, her eyes wild. "Do you want me, Logan?" Her voice is husky with want.

"More than I've ever wanted anything." I lean down to capture her lips again, but then I feel cold steel encircle my wrist.

I pull away and look down. She has efficiently handcuffed me to this old-ass furnace. *What's she playing at?* With a smile on my face, I lunge for her, trying to grab her hand, but she steps far enough away so I can't reach her. "What are you up to, wildcat?"

I'm rewarded with her breathtaking smile, the one that locks my heart up every time. "I want to know how bad you want me."

I crook my finger at her. "Come here and I'll show you."

She shakes her head and takes another step back. Her hand goes into her jeans pocket and comes out with a small key. She sets it on a table that's just out of reach, a secret smile on her face. "If you want me bad enough, you're going to have to come find me, chief." She twirls and runs out the front door.

She's too much fun. By the time I find her, I'm going to make sure she has no doubt how badly I need her and who she belongs to.

I open the white lace curtain with my free hand to watch which way she goes. She looks back to see me watching her. I can't hear her laugh, but I can see it. I know where she's heading based on the trail she's taking. Now I just need to figure out how to get out of these cuffs.

I stretch my arms out as far as I can reach, but the damn key is still a good six inches away. I smile, pull back, and stand straight, looking around. She's put some thought into this, and I know she didn't make this so I can't hunt her sexy little ass down.

A broom is propped against the wall. I lean forward, my fingertips barely reaching it. I stretch as far as I can, the cuff digging into my skin to remind me of how tightly she put it on, and brush the handle again. The broom falls to the floor, now completely out of reach.

Shit!

I glance around but see nothing close enough for me to grab. I refuse to be the man who doesn't catch my woman. I look back at the table with the key sitting there, mocking me.

Then I see my way out.

I kick the chair in front of the table and watch it tumble to its side. I maneuver it with my foot to wrap the chair's seat around the leg of the table. I sit down on my ass, and with both legs, I brace each side of the chair and pull the table across the floor toward me.

As soon as I can reach the leg, I waste no time grabbing it and pulling the table closer. I grab the key and unlock the cuff, then bolt out the door.

Harlow's a runner. It's something both of us love to do. One thing I learned during all our trail runs is that I'm a lot faster than she is. If I'm right, and I have a damn good feeling that I am, she's heading to Diamond Lake.

I veer onto a less traveled trail, one that'll get me there quicker. Sticks and twigs crunch underneath my shoes as I make my way up the hill. The night sky makes it difficult to see through the wooded path, but it doesn't slow me down. Nothing could ever stop me from catching my wildcat.

I break through the tree line and finally catch sight of her long chestnut hair flowing behind her underneath the moon. I pick up my pace but keep my footsteps silent. Right before she reaches the dock, I wrap my arm around her waist and pick her up. She squeals in laughter.

"Gotcha." I spin her around and sink my lips onto hers. Her arms wrap around my neck and she pulls me in closer. I slowly walk her backward down the dock. My fingers find the hem of her shirt and I pull it over her head.

She starts tugging at my shirt. I reluctantly let go of her to rip it off. By the time we reach the end of the dock, we're both as naked as the day we were born. I wrap my arms around her tiny body and lean forward, propelling us into the water.

The water crashes around us, but our hands never leave each other. As we break through the water, I shake my head, hitting her with more water.

"Hey!" She laughs, covering her face.

I pull her to me. The water reaches my lower chest and almost her collarbone.

Harlow looks behind me and lets out a small gasp. I turn to see what she's looking at and am taken aback. The entire lake is lighting up with small flashes from lightning bugs. Sure, I've seen them before in the fields, but never over the water like this. There are so many. There must be thousands of them.

Harlow's small hand cups my cheek, pulling my attention back to her.

"Make love to me, Logan."

Present day

Harlow.

A client called about a leaky faucet as the grand preopening ceremony festivities were wrapping up, so I swung by there before going to our cabin. Now, I'm getting home later than expected, hoping that Logan has beaten me here. After the day we had, I'm ready for some alone time with my man. But the second I walk through the door, I know he isn't here.

I kick off my shoes and notice a notepad resting on the kitchen table. I walk over and pick it up. In Logan's bold handwriting, the note reads, "If you want me bad enough, you're going to have to find me, wildcat."

I smile, remembering the exact day I said those words to Logan. I was nervous that day, but everything worked out perfectly. I went to the Lavender Lodge before Logan arrived and locked one cuff on the old iron furnace. The entire time we were working on the kitchen drainpipes, I worried he'd see the cuffs dangling there.

That night, we each lost ourselves to the other and gave one another a gift no one could ever take from us. I quickly grab my shoes and slide them back on. I know exactly where he's at. I grab the keys for the Gator off the end table... but then set them back down.

If he wants to re-create that night, then I need to run to him, just like he did. I arm the security system, walk out, and look up at the starry night sky dominated by the full moon. It's as perfect as that night so many years ago.

I take off, jogging down the trail that will lead me to the man who has made me a better person. To the man who fought for our second chance and never gave up on us. To my future.

The pebbles bounce along the trail as my shoes dig into them with each stride I take. This trail is the fastest route to the lake because it's mostly even. I know all the trails on this property like a truck driver knows all the interstates. Lately, I haven't been able to run like I used to. With all the work on the academy and Aleksei's property, spare time has been limited.

But in a moment like this, while I jog under the moonlit sky, it reminds me that every sacrifice I've made—the stress of meeting deadlines, every late night and early morning—all of it was worth it. This lifestyle isn't meant for everyone, but it's perfect for me. Perfect for us.

Not everyone gets a second chance at love, but I truly believe that if it's meant to be, it will be.

And it has. Thank God it has.

When I finally break through the woods, I gasp at the serenity of my favorite place. I slow to a walk as I reach the water's edge and look across the dark waters. A few hundred candles float there. I scan the area for Logan but don't see him anywhere. I know he's close, hiding in the shadows. Watching me.

I make my way over to the dock, which is covered with little fairy lights. I walk out to the end and take everything in. The lights remind me of the thousands of fireflies that happily hovered around us that beautiful night.

A deep, familiar voice rumbles as his footsteps sound behind me. "That was record timing, wildcat. Now tell me, how bad do you want me?"

I spin around to find Logan standing right behind me, a lopsided grin across his handsome face. I curl my hands into his shirt and pull him closer. "More than anything in the world." I rise on my tiptoes to kiss him.

When our lips meet, I let my eyes close, losing myself in this moment. The warmth of his breath mingles with mine, sweet with anticipation. It isn't just about the physical closeness; it's the connection. It speaks volumes without uttering a word.

All too soon, Logan steps back and takes my hands in his.

I smile and glance around at the enchanting scene he's set up for us. "This is amazing, chief. It reminds me of our first night together."

His eyes turn soft. He slowly lifts my hands and kisses each one. "That was the best night of my life."

"Was?"

Logan slowly drops down on one knee, releasing my hand, and drags a small black velvet bag from his pocket. He pulls out a diamond ring, dropping the bag to the dock. It's the bag I watched him pull out of the drawer at his parents' underground safe.

He bought this ring all those years ago.

My hand covers my mouth. Oh my God. I'm going to cry. Again.

"Harlow, you came into my life like a miracle I never saw coming. I don't know what I did to deserve you, but I'm taking everything I can. I regret that I can't go back in time and do this eight years ago like I originally planned."

Tears are already flowing down my cheeks as Logan clears his throat. My heart is pounding harder than it ever has. I can't count how many times I have dreamed of this exact moment.

"You are my past. My present. My future. My forever. Harlow Elizabeth Reece, I'm not going to ask you to marry me, because I won't give you a choice in the matter."

I choke out a laugh, not surprised at his choice of words. After all, there's a reason I call him chief.

"But I promise to always be there for you. To stand by your side and to love you unconditionally until my very last breath." He slowly slides a princess-cut diamond ring—simple but stunning—onto my finger.

"Logan Michael Keeyes, it's about damn time."

Hoots and hollers erupt from the trees, causing me to jump. Logan stands and pulls me to his side. Kali and Gage, Fletcher and Greg, Conner, and Aleksei all come out from their hiding places.

I look up to *my* Logan and wrap my arms around his neck. "This was perfect, chief. But..."

His brows dip down into confusion. "But?"

"You forgot one thing about that night." I lean back, and we both crash into the water beneath us.

Not every love gets a second chance. Some slip through the cracks. Some fall apart when they do. But when one holds, it becomes a quiet reminder of who was always meant to stay.

The End

ACKNOWLEDGMENTS

Harlow, Logan, and Fletcher stole my heart from the very beginning. Writing their story felt less like work and more like living alongside them. I laughed, I cried, and at times, they even surprised me. (Yes, characters really do that.)

This book wouldn't be what it is without the people who helped shape it into something I'm proud to share.

To Jessie Campbell, my brilliant editor: You've been with me through the ups and downs of the *Confessions* series, and your passion, precision, and patience never cease to amaze me. "Thank you" doesn't even come close, but I'll say it anyway... a hundred times over.

To Jeannie, my beta reader: You devoured this book faster than I ever imagined, and your enthusiasm lit a fire under me when I needed it most. Your feedback is a gift, but your friendship is the real treasure.

To James, my world: You've held me up during one

of the hardest seasons of my life. You're my safe place, my laughter, and the calm in my storm. I don't know what I'd do without you (and I won't ever have to find out).

To my family, both here and gone: You are part of every page I write. Your love and support carry me farther than I can ever put into words.

And finally, to you—the reader: You are the reason these characters come alive outside of my head. Thank you for taking this journey with me. Thank you for investing your time and heart in these stories. Your support means everything.

XO

Sneak Peek – Scarred Confessions

Chapter One

Grace.

The kitchen clock hammers loudly, counting down the minutes like they mean nothing. But every second counts. Every tick drills into my nerves, a relentless reminder of the interview that could change everything. The smell of garlic and beer clings to my clothes as I carry my full tray to the sink.

"Sorry I'm late!" Jordan says, bursting through the swinging doors into the tiny kitchen. "Adam got held up again."

A gust of air hits me as she rushes by. Her tight black curls bounce, and the smell of her sweet perfume trails her. She opens her locker and hangs up her thick red coat. Jordan was the first person I met when I unexpectedly arrived in Deer Creek three years ago. She's my lifeline here. Her boyfriend's been training late at the gym for a boxing tournament, and tonight, he's made her late for her shift. Again.

"Good timing. A new table just came in." I drop a pizza pan and plates into the sink, sliding the tray clear with the heel of my hand. The plates vibrate against the stainless-steel sink, shaking to the bass from the reggae band performing tonight. I hate this job, but it's all I've got right now.

I glance at the clock: 5:02. My heart shifts a beat faster. My interview is in half an hour. The slot they kindly agreed to so I could work around this shift. It's a video call with the local paper for a journalist position. Not many job opportunities come available in this small town. If I nail this, I'll get a paycheck that will let me do more than just scrape by. I've already stayed long to cover for Jordan, but if I leave now, I can get home in time to change and focus.

I slam the locker shut, tug my hoodie on, and bolt. "Have a good night!"

"Buy a damn jacket, girl. It's cold! And good luck!" Jordan calls after me.

Dusk is pressing in early tonight with the clouds, the sky thinning to a bruised navy. The temperature has dropped into the forties thanks to the cold front that just came through. My breath comes out in thin ghosts. I speed walk to my beat-up Cavalier, fling myself into the driver's seat, and jam the key into the ignition.

Tick. Tick. Tick.

No! *No, no, no.* I turn the key again, harder this time,

as if brute force can bribe mechanics and fate. There's absolutely no way the universe hates me this much. This car saved me once. It's ridiculous to assign it meaning, but it's my talisman. My escape. I press my lips thin and try not to cry.

Tick. Tick. Tick.

The foam underneath me sighs with a familiar flattened groan. Anger and panic knot together. For a second, I'm back in that other place: *heavy footsteps, the smell of cigarette smoke, my skin burning hotter than the sun.* I inhale sharply and hold my breath, refusing to let the memory overtake me.

I push the door back open and throw the hood up. The metal is like ice against my palms. I know absolutely nothing about cars, but I'm hoping for a miracle from God that something will stand out like a huge red flag. Turning my phone flashlight on, I jiggle the stiff, cold battery cables until my fingers sting. I slam the hood shut and rush back into the car.

"Okay, baby," I whisper, my fingers flat on the dash. "You get me home and I'll treat you to a full detail. Car wash. Wax. Everything."

I attempt one last desperate twist of the key.

Tick. Tick. Tick.

My chest tightens like someone is squeezing a fist around it. The clock glaring at me on my phone screen says I've wasted eight whole minutes. *Shit! I'm going to be late.*

I grab my purse, slam the door, and start running. If

I take the docks to get home, I'll make it on time with a few minutes to spare. The docks aren't the smartest choice at any time of day, especially in this gathering gloom, but they're the fastest.

I hug my arms tight against the cold and make a beeline for the alley. The darkening sky is falling above, a storm knocking on the door. Unfortunately, we still have over a month before the snow starts to fall around here. It's one of my favorite times of the year in Northern Michigan, but this evening, it feels hostile and unforgiving.

The cold gnaws at my skin as I move, the wind leaking through my hoodie. I increase my speed. The air smells like lake water and fried food from the diner vents I'm passing.

I pause at the alley's entrance, scanning for anyone lurking in the shadows. A yellow streetlamp buzzes and flickers overhead, sputtering shadows that dance across the cracked asphalt. My pulse climbs, loud in my ears. It looks empty.

God, I hope it's empty.

I stick close to the wall, throwing my hood over my head, and rush down the dim path. I could call my father and ask for help, but I won't. Not after everything. He would force me back into hell—back to Vegas, back to his blood money, back under his thumb. *Back into that monster's hands.* He's a high-end attorney for criminals, and I'm not interested in being part of that world again.

Voices drift from the far end of the alley, low and

muffled. I can't make out what they're saying, but it doesn't sound like a heated conversation. Fishers, probably, who got off the water a little too late. I take their voices as a good sign. No one attacks someone when witnesses are around.

I round the corner at full speed, taking two men by surprise. Both whip their heads toward me. The closest one jerks, a small black gun in his large hand glinting beneath the dim streetlamp.

I slam my body against the cold bricks of the building I just rounded. The wall bites into my back, unyielding and damp. My breathing stutters as my muscles lock tight and I clutch myself. My gaze locks on the man standing in front of me.

He's huge. Bigger than huge. A living nightmare full of rage and muscle. His nostrils flare wildly, reminding me of an angry bull ready to charge. One of his eyes is darker than the midnight sky, and the other is milky. Deep, gnarled scars web across the right side, like someone once tried to rip his face off and failed.

Terror slices down my spine. *This can't be it for me.* I don't know why, but my father comes to the front of my mind—his cold, disappointed stare. He would blame me for this, for getting myself into this situation. I can hear him now, telling me I shouldn't have run. That I should've stayed in Vegas where I would be safe.

What a lie.

Afraid to take my eyes off the giant looming over me for too long, I glance to my left. I'm five, maybe six feet away from being able to dip back into the alley, but what good would that do me? There's only one dumpster, and it's halfway down the path. I would be a sitting duck.

But I *am* the one just standing here.

I take a small shaky step to the side as the raging bull puffs out a breath, hot air coming from his nose like smoke. He raises his gun without hesitation, pointing it directly at my face.

I don't scream.

I couldn't if I tried.

I squeeze my eyes shut because I'm too terrified to witness my own death. A muffled gunshot goes off. The sound of something heavy dropping to the pavement rings loudly through my ears. My throat grows dry as chills race down my arms. I greedily suck in an unsteady breath.

I'm still standing. I'm still alive.

I slowly peel my eyes open—first one, then the other. The giant bull is lying lifeless on the cold asphalt, a single bullet hole through his head. His vacant, open eyes stare straight ahead. I've never seen a dead person in real life. It's nothing like in the movies, not even close. The blood pours out of his head so fast, you would think his heart is still beating. The gun that was pointed at me seconds ago lies only a foot away.

Oh God.

A rush of adrenaline crashes through me, almost toppling me over. I leap for the gun. The grip is still warm from the dead man's touch.

I think I'm going to be sick.

I press myself against the brick wall, wishing I could sink right into it and disappear. My stomach knots as I turn slowly, my eyes locking onto the other man a few yards away.

He stands tall—calm and unshaken. A tailored black suit clings to his frame, complete with sharp lines and clean edges. One much nicer than the one on the guy he just killed. His hair is black as night, long on the top, in a perfectly disheveled look. But it's his green eyes that arrest my attention. They're so bright, they seem to glow.

My heart is slamming in my chest, loud enough that I swear he can hear it. My legs want to run, but they feel like wet concrete. Every muscle is buzzing, tight, and braced for impact. I can't breathe right. My vision blurs around the edges, just like it used to when—

No! You are no longer the frozen girl!

My fingers tighten around the gun until it bites into my hand.

He takes a slow step toward me, like I'm fragile and dangerous all at once. I jerk a step sideways and begin walking backward, each step slow and uneven. He closes the distance with the calm assurance of someone who's done this before. My mouth is dry and my palms are slick against the gun, which now trembles with the rest of my body.

I'm so far outside my comfort zone, I don't know what to do.

"Please don't do that," I whisper. The words come out thin. My voice sounds foreign.

He doesn't stop. His steps are smooth and deliberate, like those of a pacing predator with the means to devour his prey whole. For each one I take back, he takes two forward. Silent and controlled.

I try to sound like someone who isn't unraveling. "I called the police." It's a pathetic bluff, and I hear the wobble in my own voice.

He smiles in return, like I've just told him a joke.

Cold sweat beads down my spine as realization hits me.

He's going to kill me.

I inhale the cold, sharp air and narrow my eyes. I am not the frozen girl anymore, and I will not die tonight.

I dig my heels in, pull my shoulders back, and point the gun at his chest, willing my shaking arms to steady. "Please stop or I'll shoot." I've never fired a gun before, but with his size, it would be hard to miss.

He pauses, his head tilting slightly, like I've just become more interesting. His own gun in his right hand, resting casually alongside his thigh.

I let out a slow, unsteady breath. "Thank you." My hand jerks the gun as if it were a pointer. "Now, please set your gun down slowly and kick it over to me."

He glances lazily at his weapon, then back at my face. "No," he says, his voice husky.

My brows knit together. "No?"

"No," he repeats, stepping closer.

Fear rips loose from its fragile leash inside of me. "Whoa, whoa, whoa." My voice climbs in pitch, almost unrecognizable to me. "Please stop moving."

As if to spite me, he takes one more step before stopping. He's now close enough that I can see the scruff lining his jaw, the faint scar above his brow, the way his shoulders fill out his suit like he was born in it. His green eyes don't flicker. They just stare. Right through me and into my soul.

Then he smiles. It's nothing short of confidence, control, and smugness. "You really should drop the manners," he says, his voice now amused. "At least when you're threatening someone at gunpoint."

"Excuse me?" My voice cracks.

"It gives you away. You're too innocent for this. You're not going to shoot me." He licks his lips slowly. "The odds of that are smaller than humankind living on Mars."

This arrogant asshole doesn't know a thing about me. About what I've been through. What I've survived. "Pardon me for not holding people at gunpoint daily. I'm sure your mother must be so proud."

A deep, sexy chuckle rumbles from his chest.

Oh. His laugh shouldn't make my stomach flip like that.

"Take down your hood," he says, his voice like steel wrapped in silk.

It isn't a request. It's a command.

My grip on the gun tightens. I might not know

much about gunfights, but I know letting him see me is dangerous. "No."

He chuckles again, like I'm a cute little problem he hasn't figured out yet. "I want to see your face."

"And I wish I had never seen yours. I guess neither of us is getting what we want tonight."

His jaw ticks, the amusement fading from his eyes. He must not hear the word *no* very often. Maybe never. I don't care. He needs to hear it now.

"I'll make you a deal." His voice softens. As if I can't see the wolf covered in sheep's skin. "You drop your hood, and I'll drop my gun."

I sink my teeth into my lower lip until I taste blood. If he doesn't have his gun, I have a better chance of escaping. But if he sees my face… will he only let me go to kill me another day? This might be my first rodeo, but I'm not an idiot, and I'm damn sure not going down without a fight. "No, I don't think so."

He raises his gun and aims it at me so quickly, I shriek in surprise.

"This is your other option, princess."

My stomach drops and my knees nearly buckle. My heartbeat slams in my ears like thunder. "Okay! Okay. I pick option one," I sputter, the words tumbling out too fast. I remove my left hand from the gun and yank my hood down. The gun still held tightly in my right hand shakes like I'm in the middle of a magnitude seven-point-something earthquake.

His gun slowly drops back to his side as he takes me

in, my face no longer hidden. His gaze rakes over me piece by piece, leaving me feeling raw and stripped bare. My now-exposed face feels painfully intimate. He studies every line as if he can read me.

This is the worst mistake of my life.

But it was that or get shot.

He doesn't speak. I hate how aware I am of every inch of my skin. How cold the air feels now, how the space between us seems to shrink even though I haven't moved an inch.

He licks his lips again, then steps closer.

"The gun! Your gun!" I shriek, stumbling back. "You said you'd get rid of it!"

As if he has completely forgotten about our agreement, he glances down at his gun and tosses it off to the side, then takes another step forward. I thought he was going to kick it to me, but I have a feeling he doesn't care about those details.

"Stop right there. Please don't make me shoot you." My voice breaks. I'm not even sure he hears me.

He's so close, I can smell him now. It reminds me of expensive leather and rich spices. It's only a matter of seconds before he reaches me and rips my only form of protection from my hands.

Within one beat of my frantic heart, he lunges. I don't plan. I just react. I slam my eyes shut and squeeze the trigger. The sound explodes in my eardrums. This gun is much louder than his. It recoils, slamming back into my cheekbone. Pain flares as my vision blurs.

I stagger backward as he stumbles and falls into the cold water with a loud splash.

I stand numbly, staring at the empty space on the dock where the man once stood. The gun slips from my hands and hits the ground with a dull thud.

I just killed a man.

"Who's out there? What's going on?" a voice shouts from the shadows.

I spin around. My lungs push out ragged, hot bursts of air. The dead bull still lies sprawled where he fell, a grotesque statue.

I don't think.

I run.